"CREEPIES IN THE BUILDING!" COOPER YELLED.

And then one entire wall of Ben's office blew out in a deafening explosion.

Ben found himself sprawled on his back in the dark hallway. As dark shapes moved toward him, he jerked a grenade from his battle harness, pulled the pin, and hurled the grenade toward the far end of the hall. He scrambled back into his debris-filled office just as the grenade blew.

"It's a full scale attack," Ben said to Cooper. "The Night People are throwing everything they've got at us." He looked around him, trying to see through the murk. "Anybody here hurt?"

"Just a few cuts and bruises," Cooper said.

Before Ben could reply, another massive explosion shattered the night and the roof fell in on top of everyone crouching in Ben Raine's CP. . . .

TRAPPED IN THE ASHES

IN THE ASHES OF NUCLEAR DEVASTATION,
A SMALL ARMY OF SUPER-WARRIORS
KEEPS THE BOLD DREAM OF FREEDOM ALIVE!

WILLIAM W. JOHNSTONE

ZEBRA BOOKS
KENSINGTON PUBLISHING CORP.

ZEBRA BOOKS

are published by

Kensington Publishing Corp.
475 Park Avenue South
New York, NY 10016

First printing: April, 1989

Printed in the United States of America

BOOK ONE

Love, like Death,
Levels all ranks, and lays the shepherd's crook
Beside the scepter.

Bulwer-Lytton

The logic of the heart is absurd.

De Lespinasse

ONE

The Rebels dug in deep and tight and waited. They were facing impossible odds and all knew it. But the alternative was unacceptable; all preferred death to surrender.

They had fought hard and well over the past weeks, locked inside the concrete-and-steel canyons of New York City. And their bulldog tenacity and stand-or-die tactics had cost the Night People hundreds of dead and wounded.*

Now they were cut off from the outside, locked inside New York City in the harsh dead of winter, with thousands of the cannibalistic Night People under the city, ready to pour out of the subways and tunnels, erupting like an ugly festering boil. Khamsin, the Libyan terrorist, was knocking on the door with a full division of troops.

Sister Voleta, the mother of Buddy Raines, and her Ninth Order had joined the fight against Ben Raines and her son—such was her hate for Ben Raines.

The Rebels were surrounded. To a person, they had adopted the French Foreign Legion's motto: Stand or die.

Just a few hours before Ben would order tear gas pumped into the bowels of the city, he made one more check of his people. Taking a contingent of Rebels, with

**Valor in the Ashes*—Zebra Books

Cooper his driver, Jersey his bodyguard, and Beth with the radio, Ben headed south to the tip of Manhattan Island, leaving the Russian, Georgi Striganov, in command. The war had made allies of old enemies.

"I thought they'd hit us today, Ben," Ike said, shaking Ben's hand.

Ben, tall and rangy, looked at Ike, built like a fireplug. The ex-SEAL, although pushing middle age, was still a very powerful man. "That means Khamsin is not yet in position. As soon as I complete this tour, we start pumping in the gas."

"We're ready, Ben."

"Ready, General," Danjou, the French Canadian, said.

Ben nodded and climbed back into his Blazer. They headed to the east side of Manhattan Island to meet with Cecil and Rebet, the Russian colonel.

"We're not going to have much breathing room for the next few days," Ben told him.

Both men nodded. They knew the hard bind they were all in. All the Rebels and their allies knew there was no turning back.

Ben shook hands with the men. "Good luck, gentlemen."

No one among them had any illusions from the start that the assault on New York City would be easy. But none had thought that Khamsin would ever leave South Carolina and join forces with the Night People. The Rebels had fought their way across the shattered nation to the great city. They had taken Staten Island and prepared to launch their assault on the Big Apple.

They had thought they were facing perhaps a few thousand Night People. They soon found they were up against thousands and thousands of the black-robed, unbathed, and stinking cannibals.

But the numbers of the known enemy had not rattled Ben Raines so much as once more coming face-to-face with the only woman he had ever truly loved.

Jerre Hunter.

He had not seen her in years.

Seeing her had shaken the man right down to his boots. He had put her out of his mind—almost. Far enough back in the dark reaches that she did not daily haunt him.

Now he looked at her every day. And she was still as beautiful as that day he had first met her, so many years ago. She had been a sophomore in college when the germ and nuclear bombs had hit America. Ben had found her wandering around in Virginia, and they had traveled together for a few weeks. And Ben, twenty years her senior, had realized only after she had left him that he was in love.

"Life is certainly full of bumps and surprises," Ben muttered, looking out the window of the Blazer at the cold vastness of New York City, with sudden death lurking under the streets.

"Beg pardon, sir?" his driver, Cooper, asked.

Ben smiled at the young man. "Just talking to myself, Coop."

They were on Third Avenue, just passing 116th Street, when Jersey yelled, "Stomp on it, Coop! They're all around us!"

The sidewalks had suddenly filled with creepies.

"Order the attack, Beth," Ben instructed. "All personnel into gas masks and start the pumps. Floorboard it, Coop. Run over them."

Slugs hit the armor plate and the bulletproof glass of the Blazer. It was a very uncomfortable sensation.

Cooper rammed the Blazer into a mob of black-robed creepies, crushing half a dozen under the big knobby tires. The sounds of screaming filled the interior of the Blazer, and the breaking of bones was felt more than heard by those inside.

"Turn west on One Twenty-fifth, Coop," Ben told him, consulting a map. "Then north on St. Nicholas."

"And Merry Christmas to you, too, sir," Cooper said with a grin.

Ben laughed aloud. One thing about his Rebels:

fighting while badly outnumbered, a sense of humor would help keep them going.

They cleared the few blocks full of creepies, and Ben rolled his window down. Already the smell of tear gas was sharp as it drifted down from the north.

"Masks, people," he ordered, slipping his gas mask over his head and adjusting the straps and earpieces. "Never wore one in my life that was comfortable," he muttered, forgetting that these were mike-equipped, thanks to Katzman and his communications people.

"Me, neither, General!" Cooper and Beth and Jersey all said.

They roared into Rebel-controlled territory and up to the block where Ben's CP was located just in time to see a mob of choking, coughing Night People come staggering out of a building, nearly blind from the strong gas.

"The crud had hidey-holes right across the friggin' street from my office!" Ben said. "Damn!" He bailed out of the Blazer, Thompson at the ready.

He knelt on the sidewalk and leveled the SMG, holding the trigger back, fighting the rise of the powerful old weapon.

Ben sent a dozen of the cannibals into that long sleep before he had to let off; another second more and he'd be shooting out windows on the third floor.

The street was filled with black-robed crud, as far as one could look in any direction. Coughing and staggering, they walked and ran into death from the guns of the Rebels. The air was thick with tear gas and gunsmoke and the stinking, almost overpowering odor of the unwashed bodies of the Night People.

One jumped on Ben's back, knocking him sprawling, making him lose his grip on the Thompson. Ben kicked the creature in the balls, doubling him over, a silent shriek cut off in his throat as vomit filled his mouth. Ben clawed out his .45 and shot the offensive subhuman in the face, the slug striking the man between his eyes, knocking him backward.

Ben grabbed up his SMG with his left hand and went racing up the street, Coop, Jersey, and Beth right behind him.

"We sure flushed them, all right," Ben panted.

"Flushed them all over us," came Jersey's voice through the tiny speakers in the mask.

Ben ran up the steps to his command post and through the door, running up the steps to the second floor and into his office. Jerre was crouched behind a window. She had shattered the window with the butt of her M16 and was firing into the mob of creepies. Ben stepped to a window down the line from her and knelt down to insert a full drum into the belly of his Thompson.

He lined up a row of black-robes and pulled the trigger, letting the old "Chicago Piano" roar its Wagnerian death chant. The line of choking, nearly blinded black-robes went down like fallen dominoes.

Jerre was picking her shots carefully, using select fire, and each time she pulled the trigger a black-robe hit the concrete.

Nothing like one's life being put on the line to turn a peaceful poet into a Valkyrie, Ben thought. Then he turned his attention back to the bloody street.

The fighting had subsided in this sector, the street littered with the fallen bodies of creepies. "We can't let up," Ben said, and Beth nodded her head, telling him she was receiving the transmission. "Order search and destroy to begin immediately. Hunt them down and hit them while they're still half blind."

Beth relayed the orders to unit commanders, and the Rebels left their secured positions to enter the buildings.

"Patch me through to Ike," Ben said.

"On the line, General."

"Ike. What's it look like in your sector?"

"Got 'em layin' in the streets like pins in a bowlin' alley, Ben. But they've taken to the buildings, just like we knew they would. S and D?"

"Ten-four, Ike. We can't let up now. Eagle out." To

Beth: "Get me Cecil."

"General Jefferys on the line."

"Cec. Search and destroy. Hit them hard now. Eagle out. Beth, radio all units to enter the buildings in their sector and destroy the creepies."

"Yes, sir. Engineers want to know if they are to keep up the pumping?"

"Reduce it by half but keep pumping in the gas until I give the orders to stop. We've got to push it down as far underground as we can."

"Yes, sir."

"General?" Jerre's voice entered his ear. He looked at her, irritated that she used his rank instead of his name. Another of the ways she had of annoying the hell out of him. "Have you considered the possibility that you may have to destroy this city in order to win?"

"I have. But to do it now would only mean our deaths. In case you've forgotten, we're trapped in here."

"I assure you I have not forgotten, *General!*" she popped back at him.

Jersey, Cooper, Beth, and all the other Rebels in range of the battery-powered mask mikes could do nothing except try to ignore the exchange.

"Fine," Ben told her shortly. "I was wondering if you should be hospitalized to check out that memory loss."

"My memory is just fine!"

They exchanged heated looks through the visors.

"Unfortunately," Ben said, "so is mine."

Jerre narrowed her eyes and glared at him.

The voice of Ben's son came through the speakers. "If you two don't cease this childish quarreling, your visors are going to fog over and someone is going to have to be assigned to lead you around."

Very few people would have dared speak to Ben in that manner. Buddy was one of the few.

"Thank you, Buddy," Jerre said sweetly. "Your capacity for reason must have come from far back in the Raines genes."

Ben's sigh was very audible. "What is your location, *Captain* Raines?"

Buddy laughed. "Standing behind you, Father."

Ben turned his head. His ruggedly handsome son was standing in the doorway, leaning up against the jamb. The boy could move like a damn ghost.

"I was under the impression that I assigned you to Dan's team, boy."

"Oh, you did, Father. And I have completed my assignment for the morning. Colonel Gray sent me back here to remain with you. He felt I would be more useful with you."

"Is that right?"

"Yes, sir."

Ben stood up. "Fine. Up, people. We're going to clear a building."

"Precisely why Colonel Gray sent me back here," Buddy muttered.

"I heard that, boy," Ben growled, heading for the door. He paused at his son's side, looking into Buddy's eyes. It was like looking into a mirror. While Ben was tall and rangy, Buddy was a few inches shorter and stocky. But in the face, their resemblance was startling. "Let's go."

On the sidewalk, crouched behind a rusted and long-abandoned pickup truck, Ben said, "Now the fun begins, people. We flushed them up from their holes, now we get to search the buildings."

The sound of gunfire was much more muted now, as the Rebels found the Night People in the buildings and shot them.

"Everybody hook several CS grenades on your harness," Ben ordered. "Make sure you have your asssigned fire-frags. We'll take that building on the south corner of this block. Let's do it."

They couldn't tell what type of business it had been, but Ben guessed a clothing store. It had been looted. Ben assigned several Rebels to stay on the ground floor, and found the door leading to the lower level. He held up a CS grenade, signaling Jerre and Jersey to follow suit. They pulled the pins and tossed the tear gas into the darkness.

Cursing and coughing drifted up as the gas teared eyes and tore at lungs.

Shapes came lunging up, trying to escape the choking gas. The black-robed figures ran into a hail of gunfire. The coughing and cursing ceased. Bodies lay in heaps on the stairwell. Ben closed the door and pointed a finger at Buddy, then pointed upward. The young man nodded and took the point.

The door which opened onto the second level of the building had been kicked open. Buddy took two CS grenades from his battle harness and tossed them in, one left and one right. He rolled in, staying belly-down on the floor, another Rebel following him, covering Buddy's blind side.

Footsteps echoed in the dusty and gas-filled hall. A door slammed. "Heading for the next level," Buddy said.

"Why?" Ben pondered his own question before ordering people to follow the fleeing creepies. No man voluntarily runs to his death unless he feels he can take some of his enemies with him.

"Buddy?" Ben spoke. "Direct some fire at the door leading up."

Buddy's Thompson spat lead in the hallway. An explosion followed, knocking out windows and bringing plaster and paneling down in the hall.

"Booby-trapped," Ben said. "Now go."

Buddy was back in a moment. "Hallway is blocked, Father. The explosion tore down the stairs. There's no way up."

"We can't leave them up there," Ben said. "Beth, as soon as we're clear, order a tank up here and destroy this building."

"Yes, sir."

Back on the sidewalk, a platoon leader walked up to Ben. "This block is clear, sir."

"Except for this building," Ben told him. "And it will

be shortly." He looked up as an Abrams clanked up and wheeled around in the street, elevating its 105mm cannon. The Rebels moved across the street and Ben signaled for the tank commander to start pounding the building at street level, destroying the foundation and bringing the building down.

Ben and his group walked away from the booming of the cannon.

"Sir," Beth said. "The friendlies living underground are up and have grouped on Broadway and One Sixty-third. About five hundred of them. Men women, and kids."

"I guess the gas did penetrate throughout the system. Are they finally going to join this fight?"

"Scouts report they said they would hold that area where they surfaced."

Ben nodded. "Advise our artillery to mark that area as friendly. What's the word on Khamsin?"

"Getting in position to start shelling us. Spotters report they're working on boats, New Jersey side."

"That will be a night attack. They'll eventually be able to punch through the tunnels, unless we destroy them, and I really don't want to do that. We may be forced to use them."

"General Ike on the line," Beth told him.

"Go, Ike."

"We creamed the hell out of them, Ben. I'd guess that in this area, we cut them down by a full twenty-five to thirty percent."

"About that here," Ben acknowledged. The Abrams had ceased firing. "Tell your people to get ready for shelling from the New Jersey side."

"Ten-four, Eagle. Shark out."

"General Jefferys on the horn, sir."

"Go, Hawk."

"I copied that transmission between you and Shark," Cecil said. "I figure about the same number of dead crud here. We've hurt them, no doubt about that."

After he had spoken with the mercenary, West, and with several other unit commanders, Ben turned to Buddy. "I can't help but wonder what happened to the prisoners being held underground."

Buddy glanced up. "I try not to think about that, Father."

TWO

West, the mercenary, when the battle for survival was imminent, had said, "Now it's all up to God and guns."

Ben was reminded of those words after a Scout had touched his arm and said, "We found one of the creepy hidey-holes, General." Ben noticed the man's face was pale behind the visor of his gas mask. "It's pretty grim, sir."

Ben followed the Scout to the basement of a building. Behind where packing crates had been stacked, a black hole yawned, chipped out of the concrete wall. With a strong flashlight, the Scout led the way. Down they went, into the bowels of the city, following deep tunnels that had been widened over the years. How many years was anyone's guess. Ben would guess well over a hundred years.

"I think we've found a cult stronghold," he said. "These people have been under the city for a long, long time. Many many years before the great war. I think we've flushed something much more hideous than we first realized."

They entered a large, cavelike room, and Ben pulled up short. Naked bodies of men and women were piled in one corner. They had been shot and then great hunks of meat cut from them—at least Ben hoped it had taken place in that order. He had no way of knowing.

He sighed heavily. "Well, perhaps God put them out of

their misery. Now it's up to us, behind the guns."

"What do we do with them, sir?"

"If we leave them here the rats will get them, General," Jersey said.

"Thank you, Jersey. I really needed that."

"You're certainly welcome, sir."

"Get some body bags down here. Carry them out for a proper burial." He glanced at the grotesque sprawl of death. "At least there aren't any kids among them."

"Is that a blessing?" Jerre asked. "Considering where they might be."

"You're right, Jerre," Ben conceded.

She gave him a look of amazement. It seemed to say: What? You're admitting I was actually right about something? Will wonders never cease!

"Let's get out of here," Ben said.

Back on ground level, Ben waved Buddy over to him. "We can't keep pumping tear gas into the ground indefinitely. So I want you to take your team underground with all the explosives you can stagger with. Those tunnels all connect. Follow them and start sealing them off down to . . ." He spread a map out on the sidewalk. ". . . One Hundred and Fifty-fifth Street. I'll have Ike and Cecil send teams in from their sectors and they'll be working north. It's not going to be pleasant, son. And I won't make it an order. If you refuse, I certainly won't blame you."

"Piece of cake, Father. No sweat."

"You be careful down there, boy."

Buddy smiled. "As careful as you are up here, Father."

Ben grimaced. "Git out of here!"

Buddy ran to get his team together and outfitted.

"He acts like he's actually looking forward to going down there," Jerre said, pointing to the sidewalk.

"He probably is," Ben told her. "One thing for certain: it'll be a hell of a lot warmer down there than up here."

Jerre shook her head at the pure cold nerve of the Rebels. They faced battle like thinking Viking Berserkers. They could make jokes when in the most ungodly situations.

Like now, she silently added.

She glanced up at Ben, looking down at her through eyes of love. He abruptly turned away. "Let's go hunt some trouble."

It wasn't hard to find.

Even though the Rebels had cut into the numbers of creepies, the Night Crawlers still outnumbered them badly. Ben and his little team almost walked right into an ambush. Ben had spotted dark movement across the street and shouted his people down just as automatic-weapons fire cut the cold, gas-sharp air. He had grabbed Jerre by the seat of her field pants and brought her down with him.

"Relax, kid," he told her, as the bullets zinged and popped over their heads and slammed into the body of the rusted old limo they lay behind. "I'm not getting amorous."

The pounding of combat drowned out her reply; but Ben was a fair lip-reader.

He laughed at her.

Beth radioed for help, and within a couple of minutes a Duster rounded the corner and began unleashing its deadly 40mm rounds through twin cannons. The alleyway was turned into a tiny corner of Hell.

Dan Gray came running up to admonish the general, a very exasperated expression on his face.

"General Raines!" the Englishman, ex-SAS member, commander of Gray's Scouts, and mother hen to Ben said. "Will you please return to your CP where you may be properly guarded?"

Ben got up and grinned at Dan. "Dan, if you didn't have me to fuss over, what would you do?"

"Relax!" Dan popped back. He shook himself like a big dog. "General, I have been going over some blueprints found by some of my scouts. Are you aware that there are more than sixty-two hundred miles of sewer tunnels under this city?"

"Sixty-two *hundred* miles?"

"Yes, sir. And many of them large enough for a man to walk in."

"More problems," Ben said glumly.

"Yes, sir. There is no way Buddy and the others are going to be able to effectively seal off escape routes. They'll be wasting their time and risking their lives unnecessarily."

"We can't let up on the pressure against the creepies, Dan. I think the only reason Khamsin hasn't shelled us is because the Night People have been forced above ground. But we can't go on pumping tear gas underground indefinitely." Ben was thoughtful for a moment. He turned to Beth. "Have the crews stop pumping, Beth. Let's get out of these damn masks for a time." To Dan: "Let's work out a plan to pump tear gas in a couple of times a day, at staggered intervals. Double the pump stations for more effective coverage. As long as we can keep the creepies guessing, they won't reenter the tunnels. And move the pumps around to different locations every day."

"Good idea, sir. I'll get on it immediately." Dan wheeled about and took off at a run.

"You still want teams under the city, General?" Beth asked.

"Yes. Make certain all teams have plans showing which manhole covers have not been welded closed." Ben took off his mask for a moment. The air was still bitter, but not unbearable.

"Katzman, sir," Beth touched Ben's arm.

Ben took the handset. "Go."

"My people have broken the Libyan's code, General. We can relax some; there won't be any shelling from Khamsin."

"That's good news. I never did like artillery coming in on me." He grinned. "But that doesn't mean we can't shell them, does it?"

Katzman laughed. "Damn sure doesn't, General. You want me to give the orders?"

"Yes. Shell for a few minutes, then have the tanks shift positions. We can make things damned uncomfortable for the Hot Wind and his mini-farts."

"Done, sir." Katzman broke off.

"Get the boys and girls on scramble, Beth."

She took off her backpack and changed frequencies. She would broadcast to Katzman, who would bounce the signal out to all locations. Beth handed the mike to Ben.

"All tank commanders on the west side with range capabilities commence shelling when ready. Let's make it unpleasant for the Hot Fart. All other units continue search and destroy. Let's kill as many crud as we can before the Libyan invades us. Tunnel Rats move out as quickly as possible. Good luck."

Ben checked his Thompson. "Let's go to work, people."

Buddy and his team entered a strange and eerie and almost totally silent world under the city. They entered through the hole found by Dan's Scouts. They passed the spot where the prisoners had been found, dead, and moved on into the dark unknown.

They found an elaborate system of lights throughout, leading one Rebel to comment, "They bled off the city's power. These people have been down here for no telling how many years."

"The filth is unbelievable," Buddy said, scratching at a flea bite. "I am certainly glad Chase gave us booster shots. God alone knows what kind of diseases are leaping all around us."

"Why didn't it kill the creepies?"

"Probably grew immune to it after two or three generations."

The teams placed charges as they went, some to be electronically detonated when they were once more above ground, but most of them booby traps. The charges were large enough to effectively seal off the tunnels, but not large enough to do any structural damage above ground.

They hoped.

They found communal living quarters, and the stench and filth was appalling; the stink rising above the sharp odor of tear gas.

And they found more bodies of naked and mutilated innocents.

"What do we do with them, Buddy?"

Buddy shook his head. "We're too deep to carry them out. Let's stack them close to the explosion points. The debris will cover them. I think that is about the best we can do."

The team moved farther and deeper under the city, finding a makeshift hospital where the creepies had treated their wounded—and then eaten those that died.

"Nice people," Buddy said, disgust in his voice.

They moved on through the stinking dankness, seeing no creepies and planting their charges at what they felt would be stress points.

They followed a dozen or more tunnels leading away from the main tunnel; they all led to a rabbit hole up to the city, usually coming out in some deserted building or basement. At each tunnel offshoot they laid a charge.

Some of the offshoots led to gratings and ventilation openings on subway tubes; others led into sewer systems. It was very plain to Buddy and the others that the Night People had been around a long, long time.

The team lost all track of time in the gloom, broken only by the beams from their flashlights; batteries had to be replaced often. Finally, with only a few batteries left, Buddy started looking for a way out. They pushed open a manhole cover and were startled to find it was almost night, and they were at 172nd Street.

Buddy lifted his mike. "Tunnel Rat One to Eagle."

"Eagle. Where the hell have you been, boy?"

"Exploring. Scramble, Eagle."

On the scramble frequency, Buddy asked, "Do we have any supplies cached around One Seventy-second Street?"

"Ten-four, Rat. Amsterdam and One Seventy-third. It's an oudoor swimming pool. Look around, you'll find something to eat. Have you planted your charges?"

"Yes, sir. I believe they'll be effective in closing off everything north of our location."

"Other teams report good progress, but they're on the

far end of the island. We're going to start pumping in gas now, so clear out."

"I'll bump you when we've settled in for the night."

"Ten-four, Rat. Job well done."

Above ground, Buddy and his team could hear the booming of 155s and 105s as they pounded Khamsin's position in New Jersey.

"When they hit us," Buddy said, jerking his thumb toward New Jersey, "the fun is really going to begin."

"Spookies," a team member said softly. "Down!"

The Rebels hit the sidewalk and belly-crawled behind a line of abandoned cars, many of them parked haphazardly on the sidewalk.

"I make it about twenty of them," Buddy whispered. "Question is, do we give away our position or let them pass?"

That question was answered for him as the creepies began angling across the street, heading straight for the Rebels' position.

"Spread out and let them get closer," Buddy ordered.

The five-person team of Rebels lay on the cold and still-patchy snow-covered sidewalk and waited. Diane lifted her M16 after receiving a minute nod from Buddy. She knew without being told she was to take the first four or five spookies to her left. Harold lifted his M14, set on full rock and roll; he would neutralize those creepies to his right.

"Now!" Buddy whispered, and pulled the trigger back, holding it.

The near-empty street hammered with the sounds of gunfire. The Night People, caught by surprise, for no Rebels were supposed to be in this area, went down like shattered bowling pins.

The Rebels were up and running toward the bloody scene before the sounds of gunfire had died away. They swiftly and brutally finished the wounded and took their weapons and ammo belts, then were running toward the cache of supplies, slipping away into the night just as other creepies began popping out of their hiding places, surprised looks on their hood-shrouded faces.

It was obvious that their kind had been ambushed; but where were the hated Rebels?

The bloody street lay silent before them. The Night People did not approach their dead comrades, not being in any hurry to join them in that long sleep.

Those few moments of hesitation and indecision gave Buddy and his team the time to reach their cache of supplies and settle in quietly.

Pete dug in the food packages and began handing out sealed packets of food.

"What is this stuff?" Judy asked, smelling the contents.

"Be thankful that it's dark and we can't see it," Buddy said, spooning some into his mouth and grimacing. "Now if Chase and his people could only come up with a pill to momentarily kill the taste buds!"

THREE

The tanks spat out their lethal messages all through the cold night, sending out a few rounds and then shifting positions, confusing the gunners of the Hot Wind, preventing them from getting any accurate fix.

And through the night, Ben's Rebels dug in deeper amid the buildings of the great city, cold in winter's harsh grip. It gave them more time to fortify their positions; snipers moved up several stories and set up their silent, lethal positions, waiting.

And the Night People found many of their hidey-holes and escape tunnels. But they only used them once. The first to enter were splattered all over the tunnel walls as the booby traps blew, not only killing those creepies who triggered them, but blocking the entrances and exits under tons of rubble. This was something the crawlers did not expect and were not prepared for. It sent many of them screaming and running for the surface of the city. For generation after generation, the Night People had had almost complete control of the underground; it was their kingdom. Now, all that was changing. They were being forced upward.

And their food supply was running short.

They turned to eating their own dead and any Rebel dead they might find. But those were very few.

For the first time in anyone's memory, the Night People began to sense that they might be defeated.

"Tell the tank crews to cease firing and to stand down," Ben ordered.

All along the Hudson River, the thunder ceased and the cannon smoke faded.

The first gray fingers of dawn had been replaced with bright sunlight, slowly spreading over the great city, and bringing with it an unexpected but very welcome warming. The snow began to melt, and the Rebels could peel out of some of their layers of clothing.

"Spotters stay alert," Ben told Beth. "And give me initial reports of damage to Khamsin's positions."

"Spotters report several enemy tanks burning and several hundred dead along the waterfront." Beth relayed the reports as they came in.

"Khamsin can spare them," Ben said grimly. "We can't."

"You want spotter planes up, sir?"

"No. We want to keep them as our ace in the hole for as long as possible. When they start across the river, we'll bring in the Puffs. But only then."

"General Ike on the horn, sir."

"Go, Shark."

"We sustained no hits during the night, Eagle. Hawk reports the same. West has not been in contact as yet."

"West here," the mercenary's voice crackled. "All quiet in midtown. Too quiet for me. Something's in the works, I'm thinking."

"I'm thinking the same thing. Khamsin's too good a soldier to try to cross the river in daylight. So he's probably leaving any strikes to the creepies. Our underground sensors have reported a lot of big booms down there. The creepies have found their tunnels and holes have been booby-trapped. It's probably put them in a state of panic. I'm hoping we'll have a few hours' respite before they can rally their people for any type of strike. This night is probably going to be a real lulu, though. Advise your people."

"Hawk, here, Eagle."

"Go, Cec."

"Everything is too quiet. But I think I know why. I think the creepies are scared, now. For the first time. We've invaded their underground world and they don't know what to do. We've cut off their rabbit holes and destroyed a lot of tunnels. They're not geared to fighting above ground. But that doesn't mean they won't pull themselves together damn quick."

"You're probably right. We'll use this time to dig in deeper. Hang tough, brother."

"You, too, Ben."

Ben turned to Beth. "Have you been in contact with Buddy?"

"Yes, sir. He and his team are back in the tunnels. Went back in at dawn. They know when we're going to start pumping in gas and to get out at noon."

Ben walked outside to squat down on the sidewalk. His personal escort and several of Dan's Scouts went with him. This time, Dan was making sure the general did not slip off by himself.

Jerre was with the group, but she hung back, staying away from Ben. She felt his eyes on her and turned her head, meeting the steady gaze.

"What are you thinking, General?"

Ben's jaws clenched, but that was the only sign of his temper. He had told her a hundred times since she walked back into his life to call him Ben. But she would do that only when they were alone—something that Ben tried to avoid whenever possible.

"I'm thinking about destroying this city," Ben said flatly.

All eyes turned toward him.

They stared at each other. Neither Ben nor Jerre would blink. "I thought you were opposed to that?" she finally said.

"I am. It would be only as a last resort, and only when

Khamsin and his men get on the island."

"How would we get off?"

"I don't know."

She blinked. "Do keep me informed."

Ben stood up. "You'll know no earlier than when the rest of the troops are informed." He walked away.

"One for the general," Jersey muttered, and hurried to join him.

"The soap operas must have been fun," Beth said, picking up and slinging her backpack radio. "I just remember them. But they couldn't have been any more fun than this."

"I never cared for them," Jerre said tightly.

"How much time do we have?" Judy asked, her voice metallic through the built-in gas-mask speaker.

"What happened to your watch?" Buddy asked. "You had it last night."

"I don't know. When I woke up this morning, I couldn't find it. But I'd swear I didn't take it off my wrist."

Buddy held up the patrol. The last time he'd checked they were at 164th Street, and that had not been long ago. "Those small footprints we saw this morning. The ones we dismissed as not being human but nature-made. Do you think . . . ?"

"They'd have to be very small kids, Buddy," Pete said. "And where would they come from?"

"Runaways from the breeding farms, probably," Diane answered.

"How would they survive?" Harold asked. "The canned foods here in the city have lost any nutritional value. And there are no cats or dogs in this city."

"Trapping rats," Buddy replied. "Stealing from the gardens of those around the Central Park area."

"Eating *rats!*" Diane was horrified.

"Very high in protein, so I'm told," Buddy said.

"Gross!" Judy said.

"Let's plant our charges and get the hell out of here,"

Buddy said, after thinking for a moment. "I want to go back and more closely inspect those tracks we found this morning."

"And then?" Pete asked.

"We notify the general."

They stayed in the tunnels, working their way back north beneath the city, in this strange, silent, extremely odious world that was once the kingdom of the Night People. They surfaced just as the pumps once more began pouring in the gas, seeing daylight at 169th Street, coming out through a hole in the lower part of a building.

They made their way cautiously up to 173rd, and entered into the area where they had slept the night before. The tracks were still there, and looking around, they found more. At first glance, they did not look like tracks, rather more like smudges on the concrete and floors.

Buddy got down on his hands and knees and slowly and carefully inspected the trails, finally finding what he'd been seeking: tiny pieces of cloth and thread.

He stood up. "Many of them have no shoes," he announced. "They're wrapping their feet in rags against the cold."

"Dear God!" Diane muttered.

"Yes. Assuming that they have several layers on their feet, this one," he pointed to a small track, "would be no more than three or four years old." He held out his hand to Pete. "Give me your radio." He changed frequencies and lifted the handset. "Tunnel Rat to Eagle on scramble."

"Give me a second to round him up, Rat. He's out on the street. I'll patch you through."

"Go, Rat," Ben said.

Buddy brought him up to date. He could hear Ben's sigh very clearly. "You're going to need some help searching that area for the kids."

"Send the hippie, Father."

"Thermopolis?"

"Yes."

"May I ask why?"

"Because I think the children might come to someone

like him before they'd come to us. Ask him if he'd dress as he did when he first joined us."

"Ten-four, boy. They'll be on their way in a few minutes."

Emil Hite, the con artist who had become almost a fixture in Ben's life over the years, had left Louisiana with his flock of followers to aid Ben in his New York fight. Along the way, they had run into a commune of hippies, headed by a man called Thermopolis. The hippies had agreed that it was better to join Ben and the Rebels than spend the rest of their lives running from the cannibalistic Night People. Slowly, and reluctantly, Thermopolis had found himself liking Ben Raines, personally, if not entirely what he stood for.

"Of course, we'll go," Thermopolis told Ben. "And Buddy is right: the kids will probably come to us much quicker if we're not dressed in uniforms. I'll take a few of my own people with me to aid in the search."

"Take as many as you need."

Dan walked to Ben's side. "If there are children running wild in this city, General, that casts a very different light on the matter."

"Doesn't it, though?"

The city was strangely silent as the small convoy made its way to Buddy's location. "They'll hit us hard tonight," the Rebel driver said. "We've got just about four and a half hours of daylight left. We've got to be back in position by nightfall. General's orders, people."

Thermopolis muttered under his breath and grimaced. His wife, Rosebud, caught the look and laughed at him. Her husband managed a very thin smile. Sort of like a razor blade's edge.

"They lead off in that direction," Buddy told him, pointing. "We have not tried to follow them."

Thermopolis hesitated for a moment, then laid his M16 aside. Rosebud, Santo, Wenceslaus, and the others in his group did the same. "We'll carry sidearms only," he told them. "We won't appear so menacing to the children. Let's go."

They moved out cautiously, leaving the swimming-pool area and following the hard-to-spot footprints of the kids in the fast-disappearing spots of snow. Thermopolis led the group, moving swiftly but warily. The footprints appeared again in an alley opening up on Audubon. Thermopolis waved the group down at the mouth of the alley and with them crouched behind him, studied the seemingly empty buildings across the street.

"The footprints lead straight into that building," Rosebud pointed out.

"Yes. But crossing that street is going to be dangerous. We might be watched by creepies right this minute."

Rosebud gave him a look guaranteed to curl his toenails, which it came very close to doing. Thermopolis knew it very well. "And those children over there are cold and hungry and frightened. Either you lead us over there, or I will."

"Now, Rosebud."

"Get out of the damn way!"

Thermopolis stood up. "Shall we go find the children, dear?"

"That's the general idea . . . dear."

Muttering under his breath, Thermopolis darted across the street, the others close behind him, and entered a building, noticing that the front door had been used recently. The imprint of a very small and very dirty hand was on the lock stile.

"My heart goes out to these children," Swallow said, looking at her husband.

"My heart is thumping so hard I can hear it!" Santo told her.

"Be quiet," Thermopolis told them. "We have nothing to fear from small children." I hope, he silently added. He moved toward a closed door and slowly pushed it open and stepped inside, noticing the cold ashes of a dead fire in one corner of the barren room.

Thermopolis paused as his eyes picked up on the skeleton of a rat. It had been picked clean. After being cooked he hoped. He pointed it out to the others.

Rosebud shook her head in disgust and sorrow. "We'll take the children to raise as our own, of course."

"Oh, of course," Thermopolis said dryly. "That's what I had in mind, too."

His wife's eyes spoke silent volumes, directed at him.

Overheard, on the second level, a small scurrying sound was heard.

"Too big for rats," Wenceslaus said, looking at his old lady.

"You hope," Zelotes told him.

Thermopolis led the way up the old stairs. Now the footprints were very clear in the dust. He pushed open the first door he came to.

A small girl, no more than six or seven, sat on the floor, looking at him. She also had a very large pistol pointing at him, the hammer cocked back. She held the pistol in both hands.

"Hello, dear." Thermopolis smiled at her.

"I'll blow your fuckin' head off!" she told him.

FOUR

Buddy heard the approaching vehicles pull up and stop and was only mildly surprised to see his father stroll nonchalantly up to his position.

"You just will not stay in a secure zone, will you, Father?"

"Of course not. The troops would be disappointed if I did. Thermopolis?"

"The last I saw of them they were entering that alley." Buddy pointed.

Ben squatted down and rolled a cigarette while his son looked on, a very disapproving look in his eyes. "I read a very good pamphlet about smoking, Father. Written by a man called Koop. Whoever he is, or was. You should cease the use of those things."

"Right." Ben licked the tube closed and fired up. "Humor me. You can't teach an old dog new tricks."

"That, too, is a misnomer. I once read a report on dog training. It stated that . . ."

"Boy . . . !" Ben warned.

Buddy shut up and watched his father smoke his cigarette.

Ben scratched at the uncomfortable body armor under his shirt and waited.

The girl had lowered the hammer, but kept the muzzle pointed dead at Thermopolis.

"My name is Thermopolis."

"That's a stupid name," the child told him.

Rosebud had counted a dozen kids in the room, none of them older than seven or eight, and all of them dressed in rags. None of them wore shoes; only dirty strips of cloth wrapped around their feet.

"Well, I suppose so . . . if you're not used to hearing it," Thermopolis conceded. "What's your name?"

"Kate. Are you with the army that is fighting the human-eaters?"

"Yes."

"Is the god, Ben Raines, really here in the city?"

Thermopolis started to tell the child that Ben Raines was not a god. He bit back the words.

"Did you send all that pukey-smelling stuff into the air?"

"I helped, yes." He slowly squatted down on the dirty floor, facing the child. "You can put the gun away. I won't harm you."

"You say. But you might lie."

"That's true. But there comes a time when you have to trust somebody. I tell you what . . ." And it hurt him to say it, but he knew that just the name carried a lot of weight. ". . . I'll take you to meet Ben Raines."

"You lie!"

"No, child," Thermopolis said gently. "I speak the truth."

Santo's walkie-talkie crackled. He lifted the radio and spoke briefly, then looked at Thermopolis. "General Raines is coming over here."

The kids stirred uneasily.

"Just take it easy," Thermopolis told them. "Pretty soon you'll all have clean clothes and hot food and shoes for your feet. And you'll be safe."

"We'll believe that when Ben Raines says it," Kate told him.

Boots sounded on the ground-level floor, then slowly climbed the steps. The kids drew back, huddling together in fear.

Ben stood in the doorway, tall, his face hawklike, his

eyes unreadable. He watched as Kate laid the big pistol on the floor. Ben held out his hand.

"Come, children. Let's go where it's safe and warm and get you something to eat." He smiled and his whole face changed. The kids went to him, crowding around. "You children ride with Thermopolis and Rosebud. I'll meet with you later on today and you can tell me your stories."

"You won't be far away, will you?" Kate asked.

"No. I won't be far away," Ben assured her.

After the children had gone, Thermopolis paused in the room; only he and Ben remained. "Is it always that way with you and kids?"

"Usually."

"Why? You're armed to the teeth and half the time you look like you could bite the heads off nails."

"Perhaps it's because I represent something they have never known but always wanted. Or knew some of it and yearn for more."

"Safety?"

"That's part of it."

"And so you and your people will take them to raise, and they'll grow up with the Rebel dogma burned into their brains and be good little soldiers?"

"Most of them, yes. Is that so wrong?"

Thermopolis sighed. "I don't know. I suppose not. What is it with you, Ben Raines? What is this compulsion with law and order and rules and regulations?"

"I didn't ask for this job, Thermopolis. I think destiny forced it on me."

"Disgusting!" Chase came out of the examining room, ripping off his rubber gloves and dropping them into a waste can. He walked up to Ben, leaning against a wall. "Those children have all been sexually molested. Most of them by the men under the command of this Monte person."

Ben waited, knowing the doctor was not yet through.

Chase ranted and waved his arms and cussed and kicked

the waste can before he wound down.

Ben began rolling a cigarette.

"No smoking in my damn hospital, Raines!"

Ben tossed the makings into the waste can. "Venereal diseases?"

"Some of them. But they're the treatable kind."

"AIDS?"

"We're testing them. But I don't think so. If this . . . catastrophe did any good at all, it seems to be the halt of AIDS. I've seen very few cases of it over the past ten years."

"Why?"

"Why did it stop? Hell, I don't know! I don't even know why it began. The kids are in a surprisingly good mental state, however—considering what they've been through. And what they're going to have to go through before, or if, we get out of this mess."

"We'll get out." Once again the plan he had discussed with no one entered Ben's head. He did not want to even think about it, much less put it into play, but it might be the only way out for them.

Ben became conscious of Chase talking to him.

". . . the hell is wrong with you, Ben? You have Jerre on the brain again?"

Ben smiled. "No. For once, no. Can I see the kids?"

"Some of them. Sure. In case you wondered, and I'm sure you did, why, in a city with several million pairs of shoes for the taking, the kids chose to wrap their feet in rags, they seldom got out of that two- or three-block area. They said the Night People never seemed to come in there."

"I wonder why?"

"I don't know, and neither did the kids. They did say it was a place where they had to be very careful with fire."

"Now that is interesting," Ben said softly. "That is very interesting."

Ben met with the kids, joked with them, and managed to coax some smiles from them. By the time he left the hospital, he had gained some valuable knowledge about certain areas of the city. He checked the sky. Dark in about two hours. He told Beth to get his commanders up to his CP—right now. At his CP, the meeting with his commanders was closed, the doors shut and the men and Tina alone. And that was not something that General Ben Raines did very often.

"We've got to hold the Libyan in New Jersey, people. I want everything that can toss shells the distance on the waterfront, doing so. Dan, of us all, you have the finest tastes in art, music, so forth . . ."

"Thank you, General." The Englishman smiled. "It's good to know that my talents in the finer things are appreciated."

Ike groaned and stuck the needle to his friend. "Big bore is what you are."

Dan ignored him.

"West, you run a close second to Dan." He smiled at the mercenary. "As surprising as that might seem to some people." He cut his eyes to Thermopolis, and the big rough-looking hippie smiled.

"Colonel West, you will take everything from Central Park west to the river. Dan, you'll take it from the park east to the waterfront. Both of you all the way down to Battery Park. I'll take it from a Hundred Twenty-fifth Street north. Our main objective is to kill creepies. Our secondary mission to gather up everything that might be remotely construed as art—paintings, sculpture, whatever—and master tapes or discs of music. Strip the libraries of books. Gather it all and bring it up here for storage."

"Does that include rock-and-roll and hillbilly music, General?" Dan asked, a twinkle in his eyes, knowing he was stepping on Ike's toes. And, out of the corner of his eye, he watched Thermopolis stir and frown. Dan hid his smile.

"That includes everything, Dan," Ben said with a straight face, picking up on the Englishman's joke. "Whether you like it or not, it's still somebody's idea of expression."

Ike stuck his tongue out at Dan, and the room exploded in laughter. And again, Thermopolis marveled at the seemingly undefeatable morale of the Rebels. Facing thousands of the enemy, and they could still joke. And Ben Raines . . . damn the man! He was a study in contradiction. He could talk of killing with one breath and in the other speak of saving and preserving art and literature. Even rock-and-roll music, and Thermopolis knew the man hated that type of expression. *Talk about a walking contradiction, Kris—you should see this man.*

"What's the drill, Ben?" Cecil asked. "What are you up to this time?"

Ben cut his eyes to the black general. He hesitated, then shook his head. This decision would be his alone to make. And if he chose to carry it out, history—if indeed it was ever to be written—would either applaud him or condemn him. But it would be on his shoulders, and his shoulders alone.

"Get started at dawn tomorrow," Ben told them. "I'm going to make an early run downtown. I've been delaying it, but it's time. Get back to your positions and prepare to get hit hard tonight. That's it, people."

"What is the bastard doing?" a commander questioned Khamsin, as the shells exploded around them in New Jersey.

"Keeping us out of the city," Khamsin told the man.

"Damn the savages in the city!" another commander spoke his mind. "Let's shell the city and have done with it."

Khamsin shook his head. "We do that, and those abominations would strike a deal with Raines and turn on us." He cut his eyes to the woman, Sister Voleta. "Tell me one weakness of Ben Raines. Anything we could use against him."

"He has none," the woman replied. "He has ice in his veins."

"He has one," Ashley spoke. "And I would not know of that had it not been for Big Louie's obsession with the man."

Khamsin looked at the man. "Speak."

"A woman. Jerre Hunter."

"She is in the city with him?"

"Yes, I believe so."

"And if we took the woman . . . ?" Khamsin questioned.

"I really don't know, General. I don't know what he would do. I know what he wouldn't do: he would not jeopardize a mission to save her life. But he would track the man who harmed her through Hell. And that man would spend days begging to die."

Monte shuddered. He was beginning to wish he had never heard of Ben Raines. Wished he had stayed the hell up in Canada, far, far away from Ben Raines. The bastard just wasn't human. Or so it seemed to Monte.

Khamsin was looking at him. "Monte. You will take some people into the city, cross over this night in boats, and seize this woman. And that is not a request."

"Right," Monte managed to say.

"Leave now, and make ready."

A shell crashed close to the Libyan's CP. Khamsin clenched his fists and silently rained curses down on Ben's head. He had the man trapped, and because of an unholy alliance with cannibals could not move.

But maybe if the woman could be taken . . . ?

Maybe.

FIVE

Ben sat behind his desk, his boots propped up, deep in thought. If he were in the Libyan's shoes, what would he do?

Find a weak spot and strike, of course.

And what was Ben's weak spot? He couldn't think of any.

Then he thought of one.

He yelled for Beth. She stuck her head in the doorway. "Sir?"

"Get Jerre in here right now, Beth."

"Yes, sir."

"You want me to do what?" Jerre asked, her eyes cold.

"From now on, you're my personal aide. You do not leave my side for any reason. Is that clear?"

"I don't want to be your personal aide, and I am not going to be your personal aide!" she fired back at him.

"Miss Hunter," Ben said, leaning back in his chair, "I have reached the point in my life where I don't give a good goddamn what you want." That was a lie, but Ben hoped he could pull it off and convince her it was truth. He watched her eyes turn even more icy. "I am giving you a direct order and you will, by God, obey it. Is that understood, Miss Hunter?"

She straightened up and glared at him. "Yes, sir, General Raines!"

"Thank you. That will be all. Have someone go to your

quarters and bring your gear over here. You . . ."

"I am perfectly capable of packing my own gear, General."

"Do not interrupt me when I am speaking, Miss Hunter!" Ben yelled at her. "I said: Have someone pack your gear and bring it over here. You will sleep in *that* room!" He pointed to the anteroom. "Dismissed!"

She whirled around and marched from the office, pausing at the door. "Does the general wish the office door closed?"

"No, the general does not."

"I'll get your gear," Jersey told her. "Cooper will get you a cot. Welcome aboard—again."

"Thanks." Jerre watched Jersey and Cooper leave the room, calmed down a bit and looked at Beth. "Question is: Why is he doing it?"

Beth shrugged. "I don't question the general. He's got his reasons."

Ben rose from his desk and closed the door to his office. Jerre glared at the door and mouthed a very ugly word.

"He was a strange and mysterious man when I first met him," Jerre said. "Now he's changed to just plain damn weird!"

"Don't bet on that," Beth told her. "There's a reason for everything he does. Whether or not you'll ever know the reason is up for grabs."

Jerre sat down in a chair, close to Beth. "When this is over, Beth, what do you intend to do?"

The question surprised her. She was thoughtful for a moment. "Probably go back to Illinois, to Lev. I've spoken with the general about it." She rose, poured them coffee, and returned to her chair.

"Do you love him?"

"I'm comfortable with him. I like him, and he loves me."

"Is that enough?"

"It is for me. There is an old proverb that reads: A man should always marry a woman he loves, and a woman should always marry a man she likes. If you think about it, it makes a lot of sense."

"Is that a Jewish proverb?"

The dark-haired beauty laughed. "No, I think it's Arabic!"

The Night People did not launched a full-scale attack that night. They chose instead to limit themselves to a hit-and-run operation, citywide, and that tied up the Rebels and kept them to high alert until dawn, with neither side taking many casualties.

At dawn, the creepies withdrew and the Rebels rested. Ben and the others began their search for treasure.

And that was not as easy as it sounded, for none knew what awaited them inside the buildings of the city, or what might be booby-trapped. It was slow going.

Jerre accompanied Ben, but neither of them spoke unless it was absolutely necessary, and that did not make for a very pleasant atmosphere for the other Rebels.

It soon became apparent that the Rebels had exacted a much heavier toll on the Night People than any of them imagined. And it also brought to bear just how desperate the Night People had become: for they had turned to eating their own.

By midmorning, very few of the Rebels had encountered any creepies, and the germ of worry in Ben's mind had changed into a full-grown blister. He radioed his commanders.

"What's up, people? I'm open for suggestions."

"The only thing I can figure out, Ben," Ike said, "is that they're trying to bug out. If they can get clear of Manhattan, Khamsin will pound us to pieces with his artillery."

"They can't get out," Ben said flatly. "We've got all avenues of escape blocked. So to my mind, that means they've shifted locations, en masse, and Khamsin will start hammering us one location at a time. If that's the case, it will have to be done on a systematic basis. Either south to north or north to south; it wouldn't work any other way.

He can't work from the middle to split us up; we're already split up and he knows it."

Ben studied a map of Manhattan. "Have all personnel in the south end of the island move up half a dozen blocks. All troops in the north move down a half dozen blocks. Move it, right now!"

Khamsin started his barrage at noon, throwing everything he had at the island. And Ben had pegged it right on the money.

The north and south ends of the island began to resemble Berlin at the close of the Second World War as heavy artillery knocked huge holes into buildings and started dozens of small fires.

But the Rebels sustained no serious injuries from the shelling. It's extremely difficult to hit something that isn't there.

"Message from the Night People, sir," an aide spoke to Khamsin. "They said Raines shifted his troops around. Our shelling is destroying the city but killing no Rebels."

Khamsin lost his temper and began pounding his fists on a table, screaming and cursing Ben Raines. "The man is a *devil!*" he raged. "What manner of beast is this person? How can he read my mind?"

"Sir," a field commander said. "If I may be permitted to speak my mind?"

"Speak!"

"Would it not be in our best interest to unite with General Raines against the common enemy?"

"Never!" Khamsin screamed. He ordered the field commander shot, then as he calmed, rescinded the death sentence. He ordered the shelling stopped and gave the suggestion some thought. "Perhaps," he mused aloud, "that would be in our best interest. The Night People are surely a scourge upon the earth."

"And," it was offered, "it would be a much easier way to get on the island. Once there, we could easily crush the Flesh-Eaters and then kill Ben Raines. Without Ben

Raines, his army would fall apart."

"Has Monte left yet?"

"Of course not. He says he is going this night."

"Cowardly fool! Tell him to stand down until I compose a message to Ben Raines and it is delivered. Now leave me alone. I want this message to be perfectly correct."

"Send teams in to assess the damage," Ben ordered. "And continue the searching for art and literature and music."

West had driven up to Ben's temporary position during the shelling. "Brilliant move, General. You have my compliments and my respect."

"Thank you, West. But it was just a guess on my part, that's all."

"Accurate guessing has won more battles than brilliant mental maneuvering." He smiled. "But I think you are more than aware of that."

"How'd the treasure-hunting go this morning?"

"Very well, I would say. I found a trove of priceless art. Renoir, Monet, Pissarro, Kiprensky, a few by Bower. I found a great deal of sculpture, most of them small bronzes from the Italian Renaissance period. Quite lovely." He glanced at Ben. "Did you get a chance to visit your old publishing house?"

"How did you know I was going to do that?"

"Just a guess. I would, if I had been a popular writer."

Dan walked up. "Dan, while you and the rest of the people are out and about gathering up this and that, I would like for you to gather up something else, as well."

"Certainly, General. And what would that be?"

Ben smiled. "Blow the bank vaults and gather up all the gold in this city."

Jerre sat back in Ben's temporary CP, just off Mitchell Square, and looked at the man. She still could not figure out why he had been so adamant about her becoming his personal aide. Surely he knew by now that she did not love him.

Or did she?

That was a question she had asked herself many times over the years. And she always came up with the same answer: Yes, she did. Sort of. In a way. But she respected him more than loved him. She guessed she did, anyway. Sometimes she was sure that she hated him. But those feelings had always passed as quickly as they'd come.

Was Ben trying to work his way into her heart?

No. She knew him better than that. Even over the long years, he had never once told her that he loved her. But she knew he did. He'd never even told her that he liked her.

And maybe he didn't. It was certainly possible to love someone and not like them.

Ben turned and looked at her, just as quickly averting his eyes.

She shook her head. Strange man, Ben Raines.

Ben walked out into Mitchell Square just as a runner approached him. "We're picking up signal flashers from New Jersey, General. General Ike read them. Khamsin wants to meet with you."

Ben did not change expression. "Does he now? That's interesting. I wonder why he didn't radio. It would have been much easier." He smiled at the runner. "Unless, of course, he's got a double-cross planned against the creepies."

"You trust him, General?"

"Hell, no!"

After the runner had left, Ben bumped Ike on scramble. "What do you make of it, Ike?"

"No good, that's for sure."

"You got your man standing by on ship?"

"Ten-four."

"Tell him I'll meet with him. But he's got to come to me."

"I will relay the message."

In less than five minutes, Ike was back on the horn.

"Khamsin says you'll have to come to him, Ben."

"Tell him to shove it up his ass."

Ike laughed. "With pleasure!"

Ike was back with the message in less time than before. "He says that's all right with him. Where do you want to meet?"

"Tell him I'll get back with him at dawn tomorrow. Then you get up here. Let's meet."

"He's too eager, people," Ben told the gathering. "I got a hunch he wants to talk peace while his army moves all over us. Or, perhaps he realizes that the Night People have to be destroyed before they can gain a firmer hold. Then when that's done he'll turn on us."

"I'd opt for the latter," Cecil said.

The others agreed.

"So," Ben said with a smile, "I think I'll just tell the Hot Wind to come on over. We can sure use his help in this war."

Nearly all of them were looking at Ben as if they were sure he had lost his mind. All except General Striganov. He was sitting with a faint smile on his face.

"Are you serious, Dad?" Tina asked.

"Why, of course. War, like politics, makes for strange bedfellows."

Then he started laughing while the rest of his people looked at him as if he'd lost his mind.

SIX

"I want Doctor Nate Lindgren and his PSE machine set up very close to us," Ben instructed. "Have the microphone well-concealed and have him draw up a list of questions he wants me to ask Khamsin. Of course, Khamsin will be lying when he says he wants to be our ally—that goes without saying—but I want to be as close to one hundred percent certain as I can get."

Ben had still not explained his plan to any of his commanders, and they were all, with the exception of General Striganov, more than a bit irritated over Ben's sudden trust of the Libyan.

Pulling Ben off to one side, Ike said, "What the hell is going on, Ben? You know as well as me that damned terrorist is about as trustworthy as a cottonmouth."

"Relax, Ike," Ben assured him. "Just take it easy. I know what I'm doing."

But Ike didn't relax, and wasn't all that convinced that Ben hadn't gone round the bend. He walked away, shaking his head and muttering.

Ben's daughter came to him. "Dad. You can't make any deals with Khamsin. That man and his people have raped and tortured and murdered halfway around the world. He's pure filth."

"All that is true," Ben conceded.

"And you're still going to meet with him and talk about joining forces?"

"I am."

Tina whirled around and stalked away, her back stiff with anger.

"Ben," Cecil said, "if you let that Libyan get his army on this island, we're finished. This isn't like you at all."

But Ben would only pat his friend on the shoulder and smile. "Trust me, Cec. I know what I'm doing."

The commanders, with the exception of General Striganov, went to see Doctor Chase.

"He's suffering from strain," Ike told the doctor. "That's got to be the reason for all this. The way he laughed back yonder chilled me."

"Take two aspirin, have some chicken soup and call me in the morning," the crusty old doctor told Ike. "Ben knows what he's doing, people."

"Well, maybe you'd care to tell us exactly what he *is* doing?" Dan asked.

"I don't know," the doctor admitted. "I don't concern myself with matters outside this hospital. Relax, people. You know how secretive Ben can be. Now get out of here. I have work to do."

They got, but they were not happy. All they could do now was wait, with all of them wondering if General Ben Raines had slipped an oar.

"The meeting is set for just after dark tonight," the signalman told Ben. "Khamsin will cross over by boat and meet you in Lafayette Plaza."

Ben thanked him and turned to Georgi Striganov. "Have your people secure some rooms there, Georgi. You know the drill."

"Consider it done," the Russian told him. He didn't know exactly what Ben had in mind, only that he trusted the general to do something completely off the wall and totally unexpected. Georgi knew that first-hand. During the years they had battled each other, Ben Raines had boxed him around every time they'd met on the field of battle.

The Russian knew that whatever the Libyan terrorist was desirous of from Ben Raines, it would not be what he was expecting.

Tina and Buddy stayed close to their father, in the hopes he would reveal his plan to them. But he did not.

The Night People launched attacks during the night. But the Rebels were dug in so deeply, their positions so well-fortified, all the creepies managed to accomplish was the death of more of their people. Even though the Night People still outnumbered the Rebels, they could not put them to rout.

With low curses, the night crawlers melted away with a few bloody attacks.

"Coming across," a Rebel with night glasses informed Ben. "They'll be ashore in a couple of minutes."

"I'll be in the building," Ben told him. "Please escort the Hot Wind to me."

"Yes, sir."

Ben checked the mike. "Can you hear me, Nate?"

"Loud and clear, General," the doctor manning the PSE equipment called from the room above them.

Ben sat down at the table and waited. The Libyan terrorist came into the room all smiles and good cheer. He held out his hand as Ben stood up.

"My dear General Raines! At last we meet. I am honored, sir."

Ben forced a smile on his face and shook the man's hand, sizing him up. He was stocky and powerful, and Ben guessed his age in the mid-forty range. Twenty years back, Ben recalled, this man had been one of the most feared terrorists in all the world. Hundreds of men, women, and children had died because of the bombs he had masterminded and planted around the world. Marines had been brutally massacred in Lebanon because of this man. American hostages had been tortured and starved and killed at this man's orders.

Ben resisted an impulse to tear the bastard's arm out of the socket and beat him to death with it.

"How good to see you, General Khamsin. Please, sit

down. I have tea."

"Good, good!" The Libyan smiled, but the humor did not reach his dark eyes.

The tea poured and sugared, the men stared at each other across the table. Ben's personal bodyguards stood behind him, facing the Hot Wind's bodyguards. There was no love lost in the exchange of glances between the two heavily armed groups.

Ben watched as the Libyan's eyes flicked toward Jerre. Ben had guessed accurately: Jerre was to have been a target. Probably still was. Thanks, probably, to Ashley. That turncoat son of a bitch was becoming as hard to kill as Sam Hartline had been.

Khamsin opened the dance. "I made a regrettable decision in agreeing to align my forces with the Night People, General Raines. I did not realize how dangerous they were."

That lie probably sent the graph out of control on Nate's PSE equipment.

"They must be stopped," Ben said.

"Yes. For the good of the entire world."

"And once that is done, we can make peace with each other and coexist?"

"But of course, General Raines! I am so weary of fighting. I am, after all, nothing more than a farmer. It is my desire to till the rich soil of South Carolina and live in peace."

"I can certainly relate to that," Ben said, trying hard to keep the sarcasm out of his voice. "I, too, want nothing more than a section of land to farm."

Tina almost choked on that.

Ben Raines wanted to farm about as much as a raccoon could fly a 747.

She didn't know what her dad was up to, but she certainly knew both men were lying through their teeth.

"It is agreed then, that we must join forces to defeat the Night People?" Khamsin said.

"Yes. All we need to work out is where your people will land and what sections of the city you will occupy."

Khamsin waved his hand. "Minor details, my dear general. We can work that out in five minutes."

It was agreed that Khamsin's men would cross over the next night, by boat, landing at the docks between 72nd and 86th streets. At dawn, they would strike at the Night People, with Khamsin's army controlling the middle of the city.

And cutting my people in two, Ben noted. But he agreed with a smile and a handshake. Ben made a note to wash his hands with the strongest soap he could find once this odious meeting was concluded.

"So we are in agreement, General Raines?"

"Oh, yes, General Khamsin. Complete agreement." Ben lifted his teacup in a toast.

Khamsin smiled and clinked cups.

"To a great victory, General Raines!"

"I'm counting on it, General Khamsin. You don't know how much."

Ben forced himself to be cordial with the Libyan for a few minutes more. By that time, Ben noticed the Libyan had begun to sweat just a bit and his voice held a forced note, indicating that he, too, was wearying of the sham.

Both men rose as one, shook hands, and the Libyan slipped back into the night. Ben sat for a time, drumming his fingers on the tabletop. When Doctor Lindgren came into the room, Ben stood up and waved him into another room and closed the door.

"Now what the hell!" Tina muttered, looking at Dan.

But the Englishman was just as baffled as she was. "I don't know. This is not like the General. Not at all. He's usually very open with all of us. Something is definitely up."

"There wasn't a truthful note in any of that man's statements," Nate said. "Or yours either," he added with a smile.

"Well, you knew I'd be lying."

"And I don't know what's going on, either."

"Neither does anybody else. Deliberately so. Trust me and keep all of this under your hat. Thanks a lot, Nate."

Ben turned and walked out of the room, motioning his people to follow him.

"You ready to tell me what's up, Dad?" Tina asked.

"Nope," Ben said with a smile.

Tina ground her teeth together in frustration.

Ben grinned, even with his back to her knowing what she was doing. "Careful, kid. It took me a couple of years back in the Tri-States to get your teeth fixed up. With you kicking and squalling and howling with every trip to the dentist."

She screwed up her face and stuck out her tongue at his back.

"And stop making ugly faces and sticking your tongue out at me," Ben said, without turning around. "What if your face froze like that?"

She could not help but laugh. It was the same thing he'd told her as a little girl.

The rest of the Rebels with Ben had to laugh, and to the newer members, it further heightened Ben's already overblown mystique. The man had to have powers beyond a mortal person's comprehension. How else could he know what was going on behind him without even turning around? Of course, those who had been adults before the Great War, and had some experience with kids, knew perfectly well how Ben did it. But they let the younger ones have their fantasies; it helped keep discipline problems to a minimum.

"Heads up tonight, people," Ben said, just before turning in. "The creepy crawlies might decide to come out in force."

"Damn the man!" Dan said, as Ben closed the door behind him. "What in the world is going on?"

"I guess he'll let us in on it in the morning," Tina said. "I can't believe he's actually going to link up with that terrorist."

"I guess we'll know in the morning."

But Ben was as silent on the subject the following

morning as he had been the night before. He had breakfast with Georgi, Tina, Buddy, and Dan, and never brought the subject up. He excused himself from the table and walked back to his office, Jerre and Jersey, Beth and Cooper going with him.

"General," Tina looked at the Russian. "What's going on?"

"Your father has not taken me into his confidence, Captain. But I can assure you that he is doing what he thinks is best for all concerned . . . on the side of freedom, that is."

"You and my father were once bitter enemies, General Striganov. Now you are allies, fighting together. You don't think he believes Khamsin is ready to bury the hatchet, do you?"

"Only in Ben's back, girl."

"Then . . . ?" She spread her hands in a gesture of helplessness.

"You're far too young to remember the days of Qaddafi, Khomeini, Abu Nidal, and people of that ilk. Khamsin is one of them. Nothing will appease him except blood and more blood. And even if, God forbid, he is ever victorious, he still will not be satisfied until he has conquered what is left of this shattered world."

Dan and Buddy were listening, sitting quietly.

"I have an idea what your father is going to do. He and I think a great deal alike in many subjects. I say this with all the respect in the world for Ben Raines. I think he is the greatest soldier who ever lived."

SEVEN

Ben took a contingent of Rebels and disappeared that morning, heading back to the area where the children had been found. He prowled the area, noticing the small cracks in the sidewalks and the street—cracks that had blackened burn marks. He found a board and wrapped a rag around one end of it, lit the rag and held it high over one crack. Fire seemed to materialize about five feet over the crack in the street. It flared briefly, then was gone. Ben smiled and extinguished the burning rag.

"What is that, General?" Jersey asked.

"Methane. It's often found in marshes and mines. It's caused by the decomposition of vegetable matter—among other things."

"You think it's all over the underground tunnels?"

"Probably. At least there'll be enough pockets to aid in what I might plan to do."

"Which is?" he was asked.

Ben chose not to reply.

"How come the creepies haven't blown themselves up?" Jersey asked.

"For one thing, many of them don't cook the . . . meat they eat. And since the temperature remains fairly constant in the tunnels, heating by fire is probably rare. And, I suspect, they've found the heavier concentrations and avoid them."

"Just what do you plan on doing with this methane, General?" Jerre asked.

Ben looked at her and smiled. "I might decide to have a pig roast, Jerre."

"Of course," she said sarcastically. "I should have guessed that." She turned away, muttering about smart-assed generals.

Ben chuckled and waved the group back to the vehicles. He always felt better after he got one over on Jerre. It was such a rare experience.

He ordered the short convoy to Katzman's communications center and met in private with Katzman, sending out coded and scrambled messages.

The messages sent, with only Katzman and Ben knowing the contents—and the people on the other end—Ben ordered the convoy down to publisher's row.

"Ben, god*damn* it!" Cecil's voice roared out of the speaker. "That area has never been cleared. It hasn't even been checked!"

"So I'll check it out," Ben radioed back. "Relax, Cec. I've got a platoon with me." And Ben knew several companies would soon be on the way. He was counting on it.

Ike monitored the conversation and ordered tanks into the area for backup.

Dan monitored and ordered another platoon into the area.

West sent a platoon of his people in to cover Ben.

Georgi ordered Rebet to take a detail into the area.

And Buddy and Tina led their people into the area.

"Looks like a damn convention," Ben said with a grin.

Khamsin sat in his CP across the river, monitoring the transmissions, and wondering what in the name of Allah was going on.

He shook his head at the strange goings-on and asked, "How are the boat and ferry preparations coming along?"

"Very well, sir," he was told. "We'll have enough to transport five thousand in the first wave."

Khamsin nodded. Almost half his people landing during the first push. Good. The terrorist leaned back in his chair and smiled. He must remember to say some additional prayers for success.

After all, he was a very religious man.

Ben waited until his people had cleared the first few floors of the building that had housed the offices of his old publishing company, then began the climb up to the eighth floor.

"A trip down memory lane, Ben?' Jerre asked, climbing up behind him.

"You might say that. I seem to recall that the bombs came before my royalty check did. I might find it lying about."

"Sure, Ben. Sure. And you'll just take it right down to Chase Manhattan and cash it."

He laughed. "I certainly intend to visit that bank later on."

Rebet met Ben on the eighth floor and held up a hand. "My people are still clearing this floor, General. If you would wait just a few moments more."

"Certainly, Colonel. I'd hate to enter my editor's office and find a creepy propped up behind the desk, reading one of my manuscripts."

"Right, sir," Rebet said, straight-faced.

Ben thought for a moment about his editor, and wondered what had happened to him. "Are there any bodies in there, Colonel?"

"No, sir."

When the offices had been cleared, Ben stood in the doorway for a moment, looking in. The place was surprisingly neat, although a thick layer of dust lay over everything. He stepped inside, Jerre right behind him. "The rest of you stay out here," he ordered.

"Did you personally know these people, Ben?" she asked.

"Many of them." He stopped by an open office door. "This is much more difficult than I thought."

Jerre stepped in and picked up a manuscript, blowing the dust from it. She read the first paragraph and looked up at Ben. "'It was a dark and stormy night'?"

"Snoopy must have sent that one in." Ben smiled.

They moved on to the next office, and Ben prowled through the stacks of manuscripts. "I knew this guy," he said, holding up a manuscript. He dropped the unopened mailer to the floor. "Shit!" He lifted his walkie-talkie. "Colonel Rebet, send some people in here to box up all these manuscripts."

"Yes, sir."

"I may get around to reading them someday," he told Jerre.

"I'll help you, if you like."

"I might take you up on that."

He prowled the offices, but without much enthusiasm; he felt as if he was looking at a piece of himself.

"Were you ever with another publishing company, Ben?"

"No. I signed with this one right after I hung up my mercenary boots and settled down."

"I never knew you were a mercenary."

"Soldier of fortune, really. I always fought on the side of democracy."

"Where?"

"Africa. South America. Actually, I was in the employ of the Company most of the time."

"The CIA?"

"Yes. They often had people on both sides."

"That's stupid! Why?"

"One side has to win."

"Covering all bets, huh?"

"That was the way of the world, Jerre. Looking back, I guess it was a pretty rotten world."

"And you intend to change it?"

"A small part of it. If I can." He looked at her and something invisible moved between them. But something was always moving between them. Problem was, Ben never knew the quality of it.

Or he did and refused to admit it.

She averted her eyes and walked away from him, moving down the hall, looking into the offices, each one with rat-chewed stacks of manuscripts piled all over the place. "How did they ever get anything done?"

"Beats me. I think they were just about ready to stop accepting manuscripts over the transom."

"Do what?"

"Stop accepting unsolicited manuscripts. A majority of companies already had. Moot point now," he muttered, thinking, *Just about everything has stopped, except for us on one side, and God alone knows how many on the opposing side.*

And nothing in between.

"What are you thinking, Ben? Something very profound?"

He looked at her. He never knew when she was kidding when she made remarks like that. But this time her face was serious.

"I guess so, Jerre. But profound is to the ears as beauty is to the eyes."

"And since you didn't speak your thoughts, we'll never know, will we?"

"Something like that. Let's get out of here. This place is depressing me."

"I have all your books, Ben. I've picked them up over the years."

"Have you read them?"

"No. I don't like individual violence."

Ben was still laughing and shaking his head as he left the offices. He gently closed the door behind him, and let a lot of memories fade away. His, and those of untold numbers of others.

He stood on the sidewalk in front of the building, looking around him, and making a lot of Rebels very nervous by his conspicuousness.

He looked down the street and smiled. "Let's go have some fun, gang." Then he set out walking.

"General!" Rebet called. "Where are you going?"

"To that bank. I have to make a withdrawal." Ben caught the flash of sunlight off a rifle barrel sticking out of a window and grabbed Jerre, both of them hitting the sidewalk, rolling under a truck. Ben yelled for his people to take cover.

Lead began spraying the sidewalks, bouncing and whining off as the Rebels took cover. Suddenly black-robed creepies were all around them, with their hands filled with automatic weapons.

Ben squirmed around as he sensed more than heard movement behind him. He gave several night crawlers a bellyful of lead at a distance of not more than six feet, holding the trigger back on the Thompson and sending black-robes spinning and squalling into death.

The concrete front of the building was splattered with the blood of night crawlers.

Ben pulled the pin on a grenade and tossed it through the shattered window of the building. The explosion blew out the rest of the windows and sent one creepy tumbling out onto the sidewalk, wounded but not down.

Ben finished him with a short burst and then used up the drum spraying the dark interior of the ground floor of the building.

Before he could reload, a creepy had hurled himself from the adjacent building and was on top of Ben, hatred and fury turning his ugly face into a mask of hideousness.

Ben slugged him on the jaw, rocking his head back. Ben hit him again, this time in the mouth, and felt teeth break under his gloved knuckles. He clawed his .45 out of leather and thumbed the hammer back, shooting the flesh-eater in the belly, the big hollow-nosed slug ripping out the creature's back, severing the backbone. The night crawler fell to one side, as limp as a deflated inner tube.

Ben holstered the .45 and picked up his Thompson, fitting a full drum into the belly and jacking in a round. On one knee, he turned and blew several black-robes into that dark and endless sleep, the .45-caliber slugs stopping them in their tracks and spinning them around, dancing and jerking as death touched them with a cold hand.

The tanks had begun lashing at the buildings with cannon, .50-caliber and 7.62 machine-gun fire. Flames were already shooting out of a floor of one building, and another building was sending up billows of smoke.

Below the fire and smoke, the street battle raged on, unchecked.

Night People were still pouring out of buildings like soldier ants on a rampage, and the Rebels were knocking them down almost as fast as they were charging.

Several managed to charge through the first line of Rebels and come within several feet of Jerre. She lifted her M16 and shot one creeper in the face just as Beth was knocked down by another. Ben stuck the muzzle of his Thompson to the side of the creep's head and blew the head apart. Lifting the muzzle, he stopped the short advance of black-robes. The slugs lifted one completely off his feet and sent him crashing to the bricks of the street.

"The woman!" Ben heard one black-hood yell. "Get the woman!"

Ben grabbed Jerre around the waist, lifted her off her boots, and hauled her into the grenade-shattered building behind them, yelling for his personal team to join them.

"Jersey and Cooper, get the back. Beth, stay up front with us. Heads up. They want Jerre."

Jerre looked at him, and this time there was real fear in her eyes.

Over the roar and crash and hammer of battle, she said, "You knew. That's why you ordered me to become your aide, isn't it?"

"I felt Khamsin might try to grab you. The creepies

must have had the same thought."

"You might have told me."

Ben triggered off a short burst before replying. He leaned close to Jerre and whispered, "There are lots of things I'm not telling people. You see, kid—we have an informant among us."

EIGHT

A hundred or more creepies came in a suicide run toward the building they had seen Ben carry Jerre into. The Rebel line bent, but it did not break as night crawlers hurled themselves against the line of men and women, screaming their rage and hate and frustration as they died in bloody, stinking heaps on the bricks of the street and the concrete of the sidewalks.

And for once, Jerre got close to Ben and stayed there without being told and without bitching about it.

As some unknown signal passed through the Night People, they began fading back into the buildings and alleyways, leaving their dead and wounded behind.

Ben stepped out of the building, Jerre close to him. "Get the wounded to the hospital, on the double. Sentries double; watch out for a second attack. Beth, call for trucks to haul these stinking carcasses off. And tell the engineers to send some people up here with jackhammers and diamond-bit drills and C-four."

"What are we going to do with all that, General?" Colonel Rebet asked.

"Rob a bank," Ben told him.

"Why did you suddenly decide to confide in me, Ben?" Jerre asked, as they walked toward the bank building.

"Because I've decided it isn't you."

"Thanks just a whole bunch, Ben. Your confidence in me is overwhelming."

"Nearly everyone is suspect, Jerre. But you haven't been out of my sight in over forty-eight hours, and the leaks continue."

"To Khamsin?"

"No. To the creepies. Somebody is telling them where our caches of supplies are hidden and where our small-manned machine-gun emplacements are located. And now the crawlers were tipped that you were with me and we were coming up here."

"And now?"

"We start at the top and work down. That's being done this minute at Chase's main hospital by Doctor Lindgren and his people. Once we've eliminated the top people, I can breathe a little easier."

"Surely you don't suspect your close friends? You've been together for years."

"I suspect everybody until they're cleared, Jerre. That goes with the territory. We've all been through this type of thing before. They wouldn't expect anything less from me." He looked up. "Here we are."

"You're really going to rob this bank, aren't you?"

"Gold, Jerre. Someday, we'll go back to a limited use of paper money—of some type. We have to have something to back that money. So we'll use the gold standard."

Ben waved a team of Rebels in to clear the bank, and he and Jerre crouched inside the rusting hulk of a pickup truck.

"Beth tells me she's going back to Illinois when New York City is secure," Jerre said.

Ben smiled. "Yes. She told me. Back to Lev and his cows. That's what we're striving for, Jerre. More and more people back to the land. We've gone back to opening frontiers, pushing out in all directions. Good, solid, steady people from which to build a base."

"And then you'll be president—again."

"Oh, no. Not me, Jerre. It'll be years before the nation reaches the point of electing a leader. If it ever does.

Sometimes I have many doubts about that. We destroy one outlaw band, two more pop up to take its place."

"And why is that, Ben?"

"We're well into the second decade of no public schooling, no laws to guide the footsteps of humankind. Absolutely nothing for the young to cling to, no role models for the young. In a decade and a half this world has reverted back to the caves. It's going to take many, many years to restore order."

They were silent for a time. The lower floors of the building were cleared, and they waited for the engineers to show up.

"Remember when we first met, Ben?" Jerre asked softly.

"Vividly."

"I can't believe all those years have gone by."

"Swiftly roll the ages, kid."

"Even back then, Ben, you talked of law and order and rules. The smoke from the ashes of war hadn't even settled, and you were talking about order."

"Without it, Jerre, you have anarchy."

"You'll never change, Ben."

"One thing won't." He looked at her. "But God, I wish it could."

"I wish it could, too, Ben." She touched his arm. "And I mean that."

"I know you do." He stood up. "Here come the engineers. Let's go rob a bank, kid."

"Piece of cake," the engineer said. "We won't have to blow it. We'll torch these sections." He pointed them out. "And then wrench it open. Take about an hour."

Ben left Colonel Rebet in charge, and with Jerre, headed back to his CP.

"I see now why you were so close-mouthed about Khamsin," Ike told him. "You're thinking that whoever it is tipping off the creepies might do the same for the Hot Wind, right?"

"Yes. And I don't have a clue who it is."

"Nate is working on Katzman's people right now. How far down the line are you going?"

"I'll stop it once we have the high-level and mid-level personnel checked out. I feel sure it's one of the newer people. He or she will tip their hand eventually. So far there've been no really important leaks—except for today's leak concerning Jerre."

"If there was a way to do it, I'd like to see her get gone from this island."

"I've gone over and over that, Ike. I don't see any way of getting her out of here. She's just going to have to stick close and stay alert."

Ben checked his watch. A few more hours and it would be dark. A few more hours and Khamsin would start his ferrying of troops across the Hudson River. Ike noted the grim smile on Ben's face, but said nothing about it. He cut his eyes to Cecil. The black man arched one eyebrow and minutely shrugged his thick shoulders.

Ben still wasn't talking about what he planned to do that night.

Ben lifted his eyes, looking first at Ike, then at Cecil. He surprised them both by saying, "You boys find you a good vantage point for this evening. It's going to be quite a show."

At dusk, Ben left General Striganov in charge and waved at Buddy and Tina and Dan to join him. "Buddy, go ask Thermopolis if he'd like to join us."

His son was back in a few minutes, Thermopolis walking beside him.

"Let's go, people," Ben said.

"Going to personally greet this Khamsin person, General?" Thermopolis asked.

"Oh, yes!" Ben said brightly. "I'm going to give him a very warm greeting—one befitting a man of his international reputation, you might say."

Tina and Buddy exchanged glances but said nothing.

Heavily guarded, the group drove down to 96th Street

and parked along the waterfront. Another group of Rebels met them there, having arrived several hours earlier, to secure the spot.

With the darkness, the slight warming trend of the past few days had vanished and the night had turned bitterly cold. They were all bundled up against the freezing winds.

"Khamsin is loading up now, sir," Beth told Ben.

Ben nodded and then surprised everybody when he turned to Beth and said, "Get me Base Three, please, Beth. On scramble."

The old Fort Dix airfield down in New Jersey.

"Go, sir."

Ben took the handset. "Warming them up, Chipper?"

Whatever Chipper said caused Ben first to smile and then to laugh.

"Taxi them out, Chipper. My people say Khamsin is right on schedule. You have fifteen minutes to lift off. Good luck."

"Spotter planes, Father?" Buddy inquired.

"Something like that, son. I hope somebody remembered to bring the coffee. It's cold as a well-digger's ass out here."

The coffee was poured into the cups, and the group squatted down beside their vehicles, to block the cold hard wind blowing off the river.

All of them had questions they would have liked to ask Ben. All kept away from the subject, knowing that Ben was not going to shed any light on the matter. Not yet. All felt this was to be an "eyes only" explanation.

"What time is it?" Cooper asked, for the tenth time in ten minutes.

"One minute later than the last time you asked," Ben told him. "Relax. The show is going to begin in about four minutes."

Thermopolis looked at Ben. "You brought me down here for a purpose, General. Would you like to tell me what it is?"

"Not really. You'll be able to see for yourself very shortly."

"You sure it's going to be worth the wait?" Thermopolis asked.

"It will be for me. I can't speak for you or any of the others."

Beth said, "Spotters report ferries and boats shoving off, General."

Ben glanced at his watch. "Right on schedule. The planes should be over the zone in one minute."

"To spot, of course," Thermopolis said, his tone gin-martini dry.

"Among other things." Ben smiled with his reply, conscious of all eyes on him.

"I don't think I'm going to like this very much," Thermopolis said.

"It's a long walk back to our sector," Ben said. "And you know what lots of folks say about the Big Apple: It's a dangerous city."

"If that's supposed to be funny, it isn't."

"I have a strange sense of humor."

Buddy lifted his night glasses. He could just make out the dark shapes of the boats as they made their way slowly out into the river. Far in the distance, the sounds of old prop-job planes came faintly to them.

"Those aren't spotter planes," Tina pointed out. "Too heavy. Those sound like . . ." She whirled and faced her father.

". . . Puffs," Buddy finished it for his sister.

"I have such astute children," Ben said. "Makes me very proud."

"Puffs," Thermopolis said. "I remember reading about them. They were used in the Vietnam War, weren't they?"

"Oh, yes," Ben said. "And used quite effectively, I might add."

"AC47s," Buddy took it up. "The planes are painted all black—awesome-looking. They are fairly bristling with 7.62- and .50-caliber machine guns and 20-millimeter Vulcan and 40-millimeter Bofors cannon. All weapons taken into count, the Puffs are capable of pouring out some eight thousand rounds a minute. One Puff can effectively destroy every living thing in an area the size of a football field."

"Very good, Buddy," Ben complimented him. He looked at Thermopolis. "You like rock and roll, don't you, Thermopolis?"

"Yes. I do."

"Well, get ready for some rock and roll that is music to my ears. Feel free to hum along if you like."

"Just think, General: I was actually beginning to like you."

"There are no gentleman's wars, Thermopolis. As far as I'm concerned, there never has been one. There is a winner and a loser in war. And taking into consideration what is at stake here, I, for one, don't intend to be a loser. Do you?"

"Putting it that way, no."

All along the shoreline, at spots stretching from 72nd Street up to 86th, great spotlights clicked on—the same lights that were once used for the grand openings of movies and Broadway shows.

The boats and ferries were caught in the strong beams.

Ben started whistling an old tune from back in the 1950s: "Shake, Rattle, and Roll!"

NINE

The cold night was shattered as the Puffs unleashed their fury against the boats and ferries and the army of the Hot Wind.

Thermopolis stood with undisguised awe on his face as the Puffs made their slow circles above the water, the big planes trembling as their payloads were uncorked, the deadly rain destroying everything that was in their path.

A single Puff circled the docks where Khamsin's men were waiting to be loaded on the boats. The flying tank turned the docks wet and slippery with the blood of the army of the Hot Wind.

The Puff lumbered on, all guns thundering and spitting out the deadly hail, destroying anything that came within range.

There were survivors from the deadly birds, but most were so equipment-laden they sank like bricks in the cold dark waters of the Hudson. Those who did manage to cling to some debris and make the Manhattan shoreline soon discovered that Ben Raines and his Rebels were not in the least bit interested in showing any hospitality toward an avowed enemy.

The men of the army of the Hot Wind were shot as soon as they touched shore.

Khamsin was learning a hard lesson about engaging in warfare with Ben Raines: the man was as ruthless as a grizzly bear protecting cubs. As a friend, Ben Raines was generous; as an enemy, he had no equal on the battlefield.

Khamsin, the Hot Wind, lost approximately half his army in less than ten minutes.

The boats and ferries sank beneath the surface of the river with a hiss and bubble. The Puffs winged their way back to their base, thousands of pounds lighter as their ammunition was exhausted. Only an occasional shot was fired from the Manhattan shoreline as the last of the Hot Wind's army sank into a watery grave.

"Jesus Christ!" Thermopolis said.

Ben cut his eyes to the man. "We just shortened the odds against us, Thermopolis. By just about half. Now we really do have a chance of coming out of this alive."

Thermopolis slowly shook his head. "I'm not condemning you, Ben Raines. You did what you felt you had to do. It's just that . . . I had never seen anything like that before."

Ben took the handset from Beth. "Eagle to Big Bird."

"Go, Eagle."

"Good job, Chipper. I'll have to put a bonus in your pay envelope."

Chipper laughed over the miles. "I'll settle for just wrapping up this job and seeing my wife and kids again, General. Big Bird out."

"All right, people," Ben said. "Let's go zap some night crawlers. It's going to take Khamsin several days to recover from this night."

Not only did the pounding from the Puffs stop Khamsin dead in his tracks, it had an enormous effect on the Night People, further weakening their morale. There were only a few very scattered firefights the night of the Puffs, as it came to be called. The magic dragons' brief but deadly appearance stunned everyone who had never before seen the awesomeness of the machines.

The morning after the night of the Puffs, Ben drove down to the killing area. The shoreline was littered with bodies, as the river gave up its dead, belching the bodies ashore in swollen death. Rebels were busy picking up the bodies and loading them on the barges, where they promptly froze in grotesque postures of death in the bitter winter winds.

Another front had moved in during the night, steadying the temperature for several hours and dropping a load of snow over the city. Then, at the dawning, the temperature sank like a rock and everything froze as the mercury stayed in the low teens. Adding the velocity of the winds, the chill factor was well below zero.

"What about activity over there?" Ben asked, pointing to the New Jersey shore.

"Very little," Ike told him. "It appears that last night knocked the socks off the Hot Fart."

"He'll find another pair. Bet on that. He won't try another mass moving of troops. So from now on, we've got to be on the alert for infiltrators. He'll be sending in men in small boats, at night. Ike, let's start hammering at him again. Three or four rounds, then shift the location of the tanks. Let's keep it up around the clock. It's do-or-die time for us. We've knocked him down, now let's kick him a few times."

"We'll start throwing stuff at them within the hour, Ben? That was a hell of a show last night."

"Just as long as we can keep him down and guessing, we've got a chance."

"The man has no honor." Khamsin spoke the words quietly. "None. He is void of morals. The god he worships must be from Hell."

None of the field commanders replied. Like Khamsin, they were all still somewhat in a state of shock from the previous night of the Puffs.

"We will have three days of mourning," Khamsin announced. "For three days we will pray for guidance and for the souls of our brothers. Although," he was quick to add, "we all know they are now with Allah."

Everyone agreed that was surely true. With Allah. Right.

The jarring crash of half a dozen incoming 155s sent the men diving to the floor. Khamsin was up on his boots before the dust had settled, cursing wildly. He shook his fist in the direction of Manhattan.

A runner from Khamsin's communications center darted into the room. "Messages, sir."

"What are they? Read them to me!"

"The Judges from the underground want to know why you didn't tell them of last night's invasion. They would have initiated a diversion."

Khamsin cursed louder. "Tell them . . . tell them that I did not wish to run the risk of Ben Raines intercepting the messages. My apologies," he added bitterly. "Is that all?"

"No, sir. The units close to the waterfront are asking permission to return the cannon fire."

"No," Khamsin said wearily. "We can't run the risk of harming any of our . . . allies." He spat out the last word. "Tell them to pull back. We're all pulling back; out of range of the artillery. God *damn* Ben Raines!"

"Khamsin is pulling his people back, General." Beth relayed the information to him. "The first units are already well out of range of our heaviest pieces."

"Tell the gunners to pour it on. Napalm and Willie Peter. Let's cause them all the grief we can while we can."

"Yes, sir."

The tank commanders along the Hudson began lobbing in the most dreaded of artillery: napalm and white phosphorus. The big 155 SP, capable of sending a shell screaming for twelve miles, elevated their nineteen-feet-ten-inch tubes and began sending out a round a minute. Within ten minutes, the area from North Bergen down to the New Jersey Turnpike bridge over Newark Bay was a smoking, burning hell as the long-vacant, dust-filled, and neglected buildings burst into flames.

Ben stood on a cloverleaf of the Henry Hudson Parkway and watched through binoculars as New Jersey burned. He was smiling grimly—a smile that only another soldier could understand.

"General?" Beth said quietly.

Ben turned. She was holding out the handset to him. "Who is it?"

"Khamsin, sir."

Ben took the handset. "What do you want, Khamsin?"

"I will overlook your boorishness, General, and be brief. You are a dead man. Walking around dead. I am going to destroy you. Whatever it takes, including my own life, you will never leave that miserable island of concrete and steel alive."

"There is that old saying about talk being cheap, Khamsin."

The Libyan cursed him.

Ben broke the radio connection. "He's losing his cool, gang. But he's still a very dangerous man—maybe even more so now. I cost him a lot of face, and with those types of people, that's very important."

"And now?" Jerre asked.

"Nothing has changed. We keep Khamsin on the New Jersey side of the river and concentrate on wiping out the Night People. We've got a few days; it'll take him that long to recover from the mauling we handed him and to make some plans. Let's get down to some serious ass-kicking, people!"

But the creepies had vanished. There was not one shot fired from either side all that day.

"Khamsin's been in contact with them," Ben told his commanders that afternoon. "They're cooking up something and there is no point in us sitting around worrying about it. Let's take this time and strip New York City. We'll take it block by block and treasure-hunt. We're going to take everything of value, and then I just might blow this goddamn place into oblivion. I don't know; I haven't decided yet."

"Shore would take a lot of powder," Ike drawled.

"Not as much as you might think," Ben told him. "Since I discovered a pocket of methane gas over near where the kids were found, I've had some engineers working wherever they felt was clear of crawlers. The city is sitting on top of many, many pockets of methane. I may use it. I don't know.

"For the next few days, we're going to strip New York City. Start working your sectors. Blow every bank, inspect every museum and gallery. Go into the major TV and radio networks and recording studios and take it all."

After the men and women had left his CP, Ben sat alone, behind his desk, deep in thought. He looked up as Jerre entered the room.

"Am I interrupting, Ben?"

"No. Glad to have the company."

"You looked deep in thought."

"I was thinking about all the history I would destroy if I left this city in rubble. History that future generations can ill afford to lose. Central Park, City Hall, Fraunces Tavern, UN headquarters, and a lot of other places I can't recall off the top of my head."

"Will there be future generations capable of understanding history, Ben?"

"Oh, yes, Jerre. Don't ever lose hope of that. That's what we're fighting for. Our own survival, to be sure. But much more than that, we've got to be planning for generations that will be along a century after we're dry bones in the grave."

"And that really matters to you, doesn't it, Ben?"

"Yes, Jerre, it does."

"Strange comment from a man who was once a mercenary, don't you think?"

"Maybe." He smiled at her. "But I told you, I was more a soldier of fortune than a mercenary."

"You think Khamsin and the creepies will be making more moves to kidnap me?"

"Yes. More than ever. Although it may not seem that

way to you, for the first time, we've got them on the defensive. The Night People are fighting scared. Morale must be terribly low in the Hot Wind's army. Unfortunately, we're not in a position to do much about it. We're still stuck on this island."

"But you could break out if you wanted to, couldn't you, Ben?" She asked the question softly.

"Oh, yeah, kid. That we could do."

She waited for him to elaborate. When he did not, she said, "What's the matter, Ben? You don't think I'm the informant, do you?"

"Oh, no, Jerre. Colonel Gray found him this morning."

"Oh?"

"Yes. A man who'd been with us for several years. Shows you how long the Night People have been monitoring us."

"Where is the man?"

"I shot him about two hours ago."

TEN

"Come on." Ben shook Jerre's foot. "We're getting an early start today."

She opened one eye and gave him a bleak look. "Jesus, Ben! What time is it?"

"Two-thirty. We're going to take a little trip this morning and see if we can't catch some creepies with their drawers down."

She swung out of the cot. "What a disgusting thought, especially at this time of the morning. Where are we going, Ben?"

"You'll see. Shake a leg." He began rousting out the others.

After advising them all that if they weren't down on street level, in full combat gear, in fifteen minutes, he would reassign them all to the death barges, Ben walked down the steps and out onto the bitterly cold and dark street.

Dan was waiting for him. "Good morning, sir!" he said brightly, and poured Ben a cup of steaming coffee. He handed him a sandwich.

"Do I dare ask what is in between these two pieces of bread, Dan?"

"I would not, sir. Just envision several thick pieces of bacon and try to convince your taste buds of the accuracy of that."

"I was afraid of that." He took a bite, and then his face brightened with a big smile. "I'll be damned, Dan! Peanut butter and jelly!"

"We found a huge underground warehouse fairly packed with all sorts of goodies: cheeses, powdered milk, powdered eggs, potato flakes—all sorts of things. Some of it was ruined, naturally, but quite a lot of it was still in excellent shape."

"Our luck is changing, Dan. I can feel it."

"I think so as well, General. If our intelligence was correct, we'll deal the Night People a terribly crippling blow this morning."

"I'm counting on it, Dan."

Cooper, Beth, Jersey, and Jerre came wandering out of the building, yawning and stretching and pulling at the uncomfortable body armor under their shirts.

"Grab you some coffee and a sandwich," Ben told them. "I'll drive."

"Oh, God!" Jersey said. "We'll never get there alive. Where the hell are we going anyway, sir?"

"You'll see. Get in," he said, as the Blazer was pulled around to the curb. Chuckling, Ben got behind the wheel. He frowned as three APCs pulled out of a side street and took the point.

"You really didn't think we'd let you take the point, did you, now, General?" Dan admonished him through the window.

"I could always hope. Come on, let's get this show on the road. Who is taking point?"

"Buddy. See you at the train station, General."

"Right." Ben blinked his lights a couple of times and the APCs pulled out.

"Wow!" Beth said. "These are peanut butter and jelly sandwiches." She took a big bite and rolled her eyes in satisfaction.

Ben pulled out and with a free hand, pointed to the sandwich in Jerre's hand. "Eat, kid, and be happy. How long's it been since you had peanut butter and jelly?"

"Long time, Be . . . General."

"You two can relax around us, for Christ sake!" Jersey managed to speak around a stuffed mouth. "So why don't you knock off the formalities. Makes me edgy."

"Maybe you're just horny?" Cooper suggested.

"Put a zipper on it, Cooper! And eat!"

"We have about seven or eight miles to go," Ben told them. "The others were briefed just before I ordered that early turn-in."

"I wondered about that," Jerre said, glancing at him. "You think there might be other informants among us?"

"I'm sure of it. Probably in all critical areas. Two more were ferreted out around ten o'clock. They're either still being questioned or they're dead."

"And our destination on this miserable morning?" Jerre asked, munching on her sandwich and sipping on the welcome coffee.

"Grand Central Station, gang. Actually, it was a terminal, not a station. You follow me in, and stay with me. We have very good intelligence that the place is swarming with creepies. The place is about fifty acres, that's above and below ground. The underground yard stretches from Forty-fourth to Fifty-ninth Streets. I have people already in position at Fifty-ninth, ready to go in. They've found rabbit holes the creepies have tunneled through. Buddy is hitting the main concourse first, clearing it. The terminal runs five stories below ground, and has a maze of old steam pipes. Going to be a lot of creepies among those pipes. This isn't going to be either pleasant or easy. But it has to be done. We've broken a leg from under the Night People already. Let's break the other leg this morning."

Ben followed the tanks and APCs as they turned south off 125th Street onto Park Avenue and headed south. Their unusual but tasty breakfast finished, the passengers in the Blazer tried to relax as best they could in their uncomfortable battle harnesses, loaded full with clip pouches and grenades.

"How do you know the creepies won't be alerted and waiting for us?" Jerre asked.

"I don't. But we've never launched a night attack directly at them, so it's something they won't be expecting from us."

They crossed 116th Street. They had not seen one living thing since leaving the CP. The city seemed deserted under the layer of snow still blanketing the streets. The temperature was hovering right around ten above, and with the winds blowing, the chill factor was well below zero. The chains on the rear tires of the vehicles dug through the snow and clanked against the brick and concrete of the old streets as the convoy pushed south toward the terminal.

They passed 96th Street, still some fifty blocks away from their objective.

"You ever ride the trains out of this place, General?" Cooper asked.

"A few times. I remember the main concourse. Huge place. The terminal used to be called—by some—the town square of Manhattan. You could buy a newspaper from London, have a photo taken, get your shoes shined, eat some oysters, or play tennis for about sixty-five or seventy dollars an hour."

"Lots of people used the trains?" Jersey asked.

"'Bout a quarter of a million people a day, so I was told. It's an old place. I'd guess maybe ninety years old."

They rolled past 85th Street. It seemed to the Rebels that they were visitors on a distant planet—a cold, barren, lifeless planet. But they all knew only too well that death waited around every corner, every turn, in every building, and until recently, under the very streets they now drove, the headlights searching the darkness.

"Tunnel Rat to Eagle," the speaker squawked.

Ben lifted the mike. "Go, Rat."

"Swinging over onto Lexington at Sixty-fourth."

"Pull over and wait for us, Rat."

"Ten-four, Eagle."

"Eagle to Scout Team Three."

"Three."

"Are you in position?"

"Ten-four, sir. Waiting for the commuters."

Ben grinned. "They're in position at Fifty-ninth and have the holes plugged." Lifting the mike, he said, "Hang tough and good luck."

"Same to you, sir."

The lead vehicles pulled over behind Buddy's short column. "Bloomingdale's is just a few blocks down," Ben said. "You ladies want to go shopping? Maybe buy some nighties?"

"If they model them, can we watch, General?" Cooper said with a grin.

"Cooper," Jersey said, giving him an elbow in the ribs. "I swear to God I think your brains are between your legs."

Laughing, Ben got out of the Blazer and into the bitterly cold night. He walked up to his son. "Ready, boy?"

"Yes, sir. Dan and Tina are in position on the west side of the complex, ready to go in." He grinned, his teeth flashing in the night. "General, Ike and Cecil are going to be highly irritated about being left out of his operation, you know?"

"Can't be helped. I couldn't risk the informants picking up on any transmissions and leaking it." He gripped the young man's thick, muscular arm. "Let's go kick some ass, Buddy."

"Good luck, Father."

"Same to you, son."

Back in the Blazer, Ben pulled out behind the lead vehicles and they rolled past Bloomingdale's department store. Jerre was looking wistfully at the huge store.

"You reckon they really have some pretty nighties left in there?" she asked.

"I wouldn't doubt it," Ben told her. "But in this weather, do you really want to trade your longhandles for a silk gown?"

"It's gonna be spring sometime, General. I hope."

"I feel like I've been cold for a damn month!" Beth said.

"I got news for you," Ben said with a laugh. "You have!"

They rolled past Citibank and Citicorp, past the House of Seagrams and the YWCA. "The Waldorf-Astoria," Ben pointed out.

"I bet they got beds with mirrors on the ceilings in there." Cooper grinned at Jerre.

"Cooper," she told him, "just think of your M16 as your pecker. And use it accordingly."

The column stopped at 44th Street. "Jack 'em in," Ben said, bailing out of the Blazer. "Let's go!"

The sounds of hard gunfire split the night as Buddy and his team hit the main concourse, catching the Night People at rest, huddled together against the bitter cold. The booming and thudding of grenades ripped the gloom of the city blocks around the famous and majestic old terminal.

The APCs and trucks spewed out Rebels. The tanks spun around in the snowy street, men and women manning machine guns, ready to chop down any crawlers who might try to escape the attack above ground.

The stench of the filthy hit them all hard as Ben led his team into the main concourse.

"Good God!" Jerre said, wrinkling her nose at the almost overpowering odor.

Ben lifted his Thompson and gave a black-robed bunch a short burst of .45-caliber Rebel retribution. The rattle of gunfire was echoing and reverberating in the 125-foot-high main concourse, bouncing back from its vaulted ceilings. Bullets were whining as they ricocheted off the marble floor and splattered and flattened against the walls.

"Pick your shots!" Ben yelled over the din. "Watch for ricochets!"

The move by Ben and his Rebels had caught the Night People completely by surprise. This location was deep in controlled territory, and they thought they were safe. A group of Dan's hand-picked Scouts had silently neutralized the guards moments before the attack came, leaving them sprawled in the cold and snow, knocked down and dead by silenced .22-caliber auto-loading pistols.

When several hundred heavily armed Rebels came storming into the huge terminal, the attack had further demoralized the already low-spirited crawlers. Sleepy, cold, and hungry, the Night People could do little for the first few moments except die.

And they died in stinking heaps on the cold floor of the terminal, their blood staining the filth-encrusted marble.

The main concourse was cleared in only a few minutes, and teams of Rebels began dragging the dead outside, to pile them on the street, awaiting transport to the death barges in the harbor. The floor could not be watered down, removing the blood, for the water would freeze seconds after hitting the floor.

"Gas masks!" Ben ordered. "Tear-gas cannisters into the lower level!"

The cannisters went bouncing and hissing and spewing their fumes into the levels below the main concourse.

Those who ran in panic from the blinding tear gas only ran into more tear gas being tossed down from 59th Street, and from the street entrances of their thought-to-be-safe hidey holes. Half blinded by the harsh gas, the Night People ran right into the guns of the Rebels and died in bloody stacks amid the steam pipes of the old terminal.

There was no point in trying to surrender, and the creepies knew it, and did not attempt it. They died cursing Ben Raine and his Rebels.

The battle was short, savage, and bloody. Ben did not order pursuit of the crawlers below the second level. "Blow it," he ordered. "Bring it down on them or block them off."

The Rebels made their way back out onto the streets around the old terminal and waited while the demolition teams did their work. It did not take long for them to plant their massive charges of C-4 and C-5. At their signal, Ben ordered his people well away from the terminal and told the explosives experts to drop the hammer.

The concrete beneath their boots trembled when the radio-detonated explosives blew. One section of the building, that part bordering 45th and Lexington, collapsed, sending up clouds of dust and raining down bricks and steel and mortar.

Trucks arrived to cart off the frozen dead. "No point in leaving them here," Ben observed. "Their friends would eat them."

Ike and Cecil and West roared and clanked up. Ike bailed out and began cussing and jumping up and down, yelling at Ben for being a damn fool and why in hell didn't he let them in on the raid. Then the stocky ex-Navy SEAL lost his footing on the ice and snow and did a frantic, arm-waving ballet before he thumped down on his butt in the middle of the street.

Ben and Dan were laughing so hard both men were clutching their sides at Ike's antics.

"Baryshnikov should be here to see those moves, Fats," Dan stuck the needle to Ike. "He'd be envious."

"Who the hell is that?" Ike yelled, trying to get to his feet and only succeeding in falling down once again.

Even Cecil had lost his irritation and could no longer keep a straight face.

"Who is Baryshnikov?" Dan yelled at Ike, spinning around and around on the ice in the street. "Only a redneck would ask that question, you . . . you *cretin!*"

"Redneck!" Ike squalled. "You prissy limey! Just for that, you'll never get to listen to my George Jones records."

"Who?" Dan asked.

"George Jones, you heathen! Everybody in the world's heard of George Jones. Somebody help me up, god damn it!"

"Who is George Jones?" Dan asked Ben.

"He sang country songs."

"From what country?" Dan asked, a confused look on his face.

"From America!" Ike squalled, getting to his boots, a clump of snow in one gloved hand. He balled it and tossed it at Dan, hitting the Englishman on the forehead.

And in the middle of sprawled death, standing in the freezing cold, America and England carried on the Revolution . . . with snowballs.

ELEVEN

A blizzard was raging when Ben awakened that morning. He looked at his watch. Ten o'clock. And it was cold, the wind howling through the patched-up windows of his office.

He dressed quickly and stepped into the anteroom. The rest of his crew was just getting up and dressing. "When you get some coffee and food in you, Beth, advise the field commanders to hand out extra rations and keep the troops in as much as possible. I want guards changed every hour, and advise the medics to be on the lookout for frostbite."

"Yes, sir. You want some coffee?"

"It would be much appreciated." Over coffee, Ben said, "Have the vehicles pulled inside and heaters placed nearby. Make sure all extra batteries are fully charged."

He counted heads among the crowd, making sure that Jerre was present. She caught him looking at her and as the song goes, for a moment there . . .

But she cut her eyes away and the moment was lost.

After Beth was finished with her transmissions, Ben took the radio on scramble. "It would be like Khamsin to try something on a day like this, people, so double your spotters and change frequently to keep your eyes fresh. And while we've got the creepies on the run, the fight is far from over. So stay alert and do your best to stay warm. This storm looks like it's going to be a bad one and a long one."

Ben walked back into his office and shoveled some more

coal into the small stove, vented through a window and temporarily patched. Since the CP changed frequently, the accommodations were basic at best.

Buddy walked in and warmed his hands at the stove, then turned to face his father. "I have a bad feeling about this day, Father."

"So do I, son. What's got your hackles up?"

"It would be a dandy day for a hit-and-run attack."

"Against whom?"

"You. This office. Jerre."

"Why not against yourself? Or Tina? Have you given that any thought?"

"Kidnapping a son or daughter is one thing, Father. Kidnapping the woman a man loves is quite another matter."

Ben thought about that for a moment. "It's that obvious and that well-known?"

"Yes."

"Get some additional people in here, then. And I don't mean surround the place with a battalion." Again, Ben was silent in thought. "It would be a suicide run, Buddy. The lower level of this place has been checked out and is secure. A street level attack would be stopped before they reached the sidewalk. If my intelligence is correct, they want her alive, not dead. So it's going to have to come from the roof, and I will not station people up there in this weather."

"I'll move some people in quietly, Father. We'll be stationed on the stairwells."

"All right, son. Quiet is the word."

Buddy nodded and left. Ben sat down in an old rat-chewed chair he pulled close to the stove. He looked up as Beth entered the office.

"General, this storm is really screwing up radio transmissions. The units are virtually cut off from one another."

"I was afraid of that. Heads up, Beth. I have a bad feeling about this day."

She walked to the window and looked out. Visibility

was down to near zero, and she said as much.

"They'll be coming this day. And Khamsin will, too, I'm thinking. Do we have contact with the units in our immediate sector?"

"Yes, sir."

"Advise them to go on full alert. I imagine that Ike and Cec and West have done the same. And Beth, don't sell yourself short about being on a list of people the creepies would like to get their hands on. There are a lot of things happening that, of the people in this section, only you and I are privy to."

"That has crossed my mind, General."

"Stay on top of it, Beth. When you ladies go to the john, go together. Don't go anywhere in this building alone."

"Yes, sir." She fixed a level gaze at him. "And what about you, sir?"

"I'm an old wolf, Beth. There have been bounties on my head for the past decade and a half. You can't poison me and I'm hard to trap. I'm paranoid by nature." He said the last with a smile.

"Yes, sir." She left the room.

Ben walked to a window on the alley side and peeked through the dark drapes. The building across the narrow alley had been cleared, checked, and rechecked, but Ben knew only too well the creepies could have moved in minutes after his people had made their final check.

The Night People were fighting with desperation riding on their shoulders, knowing their very survival was at stake. They would stop at nothing now. If they lost fifty percent or ninety percent of their people to win, it would make no difference to them: they could always rebuild their perverted and hideous kingdom, for their way of life was a learned thing.

Like so many of the problems that had descended upon the United States when it was whole, from drugs to crime, lack of discipline and permissiveness, and everything related to them, it was a learned thing. And it could not be treated by a pat on the head and a promise from the malcontent that he or she would do better.

Ben had always felt that the way to have a crime-free society was to have no criminals. And for many years in the Tri-States, they had no crime. One reason was they had no elaborate criminal justice system in the Tri-States that catered to the criminal instead of seeing to the needs of the victim.

Ben turned away from the window and picked up his Thompson, making sure the drum in its belly was leaded up full.

He slung it, opened his office door, and stepped out into the anteroom. He could feel the tension among his personal crew. They all were feeling that this day was going to be a bad one.

"Lighten up, gang," Ben said, his voice calming them. "Whatever comes our way, we'll handle it. We always have, we always will. History might show us to be no more than aggressive savages, trying to shove our way of life down a lot of unwilling throats. It might show us to be the only force standing between total collapse and anarchy. I don't know how future historians will treat us. And to be very honest, I don't know, really, whether I give a damn. Brute force and a driving will to survive and to build a better way of life forged this nation several hundred years ago. Generations later, the powers that be forgot that in their quest to nitpick us into a bunch of whining pansies." He smiled at the group.

"Anybody got a deck of cards? I don't think there's a one of you can beat me at gin rummy."

The day dragged on, each tick of the clock seeming to be as slow as a funeral dirge. They all heard Buddy and his people get into place inside the building. Ben pretended not to notice it.

Jerre studied his face for a moment, trying to read it. She gave up when Ben said, "Deal."

The winds howled and threw millions of bits of frozen ice against the old windows. Ben had guessed the temperature at just a few degrees below freezing, perfect for snow and sleet. And the snow and sleet would alternate with the varying thermometer reading. Come the night, Ben suspected the mercury would drop like a brick and the temperature would be unbearable, especially if these hard winds continued, and they probably would.

The game continued.

Just the faintest of foulness drifted to Ben's nostrils. Or was his mind playing tricks? He couldn't be sure. No, there it was again. It was no illusion. The Night People were very near.

Ben studied his cards, arranged them in his hand, and, with a smile, laid them down on the table. "Gin!"

"Damn, Ben!" Jerre said. "Do you have to win all the time?"

"Name of the game, kid." He met her gaze. "You know what a sore loser I am."

She narrowed her eyes, trying to read what he meant, but since she had misread his eyes for years, she finally gave up.

Ben stood up, slinging his Thompson. It drew no attention from the others. They all picked up their weapons whenever they moved around, even within the CP, and especially on this day.

"I'm going to the head, gang," Ben said matter-of-factly. "Play a round without me."

Jerre was already shuffling the cards as he opened the door and stepped out into the office.

Ben slipped his Thompson off safety and closed the door behind him. There was that terrible odor again. And it was much stronger than when he had smelled it in the anteroom of his office. He let his eyes sweep the floor for wet footprints. He could see nothing in this hall. But it was a big building, and even though most of it had been sealed off, that meant nothing. The creepies could have been working on it for days, or nights, opening new entrances.

Ben stepped back to the closed door and pushed it open.

The cardplayers looked up. When Ben spoke, his voice was just audible over the howling of the winds.

"Jack 'em in, people. Assume defensive positions. The crud are in the building." He started to close the door.

"What about you, Ben?" Jerre asked.

"I'm going head-hunting, kid. Watch your ass." He closed the door and quietly made his way up the hall. Halfway up the hall, he lifted his handy-talkie. "Rat?"

"Here, Eagle."

"They're in the building. Very close to me. I can smell them."

"Orders?"

"Come down to my hallway. Quietly now, Buddy. And be very careful."

"On my way."

Ben squatted in the dark hallway, the only light coming from the windows at the street and alley end. He turned when the fire door at the far end opened, relaxing as Buddy stepped into the hallway. Buddy signaled that he would take one end of the hall, his father the other.

Ben nodded and held up one thumb. He stood and began moving up the hallway, toward the street side of the building, his boots soft on the floor. He paused at each doorway, kneeling down and sniffing at the base of the door.

On the third door, he hit pay dirt—a pile of shit would be more like it—as the foulness assailed his nostrils. Reaching up, he clicked the handy-talkie's talk button twice, and Buddy looked in his direction. Ben pointed to the closed door, and Buddy moved swiftly but quietly to his father's side.

Ben took a fire-frag grenade from his battle harness and pulled the pin, holding the spoon down. The fire-frag is a mini-claymore, perhaps the most lethal grenade ever manufactured, filled with ball bearings that spew in all directions when the charge blows.

The screaming winds picked up in tempo, and Ben thought for a few seconds of the men and women assigned to guarding the still-open bridges connecting the island. They must be miserable. He shook those thoughts away and cut his eyes to Buddy, nodding his head at the closed door and smiling. He released the spoon.

His son returned the smile and stepped back. He kicked the door open, and Ben tossed in the fire-frag, both of them moving to one side just as the mini-claymore lashed out its lethal load and splattered blood and bone and various parts of anatomy all over the stinking room.

Ben dropped to one knee and Buddy remained standing as they moved into position and began spraying the room with .45-caliber slugs, their identical Thompsons chugging and spitting out death.

"Maintain positions!" Ben yelled up the hall. Then, as Buddy flashed a beam of light from his flashlight into the room, Ben methodically shot each creepie sprawled on the bloody floor. Insurance against a crawler faking it.

The door behind them and to their right suddenly burst open. But at the slight sound of the knob turning, Buddy and Ben had hit the floor and were hammering lead at the opening doorway, knowing that no Rebels were supposed to be in any of these rooms.

A wild scream of anguish was cut off in the man's throat as the Thompson rose with the muzzle blast and the slugs struck the night creep from his chest to his face. He was flung backward into the room just as Buddy rolled in a grenade.

One creepie was flung out into the hall by the heavy blast of the beefed-up grenade, and a section of the wall collapsed, further confusing the dimness with a cloud of dust and plaster. The explosion had prevented them from hearing the gunfire from Ben's office.

"Damn, boy!" Ben said. "Where'd you get that hand bomb?"

"Ordnance just came up with them." Buddy grinned at his father. "Great, aren't they?"

"Wonderful," Ben said, coughing from the dust and the debris. "I'll elaborate more when or if my hearing ever returns."

They listened as gunfire drummed from the stairwells and the rooftop of the building.

"They're holding their own," Ben said. "Let's secure this floor and then grab a cup of coffee." He dropped the drum and inserted a thirty-round clip into the ponderous old antique. It lightened the weight of the old Chicago Piano considerably.

Door by door, room by darkened room, father and son cleared the floor, finding no more hostiles.

The floor cleared, the men returned to Ben's office. Ben rapped on the door. "Secure in there?"

"Secure, sir!" Jersey's voice called. "Come on in."

Buddy pushed open the hall door, stepping in front of his father and entering first. The door to Ben's office was hanging on one hinge, the door bullet-pocked. Wind and snow were blowing into the office from shattered windows on the alley side.

A half a dozen dead night creepies lay sprawled on the floor.

"They crawled right up the side of the building, Ben," Jerre told him. "Using ropes and hooks. I guess they thought the noise of the storm would cover any sound they might make."

Ben nodded, and it was at that point he made up his mind on several issues that he had been vacillating back and forth on. "Buddy, take a team and clear the floor just above this one. And I mean clear it. Get me some offices about the size of this one and start setting up communications and heating. Son?" Ben looked at him. "Blow the buildings on either side of this one, and in the rear, if possible. Bring them down. As soon as we get our signals back with the other units, I'll instruct them to do the same around the CPs."

"Yes, Father."

"Let's start packing up our gear, gang," Ben told the others. "Cooper, help me with the bodies of this crud."

The two men, one at the head and one at the foot, began picking up the bodies of the dead creepies and unceremoniously tossing them out the shattered windows to the alley floor. They would soon lie in grotesquely twisted and frozen heaps.

Ben summed up his feelings, and the feelings of all the other Rebels. "If their friends want to dine on these creeps, they'll have to use a chain saw to fillet them!"

TWELVE

The storm raged on the remainder of that day and well into the night. About three hours after dark had slowly shoved light around the corners of the world, the snow and sleet stopped and the mercury tumbled. But the wind kept up its battering and howling.

With the cessation of snow and sleet, radio communications improved and Ben was able to speak with all units scattered around the Big Apple.

"Did you get hit today, Ike?" Ben asked.

"Ten-fifty, Ben. We ain't seen nothin' down here. Been tryin' to contact you all day."

Ben got all commanders on the horn and quickly explained what had happened and what he had done about the buildings bordering his CP.

"We'll start doing that this night, Ben," Cecil told him. "Are we going to raze the city?"

"I don't know, Cec. It really bothers me to think about doing it. I just haven't fully made up my mind about that."

"It may come to it, General," West reminded him.

"Yeah. I know. How about the survivors around the Central Park area, West?"

"Gene Savie and his group?"

"Yes."

"Most of them are New York born and reared. It makes them nervous to think about the city being destroyed. The

Underground People don't like them or trust them. I think Savie and his people are a bunch of candy-asses. For the most part, this sector has remained fairly quiet."

"If the weather abates in the morning, we'll all resume our treasure-hunting," Ben ordered. "At first light, we'll rotate the teams guarding the bridges. They've got to be exhausted. Maintain a sharp lookout for infiltration from the Hot Wind and his Farts. The Night People are fighting for their very existence now, and they've started desperation moves. So heads up, people. Eagle out."

Ben leaned back in the chair in his new office and tried to put himself in the role of the Night People. What would he do?

The creepies knew that the Rebels were scattered all over the city, from 220th Street in the north all the way down to Battery Park. Some of the outposts and observation teams were no more than five or six people strong.

Would the creeps try to overrun the smaller units by sheer numbers?

Only as a last act of desperation, Ben concluded—a kamikaze move when all else had failed, the Night People dying screaming out their rage and hate for the Rebels.

Trying to overrun the smaller units would prove too costly for the Night People, even at this stage of the war. For the creepies certainly had observed how carefully the smaller units had bunkered themselves in, and how deadly their field of fire was.

The Night People had small arms, a few heavy machine guns and rocket launchers, and a few mortars. Not even Khamsin could match Ben's Rebels in terms of firepower, and no known force on the face of the earth could even come near the Rebels when it came to morale.

Ben smiled when he recalled the words of that old Texas Ranger who had said, "It's hard to stop a man when he knows he's right and just keeps on coming."

Ben concluded that the Night People would keep on with their harassing actions against the Rebels—not risking too many lives in doing so.

Of course the deal they had struck earlier about the use of booby traps was down the tube. From now on the war would be as dirty and nasty and unconventional as the human mind could conceive.

Long-range and very secret patrols had reported back that Brooklyn was, for the most part, clear of Night People. They had committed everything to Manhattan. Cecil and Rebet would have to keep the bridges in their area open. Ben had plans for the old shipyard—very important plans. Plans that only he and a very few others knew anything about. Whatever else happened, those east bridges had to be kept intact.

Ben rose from his chair and looked in on his crew. They were getting ready for bed. Ben walked to his cot, sat down, and pulled off his boots, stretching out on the cot. It had been a busy day, and he suspected the following days were going to be just as busy, or more so. He closed his eyes and let sleep take him, very much aware that Jerre was in the next room.

She might as well have been in another galaxy.

Ben and his people resumed their treasure-hunting early the next morning. The winds continued to blow, and it was bitterly cold, but Ben and his people had arctic gear to wear and could stand the harshness much better than the Night People.

Several times that bitter morning, all within the span of an hour, Ben and his teams came upon Night People, huddled in stinking masses on the floors of buildings. Always before, they could seek the warmth and security of their deep tunnels to shield them from the winter—now they had nothing.

Ben and his Rebels shot them where they lay and moved on. This was total extermination of the subhuman cannibals. Everyone knew that Ben Raines and his people took very few prisoners; if you were foolish enough to fight him, you accepted that it was a fight to the death.

All over the island, teams of Rebels were stripping the

city of anything of value. They were blowing bank vaults and removing any gold they might find. They discarded the coins and paper money; they were useless.

"Might make good toilet paper," one Rebel suggested with a grin, holding up a thick wad of fifty- and one-hundred-dollar bills.

Other Rebels began stuffing their pockets with paper bills. It would also be good for starting fires.

Ben had contacted Thermopolis and his people, and the hippie leader had agreed to go with Ben and his teams.

"You know folk and rock and blues and all that," Ben told him. "If you want it preserved, come on, we need the help."

They went first to the Rockefeller Center area and began sizing up the magnitude of their undertaking.

"Some of you ladies might want to visit over there." Ben pointed to Saks Fifth Avenue. He grinned at Jerre. "Might be some real expensive nighties left."

"I just want to get out of this damn cold!" she told him.

"Okay," Ben agreed. "Buddy, you and Thermopolis take the RCA Building. I don't even know if that's where they used to record or not. Dan, you and I will take the Museum of Modern Art. There are supposed to be about a hundred thousand pieces of work in there."

"If I could find and preserve the work of Cezanne and Van Gogh," the Englishman said, "I would consider my life meaningful."

"I do hope the day proves meaningful," Ben told him, keeping a straight face. "And please let us not get so wrapped up in exploring that we forget that behind every door there might be a half a dozen creepies, waiting to blow us away."

That brought them all back to earth in a hurry. They stared at the tall buildings around them.

Cooper pointed to a statue at the edge of Rockefeller Plaza. "Is that someone important, General?"

"It's a tribute to Prometheus. From Greek mythology, I think. He stole fire from the Heavens to benefit mankind. Promethean means to be creative, courageously original, or life-bringing."

Thermopolis was looking at Ben. Every day, he thought, brings out a new facet of the man. I'd like to walk around inside his head for a few hours. Then Thermopolis thought about that for a moment and changed his mind. Might be like walking around the fringes of Hell.

"Creepies!" Jerre shouted, as she was hitting the cold concrete and squirming behind cover.

Lead began howling and ricocheting off the snow-covered sidewalk as the Rebels dived for whatever cover they could find.

"Whereaway?" Ben yelled, crouched down inside a doorway.

"That one right there!" Jerre shouted over the din of gunfire.

"RCA Building," Ben muttered.

"We're closer!" Buddy shouted. "We'll take it!"

"Have at it!" Ben returned the shout.

"Don't destroy the murals!" Dan yelled. "They're priceless."

"Right," Buddy muttered, then he and his team were off and running. They tossed a grenade to blow off the doors—or part of them—on the lower level and went in with weapons set on full auto.

But the lobby was deserted. Buddy and his team knelt down behind whatever cover they could find, and all of them stared at the immense murals covering the walls, murals done by José Maria Sert, which depicted man's progress.

"Are we gonna have to tote those things off, too?" Buddy was asked.

"I suppose. We'll worry about that later. Did you see which floor the fire was coming from?"

"Third floor," Diane called from across the wide expanse of lobby.

"Take the point," Buddy told her.

They moved toward the door leading to the stairs.

"Concussion grenade in first," Buddy ordered. "Toss

one, Pete. Diane, you hold the door open."

Diane jerked the door open and the grenade was hurled in. If anyone was in there, the force of the concussion would addle anyone within the range-force of the stun grenade without destroying anything else, such as stairs or support braces.

But the cold concrete space was empty. With Diane leading the way, the team took the steps two at a time until the now-familiar odor began to touch them. They slowed and became more cautious in their advance.

At a wave from Diane, the team stopped and flattened against the concrete walls of the dark stairway. Muted voices came to them. Diane slipped forward and looked through the small wire-reinforced glass of the metal door. She smiled and handed her weapon to Pete, then took two fire-frags from her battle harness and pulled the pins just as Buddy stepped forward and put his hand on the doorknob, slowly turning it. He nodded at her and jerked open the door.

Diane rolled the grenades in and Buddy slammed the door, all of them hitting the cold stoop and stairwell.

The mini-claymores blew, the concussion of the powerful grenades bringing down a shower of dust and shaken-loose plaster and wild cries of pain from inside the darkened hallway.

Buddy went in first, followed by Pete, Diane, Harold, and Judy. Three to the left, two to the right, their weapons set on full auto. They cleared the hall of all living and unholy things. Buddy saw a door open and quickly close. He ran toward the door and blew it off its hinges with a burst from his Thompson, then sprayed the interior with a long burst, hearing the screams from the stinking and dusty room.

Jumping to his left, he dropped the empty clip and fitted in a one-hundred-round drum. It takes a strong man to handle a Thompson for any length of time with a hundred-round drum in its belly, for the weight is approximately twenty pounds. That's more than the old

Browning Automatic Rifle.

"Coming from your left, Buddy!" Diane yelled the warning.

Buddy dropped to the floor, leveling the powerful old SMG, and held the trigger back, working the muzzle from left to right, fighting to keep the weapon from shooting at the ceiling.

The .45-caliber slugs knocked creepies spinning and sprawling and howling in pain as the big hollow-noses tore into flesh and shattered bones. The dirty, rat-droppings-littered floor became slick with blood from the dead and dying.

Judy tossed a fire-frag into a crowded room, the force of the explosion knocking one crawler out a window. He went spinning and screaming to the snow-covered plaza below. His howling ended when he impacted with unyielding concrete.

The firing ceased and the Rebels slowly rose to their boots.

"Let's clear the rest of the building," Buddy said, his voice quiet in the now calm but gunsmoke-filled air of the hallway.

He lifted his walkie-talkie and advised the Rebels at ground level that the third floor was clear.

Thermopolis and his people walked toward the seventy-story-high building.

"Have fun climbing up to the observation deck," Ben called after him. "It's on the sixty-fifth floor."

"He needs the exercise!" Rosebud called over her shoulder.

Thermopolis looked at his wife and bit back the comment forming on his tongue.

They disappeared into the lobby of the building.

Ben and Dan turned toward the Museum of Modern Art, not knowing what to expect, but both of them were expecting the worst. Inside, they paused for a moment, looking around. It was bad, but not as bad as it could have been.

Some of the paintings had been slashed with knives;

nearly all had been jerked down from the walls and thrown to the floor. A lot of them were ripped beyond repair.

"Mindless wanton destruction," Dan muttered, squatting down and looking at what was left of a watercolor. "No rhyme or reason for it." He reached out to touch the faded colors, then froze his fingers an inch from the painting.

Ben had turned, watching the Englishman. "What's the matter, Dan?"

"Don't move, General." He raised his voice. "All Rebels, freeze where you are! It's booby-trapped, General. Beth, get Buddy and his people on the horn. Advise them to back out slowly, retracing their initial steps."

"Let's go, people," Ben said. "Slow and easy."

Across the plaza, a huge explosion ripped the air, as a section of the fifth floor of the RCA Building was torn apart.

THIRTEEN

Ben and his people, safely outside the museum, waited behind cover in the plaza until Buddy and his group had exited the RCA Building and made their way across the snow-and-ice-covered plaza.

"Tapper and Robin," Thermopolis said, the emotional pain very evident in his eyes. "Two of your Rebels that I didn't know by name. At least two, maybe more. They must have touched something that was wired to blow."

"I am sorry," Ben said.

"I believe that," the hippie said. "I was under no illusions that we would all return home en masse."

"What now, Father?" Buddy asked.

Ben sighed heavily, his breath frosty in the icy air. "We don't have the time to clear the area floor by floor. Besides, we'd be sure to lose more people." He looked at Dan. "Is it worth it, Dan?"

The Englishman shook his head. "Regrettably, no. Future generations will have to be content to gaze upon pictures of the great works." He looked back at the museum. "Goddamn people who would do this. Goddamn them all to the pits of Hell!"

Ben and his Rebels, and Thermopolis and his hippie-Rebels, walked slowly away from a thousand or more years of history. They didn't like what they were doing, but all knew they had no other alternative. As for those lost in the explosion, there was nothing anyone could do. The blast had been so powerful that the living would have had to scrape up the dead with spoons.

"Before they reach the pits of Hell," Rosebud startled Thermopolis by saying, "they're going to have some Hell on Earth—from us!" She savagely jacked a round into her AR15.

"Now, dear," Thermopolis said.

"Shut . . . up!" she told him.

"Right," Thermopolis agreed.

The Russian, Striganov, listened as Ben briefed him on what had taken place that morning. "For what it's worth, Ben," Striganov said, "I would have done the same. Perhaps it's time for us to start looking more to the future, rather than to the past. We know the mistakes that were made. Perhaps that's all we can salvage."

"You may be right, Georgi. Any movement up here while we were gone?"

"Very little. My people found half a dozen or so hiding places of the odious bastards. They were destroyed where they lay."

"Intercept any communications from Khamsin?"

"Not a word. It's my guess that he is still trying to come up with some sort of plan of attack. And he's having some difficulty in doing so."

"You think the man is insane, Georgi?"

The Russian pondered on that for a moment. "No . . . no more so than any fanatic. But I think if he knew he could kill you in the process, he would cheerfully die accomplishing it."

"Yes. And that is just one of the many differences between us. Let's have some lunch and start checking out more places. The creepies could not have booby-trapped every building in the city."

"Have you made up your mind whether or not you plan to destroy the city, Ben?"

"Yes," Ben acknowledged, and would say nothing else on the subject.

The loss of two of his regular Rebels and the loss of the husband and wife from Thermopolis's group bothered him, turning him testy. His personal team knew the signs and left him alone.

Right after lunch, Ben waved his people into cars and closed-bed trucks. "Where are we going, General?" Cooper asked.

"Head-hunting," Ben told him. "Just drive. Head south. I'll tell you when to stop."

It was very slow going, even with the four-wheel-drive vehicles and chains on the tires. The snow, covered with a layer of ice, was treacherous.

"What was all that stuff I saw being loaded into the back of that deuce and a half, Ben?" Jerre asked. "It looks like space equipment."

"Flamethrowers. If you like, I'll give you a short course on the nomenclature of flamethrowers, Jerre."

"Thank you, Ben. That's something I have always wanted to learn about."

Ben chuckled, some of his bad mood leaving him. "I knew it was, kid. Veer a few blocks over to the east. I had an idea about an hour ago. There used to be a lot of places on this island that needed bringing down. I think today would be just a dandy day to do it."

Beth had been listening to chatter through her headphones. "Dan and his people are right behind us, sir."

"Yes. He knows where we're heading. Get me West on the horn, Beth." He picked up the mike at her signal. "Colonel, have you or any of your people inspected any of those old condemned buildings northeast of the park?"

"Negative, General. Damnit!" The word exploded out of his mouth and through the speaker. "You're right, of course. The last place we would think to look for them would be among the rubble of condemned buildings. You need some help?"

"Ten-fifty, West. Hold what you've got. When we start burning them out, they're going to have one direction to go: south toward you."

"Ten-four, General."

"Dan?"

"Go, sir."

"Split your people. I want the area we spoke about blocked off on three sides: north, east, and west. You and your team go in with me."

"Ten-four, General."

"Cut east for a couple of blocks, Cooper."

"To those blocks of abandoned buildings, sir?"

"Yes."

"It don't look like anybody has lived there for a hundred years, sir."

"It hasn't been that long, Cooper. And for a while, back in the eighties, Harlem underwent quite a revitalization period. They just never quite got to these places. I think that's where the night crawlers are hiding. At least, a good many of them."

"Under all that crap!" Jerre spoke. "In the basements of places they thought we'd never look."

"Right, kid. And I almost didn't think of it. If I'm right, we'll further shorten the odds against us this afternoon and night. And we will be working in this area until we've destroyed them all. I've ordered hot food to be sent to us. It's going to be a long, cold, and very bloody next twenty-four hours."

Dan's teams worked like well-oiled machinery; they were moving into position from the moment the trucks stopped. Ben turned around at the sounds of trucks laboring over the ice and snow. He smiled as Cecil stepped out of a pickup and moved toward him. The men shook hands.

"You know, Ben, when I was up here back in . . . eighty-seven, I think it was, just over there," he pointed, "I saw some of the most beautiful renovation work I'd ever witnessed. They were going to raze this area, I believe."

"Well, let's pick up where they left off, old buddy," Ben told the black man.

"Right on!" Then Ben and Cecil did some fancy handshaking while the younger Rebels looked at them and wondered what in the hell was going on between the two generals.

"That's kind of a hip way of shaking hands," Jerre explained to a couple of Rebels, both of them about nineteen. They would have been very young children when the Great War ravished the earth.

"What's hip?" the girl asked Jerre.

And at that moment, Jerre felt her age—every bit of it. "With it," she tried again.

The two young Rebels stared at her.

Jerre shook her head and took one more shot. "Being different," she said, standing out in the bitter cold.

"Why would anybody want to be any different than what we are now?" the young man said, just as Thermopolis came walking up.

Ben had heard the comment, and he caught Thermopolis looking at him, a slight smile on the hippie's lips. Ben returned the smile and said, "You think you can change him, go ahead."

"I wouldn't even try, General," Thermopolis replied. "It's not that you're such a tough act to follow, but because you've had him longer."

"Yes," Ben agreed. "There is that to consider. Where's your wife?"

"Back in quarters." Damn! Thermopolis mentally fumed. He's got me talking military now. Shit! Just being around the man is infectious.

"You understand that we're down here for the duration?"

"Perfectly."

"Fine. You work with my team, then. We can work and argue at the same time."

Killing people is work? "Fine, General." He walked over to stand by the two generals.

"You two have met, I think," Ben said, pointing between Cecil and Thermopolis.

"Good to see you." Cecil shook the outstretched hand. "Sorry about those booby traps. I know what it's like to lose friends and loved ones."

Thermopolis had learned just recently that Cecil's wife,

Lila, had been killed during the fighting in the old Tri-States.

And still they fight on, he thought. But he knew why they did it. And was glad they did. *They?* he thought. Crap, I've got my butt right in the middle of it, as well.

"Did I hear you say something about arguing, Ben?" Cecil asked.

"Thermopolis and I have been looking forward to a good debate for weeks."

"I hope you realize what you're getting into," Cecil told Thermopolis. "I've been arguing with him for fifteen years and don't recall ever winning an argument."

Beth stepped forward. "The Scouts are all in position, General. The demolition teams have planted their explosives and are waiting word."

The demolition teams had lifted manhole covers and lowered in huge charges. They had stuffed charges into drain holes and planted hundreds of pounds of high explosives into the lower levels of basements. They had worked very fast; it helped to beat the cold.

Ben hoped that the massive explosions would seal off many of the hidey-holes of the Night People, forcing them up into this area, or driving them south toward West and his people.

"Brace yourselves, people," Ben warned. "It's going to be a mighty bang. Beth, tell them to hit it."

Beth relayed the orders, and the street under their boots trembled as the charges blew. Huge clouds of dust shot up into the cold air as Ben was adjusting the shoulder straps of a flamethrower. At least thirty other Rebels were doing the same, including Cecil.

"Burn it!" Ben ordered. "If it'll ignite, fire it. Drive the bastards above ground."

Ben and his personal team were moving forward before the dust had settled, Cooper carrying extra twin tanks of fuel for the flamethrower.

Ben stepped into a building that had been long-abandoned even before the Great War. A smile touched his lips as the now-familiar stink of the creepies reached him. He could very clearly see the tracks of their shoes in the snow that had blown in through the shattered windows and empty doorframe.

The steps led straight to a black hole leading down into the lower level. Old wooden steps that widened Ben's smile.

"You enjoy killing, General?" Thermopolis asked, noticing the smile.

"Not particularly. But when I'm dealing with sub-humans such as these night crawlers, it doesn't bother me all that much, either." He met Thermopolis's steady gaze. Still looking at the man, he said, "Jersey, you and the others spray that lower level. Let's see how the creepies like ricochets."

His team stepped forward, and the empty shell of a building rattled with gunfire and the wicked whining of lead bouncing off concrete and brick. Screams of anguish rose from the stinking cold darkness of the basement as the flattened lead tore into flesh.

Ben stepped forward and triggered the nozzle of the old flamethrower, the thickened gas whooshing out, setting the wooden stairs blazing, igniting the dust of the basement, and creating an inferno in the lower level of the building.

"Toss some grenades down there, gang," Ben ordered, as the smoke began billowing up. He looked at Thermopolis. "You sure you have the stomach for this?"

Thermopolis's smile was as lean as the temperature. "You just do your thing, General. I'll be right beside you."

FOURTEEN

Twice in the next hour Thermopolis saved Ben's life by shooting creepies who popped out of the burning smoking underground and pointed guns at Ben.

Ben grinned at the hippie. "Sure you wouldn't like to join the Rebels on a regular basis?"

"Thank you, but no. After this is over, I shall have enough excitement stored in my memory banks to last me several lifetimes."

"You're all right, Therm," Ben said with a laugh. "Probably voted the straight democratic ticket back when such things were around, but you're all right."

"Goddamnedest compliment I ever heard in my life," the hippie muttered.

Several black-robes came running out of a burning building, their underground escape routes blocked by the explosions that had started this campaign.

Ben seared them with a long burst from the nozzle of the flamethrower, sending them dancing and howling into death. Ben slipped into fresh fuel tanks and glanced at Thermopolis. "Want to try this, Therm?"

The sweet smell of charred human flesh floated on the cold air and settled into the clothing of the Rebels.

"No, thank you. Pyromania has never been an overwhelming compulsion of mine."

Ben laughed at the friendly but caustic remark and moved on.

"Colonel West reporting heavy fighting in his sector, sir," Beth said. "He says his men are stacking up the creepies like stovewood."

"Good. We've been effective in blocking off most of their escape routes. We could conceivably break the backs of the creepies this day and night."

"And then all we have to deal with is Khamsin," Thermopolis reminded them all.

"No sweat, Therm," Ben told him. "Trust me."

"That's the problem," the hippie said dryly. "I'm beginning to do just that."

The cracking of burning wood, the thick, sweet-scented smoke, and the occasional collapsing of a building became familiar sounds in the waning daylight as Ben kept up the pressure.

"Set charges!" he yelled to the men and women handling the explosives. "Bring the buildings down on their heads. You others, use tear-gas grenades to flush them out." He turned to Buddy. "Son, you remember that fenced-in area we passed on the way up here?"

"The one with all the fifty-five-gallon drums stacked up?"

"That's it. Take some Rebs and some trucks and get down there. Cut the tops off of them and bring them back up here. We'll fill them with loose-packed dirt and saturate that with gasoline. We can use them for heating purposes and to give us light this night. Go, boy!"

Buddy was off and running.

"Beth, bump HQ and tell them to get a truckload of flares up here. When that's done, tell General Striganov and Ike to go to full alert—everybody up and ready this night."

"Yes, sir."

Thermopolis was curious about that. "Why those last orders, Ben Raines?"

"If you were in the creepies' shoes, wouldn't you call a close ally and ask him to take the pressure off?"

"Ahh! Yes. I certainly would."

Ben smiled and walked away, whistling an old tune

from the fifties: "Let the Good Times Roll!"

"Doesn't anything ever bother that man?" Zipper asked Thermopolis.

"Yes." His reply was slow as he cut his eyes to Jerre. "And she's standing right over there."

The demolition teams began bringing the buildings down, the shattering crashes sending huge clouds of dust swirling upward, joining the dark smoke from the burning building.

Buddy and his teams worked swiftly with the barrels, filling them with dirt and saturating the dirt with gasoline. The barrels were placed half a dozen to a short block, more to a longer block, and into buildings the Rebels would occupy that cold winter night. Portable coal-burning stoves were brought down with the hot food, the Rebels taking shifts eating and sipping scalding hot coffee. The food and the coffee chased away the weariness brought on from the frantic work of that afternoon.

All of the Rebels longed for a hot bath, but all knew that was impossible. Maybe tomorrow. Maybe. For now, they would tolerate their grimy hands and faces and the stale smell from their bodies.

South of Ben's area, the elusive, seldom-seen but friendly Underground People had taken up positions in Central Park. Gene Savie's people were scattered along a dozen-block area, and Colonel West and his mercenaries had sealed off 86th Street, west to east, over to the Carl Schurz Park. The Rebels had placed many of the creepies in a box, and Ben was determined to put the lid on the box, nail it shut, and bury it.

Then he would deal with Khamsin.

The still-burning buildings cast weird dancing shapes and shadows flickering across the snowy street as demolition crews worked in the night, planting more charges and bringing down more of the old long-abandoned buildings. As the Night People tried to make their escape above ground, their underground tunnels blocked and collapsed, the Rebels shot them as they ran.

Those creepies who actually made it out of the ruins had but one direction to run—south—and when they did, they ran smack into Savie's survivors, the mysterious Underground People, and Colonel West and his mercenaries. The few night crawlers who made it into the park in the curve of the East River were hammered to the cold earth by lead from hidden machine-gun emplacements.

Ben sat in the relative warmth of a ruined building, sipping on a mug of coffee, smiling, savoring the sweet aroma of hot coffee and the equally sweet taste of victory. He knew there would continue to be battles between his forces and the Night People, probably right up to the moment he would lead his forces out of New York City—and he would lead them out—but the back and both legs of the cannibalistic creepies had been broken.

Thermopolis sat a few feet from Ben, watching the man munch on a biscuit and sip his coffee. "I don't suppose," Thermopolis said, "now that you feel the Night People have been routed, you'd care to tell us how you plan on dealing with the Libyan?"

Ben met his eyes. "He'll have to come to us."

"Why? Why can't he just sit over there in New Jersey and starve us out?"

"For one thing, he doesn't have the food to outlast us. I'm betting I'm right on that. Neither does he have the patience. Those people aren't accustomed to harsh winters, and this winter is a long way from being over. He knows we have him outgunned with long-range artillery. He has two very shaky allies in Monte and Ashley. He's going to have to make his move very quickly, or those two will cut and run. Sister Voleta—and keep in mind that she is a nut—and her followers, all trash and scum, will soon weary of the waiting; I've dealt with them before. Therefore, to keep his army intact, Khamsin will have to come to us." *Especially after I put the needle to him,* Ben thought.

"You want him to come to us, don't you?"

"Yes. Now that his forces have been cut in half."

Thermopolis sipped his coffee—real coffee, now that a large warehouse had been discovered in the city—and studied Ben Raines. Jersey and Beth and Jerre were all huddled together. He didn't think they were asleep, but they weren't far from the arms of Morpheus. Cooper and Buddy and a few other Rebels were watching and listening to the exchange.

"You could get us off this island right now, couldn't you, Ben Raines?"

Ben smiled at the man. "Now why would you think a thing like that, Therm?"

"Because you're sneaky and calculating and would never let yourself be put in a box without an escape hole, that's why."

But Ben would only smile and offer no comment.

"If you have a plan," Thermopolis pressed, "and something were to happen to you, how would the rest of us know what to do?"

"Assuming I have a plan, there will be others I will have taken into my confidence. Relax, Therm, we're going to win this fight."

"And the next one and the next one and more after that, right, Ben Raines?"

"Sure. Many years of fighting face us. You and your bunch better stick with us, Therm."

"Why?"

"Simple. You're marked now. All up and down and across the nation, the word has gone out among the filth and crud and warlords and what-have-you: the hippie has traded his peace symbol for a gun. . . ."

"But we've always carried guns."

"But you never before linked up with me, Therm. You were pretty much left alone because you people would fight if pressed into it. Now look at you. Combat boots, body armor, battle dress, and you're commanding your own detachment, a part of a larger army. Ben Raines's Rebels. And whether you like it or not, you'll leave here knowing a hell of a lot more about survival than you did coming in. And you'll put it to use."

"So?"

"Other small groups of people who think like you—and I'm not saying your way of thinking is wrong, because it isn't—will join your group, your commune, whatever you call it. Your ranks will swell and you'll have a settlement, a town, with schools and medical facilities and so forth. And others of a different ilk will try to take it from you. And what will you do?" Ben shrugged. "Fight . . . it's human nature." He smiled at the hippie. "Welcome aboard, Therm."

Thermopolis did not return the smile. "All that you just said need not necessarily be true."

"Ah, but it is, my friend. You're not going to allow what you have built and what you will build to be taken from you. For all your beads and long hair and noble words, you and I are not that much different."

"The hell you say!"

"Don't you have rules within your commune?"

"Of course," Thermopolis said indignantly, but with a sinking feeling that he was going to lose this debate. Bastard was tricky.

"Why do you have rules if you're such a free spirit?"

Thermopolis pointed a finger at Ben. "We have rules, not inflexible laws like you and your group."

"Bullshit, Therm. What do you do when one of your group turns bad and rapes or kills or steals?"

"That has never happened since we've been together." The son of a bitch is about to trap me again, Thermopolis thought.

"Why hasn't it happened, Therm? If your society is so free and open and so forth? You just let in anybody who comes wandering up, right?"

"No, Ben Raines, we don't do that."

"Ah! You don't. So you must have a certain code, or set of laws—*rules*, since we're playing semantics here—that you go by, right?"

"Yes, Ben Raines," Thermopolis said wearily. "We do." Bastard!

"You have schools, Therm?"

"Of course, we have schools!"

"We have schools. You have medical facilities?"

"Of course, we do!"

"So do we. Is there a system of government within your organization? Someone to whom people come to make the final decisions."

"In some cases, yes."

"And that person is . . . ?"

"Me, Ben Raines!"

"And there are basic . . . *rules* that anyone joining must agree to abide by, right?"

"Yes," Thermopolis sighed.

"Do you have a system worked out as far as who does what if you are attacked?"

"Yes, Ben."

"So you have an army. I'm sure you call it a home defense force, or something like that. Maybe it isn't even named. But you have, nevertheless, people who give orders and people who take them, right? If you didn't, the force would be unworkable, right?"

"Yes, Ben."

A crashing explosion and the following sounds of a building coming down halted the exchange momentarily.

"Are you and your group stagnant, Therm?" Ben picked it up.

"What do you mean?"

"Are you content with the status quo? Do you experiment with food crops, seeking ways to grow more and better food, say, without the use of chemicals that ultimately poison the earth?"

"Yes, goddammit!"

"So do we. Do you believe now, or before the war, that animals of the forest should be hunted for sport?"

"No, Ben Raines. I never thought of that as sport."

"Neither did I. Are you or were you opposed to the trapping of animals?"

"I used to destroy traps whenever I found them. I think trapping is cruel."

"Well, now, isn't that quite the coincidence? So do I.

Damn, Therm, if we keep going this way, agreeing on everything, we're likely to discover that we're soul-mates, or something like that."

"Good God, spare me that!" Thermopolis's comment was Mojave-dry.

"Oh, we'll always have something to argue about, Therm. But there isn't fifteen cents' worth of real difference between us."

Thermopolis looked at him, clearly disgusted with himself. "Music!"

Ben laughed. "I don't care what kind of music you listen to, Thermopolis. Just as long as you don't try to force me to listen to it."

"I give up," Thermopolis said, waving his hand. "You may be a bastard, but you probably can't help it."

Ben jerked his .45 out of leather, jacked the hammer back, pointed the muzzle at Thermopolis, and pulled the trigger.

FIFTEEN

Thermopolis felt the heat of the big slug as it passed within an inch of his right ear. The events had taken place so swiftly he had not had time to exit the backless chair in which he'd been sitting.

He heard a choked-off scream behind him and looked around. A black-robed creepie was draped over the windowsill, blood leaking out of his bullet-torn throat. The creep bubbled and gurgled and then was jerked out of the window by a couple of Rebels. He was finished with a single shot to the head.

"Sorry about that, Therm," Ben said, easing the hammer down on the .45. "But I didn't have time to warn you."

"Perfectly all right, Ben Raines." He rubbed his right ear. "I thought I'd said something to irritate you."

Ben smiled and shook his head. "Let's get a few hours' sleep while we can. I have a gut feeling that Khamsin is going to pull something this night."

"Let them come, let them come," Ike whispered into his headset mike, as his eyes pierced the darkness through night glasses.

The tanks had lowered their cannon to the minimum elevation. Rebels knelt and lay behind .50-caliber machine guns. Mortar crews were constantly changing angle, matching the slow movement of the dozens of light boats being paddled and oared across the Hudson from the slips at Hoboken to the docks along Eleventh Avenue, Manhattan side.

"Flares!" Ike ordered.

A dozen flares were fired into the air, their brilliance lighting up the night sky and trapping the Hot Wind's men in a blaze of artificial light.

"Fire!" Ike yelled.

From 14th Street all the way down to Clarkson the shoreline trembled and thundered with gunfire.

"Flares!" Georgi Striganov ordered, from his position on the river's edge at 155th Street, miles north of Ike's position.

And Thermopolis lay in his sleeping bag and looked at Ben. The general was sitting up, rolling a cigarette and chuckling softly.

"Is all this a joke to you, General?"

The others, including Buddy, lay awake in their sleeping bags, listening.

"Oh, no, Therm. War is never a joke. But victory is very sweet. I would imagine the Hot Wind tried to put a thousand men on the island this night. He lost them all. That knocks the odds down to just about even."

"And now what, Ben Raines?"

"Well, Thermopolis, in the morning, we put it to a vote among all the Rebels and the Russians and the Canadians and the hippies and Emil's group and the Underground People and Gene Savie's bunch."

"Put what to a vote?"

"You're going to be amazed, Therm." Ben ground out his cigarette and slipped back into his sleeping bag, closing his eyes.

At dawn, the shoreline was littered with the washed-up bodies of the men of the Hot Wind. They lay frozen and stiffening in the cold air.

"Beth," Ben said, "get me all commanders on the horn."

"On scramble, sir?"

Ben paused. "No. Let Khamsin hear this. As a matter of fact, broadcast some bullshit for a few minutes to make sure they've got us."

Beth opened the frequency and proceeded to say a large and very profane number of highly uncomplimentary things about the Hot Wind, his mother and father, and any brothers and sisters he might have had, and even insinuated some unhealthy relationship between Khamsin and a goat, back when Khamsin was a boy in Libya. Then, with a satisfied smile on her lips, she contacted all commanders and handed the mike to Ben.

"You amaze me, Beth!" Ben said. "I didn't even think you knew words like that!"

"Our countries may no longer exist, General, but I'm still a Jew and that lousy no-good bastard across the river is still an Arab terrorist." Then she spoke in very fast Hebrew.

"What did you just say?" Thermopolis asked her.

"I prayed that a camel would chew off his testicles!"

"My word!" Dan said, pausing in sipping his morning tea.

Ben sat down in a battered old chair, threw back his head and laughed.

He wiped his eyes and picked up the mike.

Khamsin had been notified and was listening, shaking, livid with rage. He muttered dark threats about what he would do to a certain Jew bitch if he ever got his hands on her.

"This is General Ben Raines," Ben began. "From all reports received over the past twelve hours, it's apparent that we have broken the backs of the Night People. That does not mean that we have wiped them out. We'll be fighting them for some time to come. But they are no longer the main threat.

"Our main concern now is that silly bastard across the river in New Jersey. The Hot Fart."

Khamsin began jumping up and down, screaming curses upon Ben's head.

"We could roll right over into New Jersey and kick his ass, but the man has no honor and none of us could trust him if he said we would be allowed safe passage across the bridge."

"No honor!" Khamsin squalled. "Kick my ass!" He picked up a chair and hurled it across the room.

Sister Voleta was listening in another section of the battered city. She had called for a meeting with Monte and Ashley. Both men had crossed back into New Jersey to join Khamsin and his people. Sister Voleta listened and shook her head.

"Typical Ben Raines," she said. "Don't fall for it, gentlemen. I know the man. Buddy Raines is my son."

Both knew that, but still found it hard to believe. Sister Voleta was a pure basket case, but as is often the case, a highly intelligent one.

"Ben is playing with Khamsin. And if Khamsin buys it, Ben will destroy him. Bet on it. You just listen, and you'll see what I mean."

"So, to all forces fighting under my command, here it is; put it to a vote. That's the Rebel way. If the Hot Wind wants this city so badly, all right, we'll just invite him over and he can damn well try to take it. Personally, I don't think that ignorant heathen has the balls to do it. So we'll see. Vote on it, people. Let me have your reply by noon. Eagle out."

Khamsin was screaming his rage, pacing the office, waving his arms, yelling curses.

"If he takes Ben up on his offer," Sister Voleta said, "we don't go. With our people, we can lie back and wait until Ben kicks Khamsin's butt—and he will. Believe it. But Ben will lose some people doing it. Then, as Raines tries to leave, we ambush him."

"I like it!" Monte smiled.

"So do I," Ashley said.

Sister Voleta smiled.

"Heathen!" Khamsin screamed, slamming both hands down on a tabletop. "How dare that filthy rabid dog call me a heathen!"

Ben looked out over the ruined and still-burning sector of the city. Bodies of night crawlers lay like huge roaches, sprawled on the dirty, sooty snow. "Collect all weapons and ammo," Ben ordered. "We're going to need them."

"The bodies, General?"

Ben hesitated. The death barges were full of frozen creepies, and his people were getting tired of hauling away dead crud. "Throw them on what's left of the still-burning buildings. Burn them."

The cold winter air stank of death, the smell was trapped in their clothing and seemed a permanent stink in their nostrils.

"Have you received a report from West on last night's fighting, Beth?"

"Hundreds of dead creepies, sir. Tina's working it up right now. Buddy and Thermopolis are working up a guesstimate of the dead up here."

"Our losses, Beth?"

"Five dead, fifteen wounded. one seriously. Most of the wounded were transported to the hospital."

"Give the orders to wrap it up here, Beth. Let's head back to the CP for a warm bath and a change of clothes."

A smile creased the woman's grimy face. "No one's going to gripe about that order, General."

They bathed in warm water and then rinsed off under a cold shower—quickly. The smell of smoke and dirt and death was tossed out into the streets and into the alleys and quickly froze.

Jersey tapped on Ben's door just as he was finishing shaving. "Come."

"Report from the Underground People, sir. They say the Judges left the city early this morning. Before dawn. I don't know how they'd know that. But they were pretty positive about it."

Ben slapped on some expensive after-shave he'd found in a department store. Jersey stood staring at the bullet scars that pocked Ben's hide. Ben slipped into a thermal undershirt and then into a field shirt, hooking his body armor over that.

"If it's true, and I have no reason to doubt it—those Underground People are a strange and mysterious bunch —it means the creepies are just about finished. We'll have little potboilers with those left in the city, but for the most part, it's over with them. Any word yet on the voting?"

"I haven't heard, area-wide, sir. But up here, including the hippies and Emil Hite's bunch, it was unanimous that we stay and finish it with Khamsin."

Ben turned to face her. "Not one negative vote?"

"No, sir."

"I figured Thermopolis would cast a negative vote just to be ornery. He got hot the other night when I told him that back in the days when this country was more or less whole, if a person didn't vote, they had no right to bitch about what was happening within and without their government. Of course, I didn't believe that then and don't now, but I enjoyed getting his goat."

Tina stepped into the office. "Voting is in, Dad. The only people who voted against inviting Khamsin in and kicking ass were Gene Savie's people."

Ben nodded his head. "I expected that. Hell with the Savies. Jersey, have Beth call for a meeting with the commanders, up here." He looked at his watch. "As quickly as possible."

For the first time, Ben met with a representative of the Underground People. The man was very pale and wore dark glasses against the reflected glare of wan sunlight off the snow. But he looked to be in excellent physical shape.

"Paul," he said, introducing himself and shaking Ben's hand. "Are you going to destroy the city, General?" Paul came right to the point.

"I don't know, Paul," Ben lied. "If I did, how much of a hardship would that be for you and your people?"

"Very little. There are many cities. You realize, of course, that you have not destroyed the Night People?

There are several thousand still in the city, and that many more in other boroughs."

"Yes, I believe that. Leaderless and confused. They'll still present something of a problem. You're sure the Judges have left the city?"

"Oh, yes. They went up into Canada. Montreal, I would think."

Striganov, Rebet, and Danjou stirred at that news.

"To start a new colony of creepies?" Ike asked.

"No," Paul said. "To join the one already there. It's worldwide, ladies and gentlemen. The perversion began more than a hundred years ago. It skyrocketed after the Great War. I would guess there are several million of them around the globe. Believe me when I say that Hawaii is now anything but a paradise."

"I think you said the same thing, Dad," Tina reminded her father.

"Yes," Ben remembered. "Well, right now let's talk about defeating Khamsin."

"Why did you throw down such a challenge, General Raines?" Paul asked.

"Khamsin has long-range artillery. We have more, but his is ample. Now that he no longer has to worry about harming any allies in this city, he could do us some damage if this thing settled into a battle of cannons. I'd rather have him over here for several reasons. One, by now, we're all familiar with this city—we're dug in deep and tight. Two, Khamsin does not know the city. Three, Khamsin is not a street-fighter; every time we've got him in a city, we've kicked his butt. He's a terrorist and not a very good field tactician. Not when it comes to moving around big armies.

"Now then, I've got people working right now planting charges on all the bridges connecting this island. I have other teams working at making certain there won't be a boat or a ship or a barge or a ferry left that'll float when we decide to pull out. And when we do pull out, it's going to be a wild, mad run for it."

"Are you going to tell Savie and his people about this

plan?" Paul asked. "I see they have no representative present."

"No, Paul, I don't intend to inform them of anything. I don't trust them."

"That is a wise decision," Paul said.

"West, what is your opinion of Savie and his group? You've been working fairly close with them for a few days."

West sighed. "I just don't know, Ben. You remember that Savie told you that originally there were thousands of people like him. I don't believe that. There is no sign that the park has ever sustained more gardens than it has now. I think he told you a bald-faced lie about that. Also, they never seem to mix it up with the Night People. Not directly. They burn up a lot of ammo, but account for damn few bodies. They're either the worst shots in the history of warfare, or they're deliberately missing."

Ben looked at Paul, the man's eyes unreadable behind the dark glasses. "Your opinion, Paul?"

"Like Mr. West, I don't know. I've never fully trusted any of them. But I do not think they are in any direct cahoots with the Night People. Not anymore. I . . . well, I think they're just very self-contained and selfish people. Very snobbish people. As to them not being able to hit anything with weapons . . . I think they have never had to become proficient with weapons, and now—for some reason—they have become very frightened people. I also think that they, long ago, made a deal with the Night People. Perhaps that agreement fell through some months ago. I've given that some thought over the past weeks. That's what I lean toward."

"You mean, sort of a live-and-let-live policy?" Ike asked.

"Yes. Precisely. Then the Night People—this is conjecture, please understand—became greedy, or regretted their agreement, and began turning on Savie and his people. But as I said, over the past few months, my people seldom ventured above ground."

"If they collaborated with the cannibals, then that

makes them just as bad as the creepies," Tina said, her expression that of someone who had just tasted something very unpalatable.

Several others muttered about what ought to be done to those so-called survivors around Central Park.

Ben held up his hand for silence. "We have no proof, people. Let's don't condemn them without some proof."

Thermopolis stood up. "Ben Raines, it isn't reasonable that a small group of people could survive in this city for almost fifteen years—not only survive, but live well—surrounded by thirty or forty thousand of these cannibals."

"Just relax, people. I've had my own suspicions of Savie and his people since long before I first met with them. But we're not going to do anything just yet. I might decide to use them as grist for the mill. So to speak," he added dryly.

They all knew better than to push for any further details. But they all knew that Ben Raines could be a very vindictive man if pushed. None wanted to be in the shoes of Savie's group if they had collaborated with the Night People.

"We're going to let Khamsin bubble in his own stew for a few days," Ben said. "And while he's doing a slow burn," Ben smiled, "and he will be doing a slow burn, we'll take that time to formulate plans, resupply, rest, and go over equipment." He stood up. "Now let's get down to the bolts of this operation. We got the nuts waiting for us across the river."

SIXTEEN

"Emil," Sister Sarah said to the little con artist, "what did our friend Thermopolis say after returning from the meeting with the Great General Raines?"

Emil glanced at the woman. Since he had been in New York City, he had almost forgotten about his scam and his fictitious god Blomm. Time to be thinking about that. For if Ben Raines said they would be home by spring, they would be home by spring. Time to crank up the old scam machine, he reckoned.

"We shall be home by spring, Sister. Just in time for the planting of our gardens."

"I will be glad, Brother Emil. This place is so dreary. And I do miss your sermons and dances of praise to the Great Blomm."

God! Emil thought. *I hope she don't ask me to dance today. All this snow and ice and I'd bust my ass for sure.* "And I miss doing them, Sister. But I have been in touch with Blomm in private—it's the best I can do with all the action around us. He has not forgotten us. Now run along, my little chickie. I must pray."

Thermopolis and Rosebud had been standing close enough to hear the exchange. After Sister Sarah had gone her way, Thermopolis smiled and said, "How long have you been running this scam, Emil?"

Emil looked around frantically and put a finger to his lips. "Shush that talk!" he whispered hoarsely. "You'll call down the wrath of Blomm upon your head."

"Blomm's butt!" Rosebud said.

Emil cast his eyes Heavenward and clasped his hands together. "Forgive them, O Great One. They know not of whom they speak."

"It doesn't take you long to get back into your act," Thermopolis told him. "I ask again: How long have you had this scam running, Emil?"

"Oh, piss on it!" Emil muttered. He walked to the couple. "Years."

"Oh, I'm not condemning you, Emil. Whatever works for you." Thermopolis smiled at him. "I ran into an old friend of yours earlier this summer."

"Oh?"

"Francis Freneau."

"Crap!" Emil said. "Long Dong himself."

"I didn't tell him that so-called 'Heavenly explosion' that sent him galloping out of Louisiana was a rocket fired from Big Louie's camp out in Kansas."

"Thank you. How in the hell did you know that, Thermy?"

"Friends of ours have a small commune out there. We talk back and forth by shortwave equipment."

"How is that jerk, anyway?"

"Doing well. He has him a small group of followers up in the hills and hollows of Kentucky. He's gone into snake-handling."

"Good! I hope one bites him on the d . . ." He looked at Rosebud and clamped off the last bit. ". . . elbow," he finished it.

She laughed at the expression on his face.

"Snake-handling!" Emil shuddered. "I knew he was crazy. I didn't think he was ignorant!"

"He's defanged the ones he handles."

"I should hope. What's he have to say about me?"

"Glowing praises. And that's the truth. He says as long as you leave him alone, he'll leave you alone." Thermopolis laughed. "He told us that after that rocket blew—and he still isn't convinced that it wasn't the god Blomm—he couldn't get it up for a month."

"Serves him right. With what he's got to offer, he needs a rest."

Rosebud shook her head and laughed. "Hasn't anybody ever told you that it isn't the size of the boat, but rather the motion of the ocean, Emil? And," she added, "a certain emotion called love has a lot to do with it, too."

"Love, baloney. I been in love lots of times." He sighed and his shoulders slumped. "No . . . that's a lie. I don't think I ever have. I been too busy chasin' women to fall in love. In heat, yeah! Love, no."

"You're going to look up one of these days, Emil, and there she'll stand. The girl of your dreams."

"Tell you good folks the truth, I kind of like things the way they are now." Sister Susie walked by and smiled at him. Emil grinned as he eyeballed her posterior. "See what I mean? Ta-ta, folks. I think Sister Susie needs some counseling." Emil went tripping off behind Sister Susie.

"He's incorrigible!" Rosebud said.

"True. But it's like Ben says: His followers know it's a con, and Emil doesn't hurt anybody."

"How is the, ah, situation between Ben Raines and Jerre?"

"No better. It never will be any better, and Ben knows that, I think. I think right now the both of them are having a good time snarling at each other."

The tension was, as the saying goes, thick enough to cut with a knife.

Ben sat in his CP, alone with Jerre, who had been given the job of figuring out how long their existing supplies would last, and it wasn't a job she was particularly thrilled with. She made that clear by muttering under her breath from time to time.

Ben looked up from a city map. Jersey and Beth and Cooper were in another office, the door closed. The silent but stinging vibrations—mostly bad—that had been bouncing around between Ben and Jerre had gotten too much for them to take.

"Jerre, if you don't like that job, give it to someone else to do. But please stop with the mumbling."

Silence from the outer office.

"That's better. Thank you." Ben returned to the studying of the maps. The George Washington Bridge could not be used. So that meant that Khamsin—if he crossed over onto the island—would have to go all the way up to the Tappan Zee Bridge, or come all the way down to Staten Island and cross over into Brooklyn, then use one of the three bridges at the lower end of Manhattan.

And Ben didn't want that. He wanted Khamsin to come in from the north.

But how to get him to do that?

Mutter, mumble from the other room.

With a sigh, Ben pushed back from the desk and walked to the open door. "Why don't you just give me a ball-park figure as to supplies, Jerre?"

She looked up for a few seconds, then read from a legal pad. "About twenty-five thousand rounds of ammo for each Rebel. Several hundred grenades per Rebel. Enough food to last for approximately a year. Approximately twenty thousand AK47s taken from the dead creepies, and half a million rounds of ammo." She plopped the pad onto a desk. "You want more?"

"No, that will do. That pretty well matches up with the first report."

She glared at him. "You mean . . . you already had these figures?"

"Of course. I always have someone do a second report. That cuts down on the chance for error."

Another round of low muttering while Ben stood and smiled at her.

Dan entered the offices and almost took a step back as the vibrations from the man and woman struck him. "We found what you requested, General. Some of them are a bit rat-chewed, but most are in good shape."

"Very good, Dan." He looked at his watch. Plenty of time. "Let's start getting them up and flying. That should really set the Hot Wind to puffing and blowing."

From Castle Clinton in Battery Park, all the way up to the Bronx County line, flags began going up. American flags, Canadian flags, and Russian flags. Dan had sent people over to the UN building and found enough flags for the duration. The entire waterfront began to resemble a Tri-Country flag day celebration as the multicolored banners fluttered in the cold wind.

On the New Jersey side, this was pointed out to an already highly irritated Khamsin. It did nothing to improve his dark mood.

Ben had asked Thermopolis to write a song, and he had swiftly composed a little ditty that, if the countries still existed, would have done absolutely nothing to improve relations between America and the Arab world, since the song was about several past Arab leaders and compared them to what normally falls behind certain disagreeable pack animals of the desert.

Then Ben set up broadcasting equipment and Thermopolis, strumming a guitar, began serenading Khamsin and the troops of the Hot Wind.

Since Khamsin's idols were such wonderfully noble and deeply religious people as the Ayatollah Khomeini, Muammar al-Qaddafi, and other terrorists, and since Thermopolis used words that were somewhat less than complimentary in describing those people, Khamsin almost had a stroke when Thermopolis's voice blasted out of the speakers.

Khamsin immediately ordered all radios to be turned down and ordered all troops into prayer, beseeching Allah to strike Ben Raines dead on the spot. Please?

Allah must have been taking a nap that day, for Ben Raines remained very much alive and well in Manhattan and was thoroughly enjoying sticking the needle to Khamsin.

Even Jerre's mood improved as she listened to Thermopolis sing his songs, many times making them up as he went along. Emil wrote a little ditty about Khamsin, and he and Thermopolis joined voices and words. Then everybody started writing songs about Khamsin, and the airwaves were filled with song. Not a whole lot of talent, but everybody seemed to have a good time. On the Manhattan side of the Hudson, that is.

Ben ordered that the songs be taped so they could be played around the clock.

"Get Khamsin on the horn, Beth," he requested.

But the Hot Wind was so angry he refused to speak with Ben.

"Just as well," Ben said. "Beth, how about you and some of the others getting together and serenading the Hot Wind and his troops with some happy Jewish songs. That ought to really set his cork to popping."

Upon hearing Beth and other Jewish Rebels singing songs in that hated language, drifting across the cold waters through massive speakers set up along the waterfront, Khamsin ordered his people to pull back, out of range of the concert speakers.

Khamsin went to sleep that night with the unholy melodies still rambling around in his brain. He ground his teeth together and cursed Ben Raines in his fitful and restless slumber.

But not all the Rebels took part in the serenading of Khamsin and his army. Many worked through the day and night reinforcing positions, mining bridges, and laying electronically detonated charges all around the city, smiling and humming as they worked.

Ben went to sleep that night smiling. And not even the ever-present image of Jerre before his eyes could erase the smile on his lips.

He awakened abruptly as the sharp stink of Night People filled his nostrils. In the darkness, Ben rose and quickly dressed, buckling his body armor in place. He picked up his Thompson, clicked it off safety, and slipped into the anteroom. The smell faded as he left his office. He looked around at the sleeping forms. Ben touched Buddy on the shoulder and the young man came awake instantly.

Ben knelt down and whispered, "Slip into my office and take a good whiff."

Buddy was back in a few seconds. He sat on the edge of his cot and pulled on his boots. "Creepies in the building for sure," he whispered. "I think they've managed to work their way into the closed-up rooms next to your office."

"Probably scaled the building." Ben woke the others and alerted them with soft whispered words. "Heads up, gang. We got creepies in the building."

Before everyone could dress, one entire wall of Ben's office blew out in front of a massive, almost deafening explosion. Had Ben not awakened, he would have certainly been killed.

The explosion knocked everyone sprawling as small items became lethal objects, hurled in front of the blast.

Ben was knocked through the closed hall door and found himself sprawled on his back in the dark hallway. He had lost his grip on his Thompson.

As dark shapes moved toward him, their body odor leading the way, Ben shook his head to clear the cobwebs, and clawed out his locked and loaded .45. He emptied the weapon into the knot of creepies, then jerked a grenade from his battle harness, pulled the pin, and hurled the grenade toward the far end of the hall.

He scrambled on his hands and knees back into his debris-filled office and found his Thompson just as the grenade blew. Screaming bounced around the dark and deadly hallway as automatic-weapons fire cut through the bloody gloom.

Ben found Beth, frantically trying to contact somebody by walkie-talkie. "Big radio took a chunk of something, General. It's out."

Ben listened for a moment; it seemed that gunfire was all around them, from the street level up. "It's a full-scale attack, Beth. The creepies are throwing everything they've got at us. And it's considerable. Tell the people to stand and hold."

"Yes, sir."

"Anybody hurt?" Ben asked, looking around him, trying to see through the murk.

"A few cuts and bruises, is all," Cooper said.

Before Ben could reply, another hard explosion shattered the night and the roof fell in on top of those in Ben's CP.

SEVENTEEN

Ben was driven to his knees when a chunk of debris hit him on the back. It knocked him off balance more than hurt him, and it pissed him off that the creepies could still manage to penetrate Rebel security. And his Thompson was buried somewhere under all the rubble. He grabbed up an M14 and an ammo pouch—the ammo hopefully for the old Thunder Lizard—and swung the muzzle around just as a horde of black-robes came running through the ruined wall of his office.

"The woman!" one shouted. "Get the bastard's woman."

Ben leveled the M14 and held the trigger back, filling his shattered office with .308 slugs and knocking creepies in all directions.

"Jerre!" he shouted, over the rattle of weapons.

No reply.

"She's over there, Father," came Buddy's calm voice. "Buried under all this crap. She seems to be all right. Just knocked out."

"Grenades," Ben ordered, pulling an HE grenade from his battle harness and jerking the pin just as Buddy and Cooper were doing the same. Jersey and Beth were covering what was left of the doorway leading to the hall, and there wasn't a hell of a lot left of the hall.

The grenades blew, and the screaming that followed told the Rebels they had landed right on the mark. Buddy sprayed the darkness with .45 slugs and ended the screaming.

"It's happening all over the city, General," Beth told him, as her walkie-talkie ceased its transmission. "Scattered, but very intense."

Flames were spreading from two rooms over as Ben found his Thompson and slung it. He crawled over to Jerre, who was sitting up with the aid of Jersey. "Get her out of here," Ben told some Rebels who materialized in the shattered doorway. "Take her to Doctor Chase. And don't leave her side for any reason. That is a direct order."

"Yes, sir!" One slung Jerre over his shoulder and they were gone.

"Grab whatever you can salvage," Ben said. "Then let's get the hell out of here."

Working as quickly as they could in all the rubble, the Rebels grabbed up whatever they could find and left the building just as the flames were spreading all around them. They hit the street and ran right into a firefight.

They darted away from the burning building, and Ben spread his thin line of Rebels out behind vehicles. Lying on the frozen snow, the Rebels went to work.

"Here they come, gang!" Ben yelled, as he shouldered the butt of the M14 and let it rock and roll.

"Stand firm!" Thermopolis yelled, bringing his M16 to his shoulder. He grimaced, knowing he was beginning to sound like Ben Raines.

"Oh, Blomm!" Emil yelled. "Hear our pleas and strike these heathen dead!"

A wall of a long-abandoned building chose that time to give it up, collapsing on a dozen or more creepies, burying them under tons of brick and stone.

Rosebud looked at Thermopolis, questions in her eyes. He lowered the M16 and shrugged a "who the hell knows" gesture.

Then none of them had time to think about Blomm or anything else except survival as the creepies swarmed all over their position.

Rosebud smacked a creepie in the face with the butt of her Mini-14, and her husband shot him in the chest as he was falling backward.

Brother Sonny clubbed one on the noggin, and Sister Susie buried a camp axe into his skull. "Filthy Godless bastard!" she said.

Emil was rolling around on the dirty floor with a night crawler, both of them screaming like deranged banshees. Emil finally rolled on top of the stinking crud, a brick in his hand, and clubbed him into unconsciousness. He grabbed up his M16 and crawled back to his position just in time to have another creepie hurl himself through the broken window and land right on top of Emil, sending them both rolling around on the floor.

"Ye Gods!" Emil squalled. He jammed his fingers into the creature's eyes and then drove the stiffened fingers of his other hand into the man's throat. The night crawler fell to one side, choking and gasping for breath. Emil grabbed up his M16 and ended the gagging sounds.

"One more time," he muttered darkly, returning to his position, wary of anything that might be lurking out in the darkness, waiting to leap at him.

Emil turned to look into the eyes of a dark-haired French Canadian girl who had been cut off from her unit.

ZING!

With lead flying all around them, the screaming of the dying filling the cold night, death all around them, Emil fell in love.

"This building is cleared, General!" Dan called from across the snowy, body-littered street. "Lay down a covering fire for the general's party!" Dan yelled to his Scouts. "Come on, General!"

While the Scouts laid down covering fire, Ben and his people zigzagged and slipped and slid and almost fell down crossing the icy street. They made it intact to the dark and somewhat warmer ground floor of the old building.

"You got a radio that works, Dan?" Ben panted.

"Here, sir," Dan's operator called.

Staying low, Ben made his way over to the Rebel and took the mike. "This is Eagle. All units give me a report."

"Northernmost unit under heavy attack but holding, sir," the strange female voice, slightly accented, came out of the speaker.

"Who is this?" Ben asked.

"Michelle Jarnot, General. Part of Major Danjou's unit. I got cut off."

"It's love, love, love!" Ben heard someone shout.

He looked at Beth. "Someone is yelling that they're in love."

All heads turned to look at him.

"Did you say love, sir?" Dan asked.

Ben listened as someone began singing "Love Me Tender." Fans of Elvis had no cause for alarm.

"Yes. Love. Michelle, do you have any wounded or dead up there?"

Whoever it was up there smitten with Cupid's arrows began singing "We've Only Just Begun."

Ben flipped the toggle switch from earphones to speaker.

"Not in this unit, General. But there is going to be someone with a fat lip if they don't keep their hands off of me!"

All heads turned toward the radio.

"Somebody kindly keep their eyes to the front," Ben said. "We do have creepies out there, people."

A man's voice came out of the speaker. "This is Thermopolis, Ben Raines. Creepies are withdrawing. Our situation has stabilized. Which is more than I can say for Emil," he added.

"What's wrong with him?"

"He's in love!"

"Ten-four, Thermopolis," Ben said with a chuckle. "The situation here has also calmed. Good luck with Emil."

"Thank you, General."

Ben checked his watch. About three hours until dawn. He looked at Dan's radioman. "Check with all units. I want a status report from each."

"Yes, sir."

Ben made his way back to the front of the building. "I believe it's over. But stay alert. Fires at the rear of the building only. Take shifts warming up."

The last dark hours of morning passed slowly, with only an occasional shot blasting the darkness. From their position in the storefront, the Rebels could see the bodies of Night People sprawled in death on the bloody, trampled snow.

Dan counted heads. "Where is Miss Hunter?"

"In the hospital. I don't think she's badly hurt. When the roof caved in on us she got a bump on the head that knocked her out." Ben explained what had taken place in his office.

"Last-ditch desperation attack on their part," Dan said. "I don't think they've got the people to do it again."

"Nor do I. I think from now on it'll be minor skirmishes. But," he added, "we've said that before."

"Quite right."

As the first fingers of gray dawn began tearing away the night, the Rebels began moving stiffly out of their positions, some of them jogging in place to warm up cold-tightened muscles and get the heart rate up and the blood surging.

"Well, I guess I look for a new CP," Ben said. He turned to Beth, who had scrounged around and found another radio. "Advise Doctor Chase to get ready to move, Beth. Tell him to move everything down to the old NYC Medical Center on the East River." He turned to Dan. "Make damn sure the Brooklyn Bridge, the Williamsburg Bridge, and the Manhattan Bridge appear to be disabled, from ground and air. Khamsin has got to come at us from the north. Once he's committed his people, we throw up a line at Eighty-sixth Street. And that's where we hold him, Dan."

"Yes, sir. Your CP?"

"I don't know."

"I would suggest somewhere around the old UN Headquarters, General. I can guarantee that area is free of creepies."

"All right, Dan. Find me a place. With windows," he added, smiling.

"Yes, sir. I already have one picked out, cleared, and set up for you."

Ben's new CP was in an office building one block over from the UN Plaza. It was on the second floor, facing Second Avenue, with a good broad view. Ben inspected the windows and found they had been replaced with bullet-proof glass. Obviously, Dan had had this place in mind for some time.

On the morning of the second day in his new CP, Ben looked up as Jerre appeared in the doorway.

"Did Chase release you or did you run away?"

"He released me. I'm all right. I don't even have a headache." She looked around. "Nice place."

Ben pointed to her right. "Your office is right there. You'll be helping me mark locations of our units as we begin to shift them."

"All right, Ben."

"Chase get moved?"

"He's almost finished. He approves of the new choice. Is it about to hit the fan, Ben?"

"A few more days. I'd say five days at the most. Intell states there is a lot of activity over Khamsin's way." He leaned back in his chair and smiled. "Khamsin is moving his people north, so it looks like he's taking the bait without us having to taunt him any further."

She moved to a huge wall map and studied it. "So he'll cross over here." She placed her finger on the Tappan Zee Bridge.

"Yes. That's the only logical choice. He'd have to go miles out of his way to cross over any farther north. When he reaches the southern end of Bronx County, he'll have his choice of two bridges to use entering Manhattan. I don't care which one he uses. Certain units will be fighting a holding action as he comes over. Just hard enough to make him think he's facing our full force. When he's got his people over, probably after a couple of days, those two bridges up north will be blown, electronically, so none of our people will be trapped."

"How about this railroad bridge?" She pointed it out.

"That will go up with the others."

"All these other bridges linking Manhattan, all the way down to the footbridge?"

"They'll be blown. At least one section of them will be knocked out, thus making them unusable for any type of vehicular traffic."

"These three bridges at the south end of Manhattan? What about them?"

"That's our way out of here, Jerre. They'll be rendered useless as we bug out—when the time comes."

"Then . . . you're going to trap Khamsin in Manhattan?"

"That is my plan, yes."

"And . . . ?"

"And, what?"

"They'll eventually get off the island, Ben."

"No, they won't. At least, not very many of them."

She sat down in a chair facing his desk. "The tunnels under the river—rivers?"

"Blown. Destroyed. Blocked."

"Of course, all your top people know of this plan?"

"As of late yesterday, yes."

"And now you're telling me. You trust me that much, Ben? I didn't think you trusted me at all."

Ben shrugged. "What reason do I have not to trust you? Besides, within two or three days, every Rebel in this command will know about the plans. You know how fast camp talk spreads."

"You're that sure that the creepie informants have been . . . well, taken care of?"

"Yes. Dan is very good at that sort of thing." He stood up. "Would you like some coffee?"

"Yes, thank you. It's hard to believe that we've been

alone for five minutes and we're not arguing. It's almost like old times, back in Virginia. You remember, Ben?"

"I remember." He sat back behind his desk and sipped his coffee, looking at her beauty.

She met his gaze. "And what about New York City, Ben?"

"What about it?"

"When we bug out, I mean?"

He met her gaze, locked with it. Neither one of them blinked.

"You're going to trap Khamsin and his troops in Manhattan and then destroy the city, aren't you, Ben?"

"Yes," he said softly.

BOOK TWO

The angel of death has been abroad throughout the land; you may almost hear the beating of his wings.

John Bright

ONE

Ben's spotter planes tracked the movements of Khamsin and his army as they made their way north, proceeding up the Garden State Parkway, staying well out of the range of the Rebels' guns.

And Ben didn't know yet whether Khamsin had any intention of taking him up on his offer to butt heads in the city.

He suspected that Khamsin himself wasn't sure just yet. That was why he was moving so slowly, trying to make up his mind.

But that was all right with Ben and his people; the relative lull in the action—with only an occasional firefight with the creepies—was giving them all some much-needed time to rest and for Ben to reposition his units and to have his people lay more booby traps and more barricades and to dig in deeper.

Weapons were taken down and carefully cleaned and oiled. Cases of Chase's MREs were handed out and stored, for when this battle began, hot meals were going to be the exception rather than the rule. Every member of Ben's Rebels would be placed on the line, except for the doctors, their staff, and a few communications people.

And Ben had placed spotters on the top floors of half a dozen skyscrapers along his northernmost area of control, from the Hudson to the East River.

They would be his eyes above the streets, silently

watching and reporting to the Rebels the movements of Khamsin and his troops.

And the first day they were up, the spotters reported some very interesting news to Ben.

"A lot of movement over in New Jersey, General. Looks like the Hot Fart left several battalions behind."

"Keep an eye on them," Ben ordered. "I don't think those are Khamsin's people. I'll get back to you."

Ben leaned back in his chair and cut his eyes to Ike, telling him of the spotter's news. "What'd you make of it, Ike?"

"Those aren't Khamsin's people. I agree with that."

Ben looked at the other commanders; they all nodded their heads in agreement.

"Okay, then it has to be Monte and Ashley's troops and Sister Voleta's people," Ben said. "But why did they stay behind?"

"Because," Buddy said, "remember that my mother knows you well, Father. And she probably guessed that you were deliberately taunting Khamsin, to draw him over into Manhatttan. My thinking on this matter would be that she has convinced Monte and Ashley to join her, and not to accompany Khamsin."

"So what's she got in mind, son?"

"Killing you would be uppermost on her mind. But as to how she plans to do that . . . ?" He shrugged. "Bear in mind at all times that my mother is brilliantly insane and quite cruel."

"Why did you stay with her so long, Buddy?" West asked the handsome young man.

"I had no other place to go. And I never knew that Ben Raines was really my father until the Old One—my grandfather, I think—confirmed it just weeks before I left my mother's camp."

"Whatever your mother is up to, Buddy—and she is your mother, don't forget that, crazy or not—I won't assign you to fighting her or her people."

"You may not have a choice in the matter, Father," the young man reminded him. "She may be plotting some sort of ambush."

"She would have no way of knowing how we plan to bug out of here, son."

But Buddy shook his head. "I don't know, Father. Her hatred for you is so strong I sometimes think she can see through the miles. I've seen the woman do some things that bordered on the supernatural. She was a practicing witch, you know?"

"A witch?" Tina looked at her brother.

"Yes. Before the Great War. She belonged to some sort of satanic cult. She was some sort of high priestess." Buddy looked at the expression on his father's face and burst out laughing.

Ben shook his head. "She told me she loved my horror stories. Had all my books. She even had the bloodiest scenes committed to memory. I should have guessed that she might be a little strange. Over the months a lot of that . . . brief encounter has come back to me."

"Hell, Ben," Cecil said, "maybe she does possess some supernatural abilities. None of us can afford to discount anything anymore."

What the hell do I do? Ben thought. *Walk around carrying a silver bullet or a sharpened stake to drive through her black heart?* He sighed. "All we can do is keep an eye on those left in New Jersey and direct most of our attention to Khamsin. But advise the spotters closest to New Jersey to keep an eye out for any movement from Sister Voleta. You suppose that motorcycle bunch came up north with her, Buddy?"

"I'm sure they did. She's probably five or six hundred strong. Just her group."

"Maybe fifteen hundred then, max, counting the men with Monte and Ashley. No more than that, 'cause we've creamed the hell out of that crew," Ben mused aloud. "Enough to cause us some grief in an ambush, though."

Ben once again cut his eyes to Ike. The ex-SEAL was in charge of planting the explosives around the city. "How are the explosives holding out, Ike?"

"We'll have enough to do the job we talked about, Ben.

Especially if those methane pockets run deep, as I think they do. We've tapped into every gasoline storage tank in the city. We'll open the taps and flood the tunnels with raw gas just seconds before we bug out. Then we'll blow the big boys. I've planted chemicals in what I think are strategic locations—most of it highly concentrated and short-lived blister gas. Effective disabling time something around fifteen to twenty minutes."

"We're going to be cutting it close, gang," Ben said. "Real close. Uncomfortably so. If we stick to the original plan. And if the wind is wrong, we're really going to be in trouble."

"Do we have a choice?" West asked.

"Not really. But we have got to clear the Narrows before we hit the button, and those ships are going to have to be hauling ass, people. We're going to have to leave the tanks and the big SP artillery. But that's no big deal; we've got tanks and long toms running out the ying-yang. We can run the jeeps and light trucks right on the ferries. The rub comes in if Sister Voleta and her people set up any kind of ambush once we're back on land. We're going to be short on heavy artillery."

"Our mechanics have checked the engines on those ships, Ben," Striganov said. "They've got them purring and we certainly have the fuel for a long sea cruise."

"There is something else," Tina said. "Dad, have you considered returning to pick up our vehicles once the danger time has elapsed?"

"Yes. And I still haven't discounted it. We very well may have to return, mount up, and head up into New York State, then cut over. We have electronic air sensors we can plant before bugging out. We can monitor them for readings." Ben met the eyes of each person in the room. "Anything else, gang?"

They shook their heads.

"Tell your forward teams to move out this afternoon and get into position at One Hundred Eighty-first Street. I want Khamsin stopped cold right there for at least two days. Three days would be better, but tell your people not to hang in so long they risk being overrun and captured. Then bug out and fall back, fighting all the way. Suck him in here. When he's got all his troops on the island—and we'll know from spotter planes—blow the bridges behind him. I'll meet with the forward teams before they pull out. That's it, people. Let's go."

Khamsin crossed into Rockland County, New York, pulled his long columns onto the New York State Thruway, turned east, and then stopped.

The pilots of Ben's spotter planes reported that the Libyan terrorist's army seemed to be setting up a bivouac area about fifteen miles from the Tappan Zee Bridge.

"Come on, you bastard!" Ben muttered, staring at the huge wall map in his office.

Even Ben's Rebels were getting edgy. They were all well rested and ready for a fight. So let us get it on! was the generally shared opinion.

But Khamsin wasn't quite ready to attempt taking a bite out of the Big Apple.

"The pig is pulling something," Khamsin told several of his most trusted senior officers. "He has some sneaky and totally dishonorable plan up his sleeve. I do not trust that man at all."

"So we wait?" he was asked.

"For another day or so. I must pray for guidance."

Restless, Ben began a day-long tour of his troops, starting at the westernmost position on the parkway up the Hudson River. Colonel West and his mercenaries would defend from the parkway over to Amsterdam. Rebet and Danjou would take Amsterdam to the edge of Central Park. Cecil and the Underground People would have Central Park. Ike would take the edge of Central Park over to Third. Striganov would hold Third to York, and Buddy and Dan would take York to the East River. Ben and his people would stand in reserve, ready to plug any suddenly appearing hole in the line of defense.

It was the dead of winter in the Big Apple, but the day had started out surprisingly pleasant, with most of the snow and ice melting; the temperature during the night had not dropped below freezing.

"I'm sure that Khamsin has been praying," Ben told West. "And he'll probably take this warm spell as some sort of sign from Allah. I expect him to cross over the bridge today and hit us tomorrow."

"I have been thinking along those same lines. So even if he should cross over into Manhattan tomorrow, we still have a couple more days of this damn waiting."

"Yes. The meteorologists say this warm spell is just a prelude for a major winter storm, coming in right on its heels. If they're right, and they usually are, just about the time we blow the bridges, there'll be a blizzard hitting us."

"And we're accustomed to them and Khamsin is not."

Ben smiled. "That thought has crossed my mind. I've moved a lot of Abramses up to within shelling distance of Khamsin—when he crosses over, that is. We're going to sit back here and not make a move. The forward tanks will be well behind our front teams. The commanders have worked out the areas where the shell trajectory will clear the lower buildings. After we're all back here on the main lines, artillery can shell and let them fall wherever. Khamsin has never fought in a city like this. When the tops of buildings start coming down on their heads it's going to be a real morale-buster."

"And for us as well," West pointed out.

"Yes. Taking everything into consideration, it's going to be a miserable little war for both sides."

Ben drove over to Rebet and Danjou's sector. The two field commanders were standing together, smiling as they watched Emil Hite trail Michelle Jarnot around the area. From the look on Michelle's face, it appeared that she wished the damn war would hurry up and start—anything would be better than this.

"I will shower the ground before your pretty little feet with rose petals!" Emil wailed.

"I hate roses! They make me sneeze! Go away, Emil. Please!"

Michelle ducked into a building, with Emil right behind her, singing "Some Enchanted Evening." He sounded like Bloody Mary with a cold. *South Pacific* would never again be the same.

"How long has that been going on?" Ben asked the two men.

"Ever since Michelle got cut off from her unit the other night," Danjou replied.

"I certainly have to compliment his taste in women," the Russian said, trying to keep a straight face as Emil changed songs and the sounds of "On the Street Where You Live" came drifting out to them. "He is loving well if not too wisely."

Ben knew that feeling from personal experience. In a way, he could empathize with Emil.

"Jesus Christ, Emil!" Michelle yelled. "Will you please cool it? You're driving me bananas."

"I love you, Michelle!" Emil shouted for all the world to hear. Or at least a couple of blocks. Then he burst into a ragged rendition of "Stand By Me."

Ben chatted with the field commanders for a few moments, until Emil's singing got the best of him. He moved on over into Central Park and found Cecil.

"I hear Emil has been shot with one of Cupid's little arrows," Cecil said with a smile.

"Yeah. And I think it shot him right in the head. Now that you've had a chance to meet the Savies and their group, Cec, how do you rate them?"

"I don't trust them," the man said flatly. "Quite frankly, they make the short hairs on my neck stand up."

"You think they have any idea at all about what's going down?"

He shook his head. "No. They came around, asking questions. But my people just ignored them. I haven't seen them since late yesterday."

"Don't count on them, Cec. I don't think they know, yet, what side they want to be on. Except for the winning side.

You seen the Underground People?"

"No. But they're around."

"Bet on that. They'll stand."

Ben drove over to Ike's sector. "I won't add the activating agent to the gas until just before we pull out, Ben," Ike told him. "That's just in case one of the areas where they're planted takes a hit."

"Good. Let's take as many potential backfires out of this plan as possible."

"I'm thinking if this warm weather holds, Khamsin and his boys will come across tomorrow."

"Everyone I've spoken with agrees with that assessment, friend. Hang tough, Ike."

Ben moved east a few blocks, reaching Georgi Striganov's sector. The Russian had dug his people in deep, and his very capable troops were ready and waiting for a fight.

"Savie and a few of his bunch came around early this morning," the Russian said. "I don't trust him, Ben."

"No one else does either. But I think out of pure desperation they'll be forced to join us. If they don't fight, and fight well, their butts are going to be left in New York when we bug out."

"That wouldn't bother me at all," the Russian bluntly stated.

Ben moved over to the easternmost sector, near a small park on the East River. As usual, Dan had dug his people in deep and camouflaged them well. A master of ambush, Khamsin's men were going to be in for a very brief and very deadly encounter when they bumped into Dan and Buddy.

"Not long now, General," the Englishman said. "Tomorrow, I'd wager."

"Ten o'clock," Buddy said.

"Noon," Dan countered.

Ben left them in a friendly argument and went back to his own sector. Spirits were high among his people, and they were more than ready to mix it up and get this fight over with.

There was no sign of any Rebels in this area, as in all the sectors Ben had just inspected. His Rebels were staying low and quiet. He walked into the building where he knew Thermopolis and his people were housed and waved the man over to him.

"You have any stroke with Emil, Thermopolis?" Ben asked.

"Well, he will listen to me on occasion."

"He's making a fool out of himself over in Danjou's sector. Go get him for me, please, and haul his ass back here. Tell him I said to stay put."

Rosebud laughed and stood up. "Come on," she said to her husband. "I wouldn't miss this for the world."

TWO

"Oh, rejection!" Emil wailed on the drive back from the western edge of the park. "Death, where is thy sting? I would rather die than live without her!"

"I have a suggestion, Emil," Rosebud said.

"You have a plan?" He perked up immediately and stopped moaning about dying.

"No. I said I have a suggestion. Ignore her."

"But I love her!"

"So ignore her and see what she does. Women hate to be ignored. After a few days of being ignored, if she starts to wonder what the matter is and looks you up, then you'll know if she really cares about you." Rosebud was aware of her husband's incredulous look as he stared at her. She ignored him.

"But in a few days we might all be *dead!*" Emil moaned.

"Well, then it won't make any difference one way or the other, will it?"

Emil thought about that. "You're right. I shall ignore her. As a matter of fact, I shall make it a point to ignore her."

She glanced suspiciously at him. "What do you mean by that, Emil?"

But Emil would only smile mysteriously.

After dropping Emil off, once more back in the bosom of his block, Thermopolis and Rosebud went to Ben's CP and reported that their mission had been accomplished.

"Emil gave in that easily?" Ben shook his head. "I may make you his permanent keeper. How'd you do it?"

"It was all Rosebud. But I figure in about twenty-four hours we're all going to be so busy just staying alive that Emil won't have that much spare time to be thinking about Michelle."

"You're right about that," Ben acknowledged. "Spotters just confirmed that Khamsin has crossed over the Tappan Zee Bridge. They're on their way."

"I guess we're as ready as we'll ever be, Ben Raines. You think we'll be home in time for spring planting?"

"I guarantee it, Thermopolis." He smiled at the man and wife. "Either that, or none of us will ever have to worry about planting anything again."

"You're such a spirit-lifting person to converse with, Ben Raines."

Ben's forward teams watched as Khamsin sent people across the bridges, inspecting for mines. They found nothing, since Ike's people had planted the massive charges below the waterline.

"They're comin' across!" a team leader said. "Let's boogie out of here and let them come."

The Rebels headed south, letting the Hot Wind and his troops have the northernmost tip of Manhattan.

But Ben Raines had made Khamsin a very wary man. He was not about to be suckered another time. His troops advanced very slowly, carefully inspecting each foot of ground before they moved an inch.

Staying several blocks ahead of Khamsin's troops, a team leader radioed back to Ben, "They keep this up, and we'll be here for ten years waitin' for them."

"They'll pick up steam, Scout. It's a natural human reaction as they find no danger. Head on south and let them come."

"Yes, sir."

The forward teams got into position and waited. It was late in the afternoon before Khamsin's troops reached

Dyckman Street, and it was there the Rebels struck the first blow, hitting a hard one-two combination of automatic-weapons fire and rocket launchers.

The Libyan responded with cannon fire from tanks that were stretched out from Henry Hudson Parkway over to Tenth. The Rebels fell back two blocks, fighting as they withdrew. Khamsin studied the stituation for a few moments and then ordered his people to hold what they had taken and not to follow, fearing a trap.

The Rebels had been placed much like a series of upside down *T's,* with the bottom line growing stronger every several blocks. Khamsin faced no more than twenty-five widely scattered Rebels at Dyckman. As the Rebels fell back, they joined twenty-five more at Ellwood; twenty-five more waited at Fairview. So by the time Khamsin and his men advanced down to 181st Street they would be facing several companies of Rebels. By the time they reached 171st Street, Khamsin would be committed and Ben would start blowing the bridges, from the northernmost tip of the island all the way down to and including the High Bridge.

By that time, Khamsin would realize what Ben was up to. He would also know that he had been boxed in and that this was a fight to the death.

Khamsin crossed Dyckman and advanced only two more blocks that day. He had no desire to face Ben Raines's Rebels in the darkness of deadly night. Khamsin was fully aware of how vicious the Rebels were, how coldly and impersonally they killed. He ordered his troops to seek shelter and keep their heads down.

They would be safe this night. Ben had ordered no booby-trapping this far north. He wanted the Hot Wind and his mini-farts to get deeper into Manhattan and be totally committed before they truly discovered the horrors of guerrilla warfare.

The slowly retreating Rebels knew which buildings to avoid as they withdrew. Khamsin and his men, of course, did not. If Khamsin thought his fanatic mentors were experts at terrorism, he was only a few days away from looking into the cold eyes of the Grand Master.

Ben Raines.

"Khamsin has ordered his people in for the night, General," Beth relayed. "They've bivouacked at Thayer and Arden, with some of them stretched out from the Hudson to the Harlem rivers."

"He's playing it cautious. I'm sure memories of Atlanta are fresh in his mind."

"Orders, sir?" Beth asked.

"Tell our northernmost teams to step down one alert and get some rest. Tell them I compliment them on a job very well done."

Ben returned to his desk and began studying maps of the city. Khamsin still had several miles to travel before Ben and his troops would cut loose with the full fury of Rebel-style warfare, and Ben knew the Libyan would take those miles very slowly and very cautiously. But Ben also knew the man's confidence would grow with each block. But Khamsin could not be allowed to take those blocks easily. He would have to pay for them in terrorist blood, but not too much blood.

Ben and his people were walking a tightrope in luring Khamsin into Manhattan; one misstep and the Rebels would fall. And there was no safety net below them. Only death waited for them in the impersonal and seemingly barren city streets.

Ben suddenly realized he was hungry and that he had skipped lunch; he had been too busy monitoring radio reports coming in from the forward teams. He picked up his Thompson and went down to the makeshift kitchen that had been installed in the floor just below him and fixed a sandwich and a cup of coffee.

"Want some company?" The voice came from behind him.

Ben did not have to look up or turn around from his sandwich-making; he knew who it was. "Sure. You want something to eat, Jerre?"

"A sandwich would be nice, thank you." She sat down at the table. "This waiting is getting to me."

"They'll be on us before you realize it." He placed a sandwich and a cup of coffee before her. "Then we won't have time to think about anything except staying alive." Ben sat down across the table from her.

"How about all the subway bridges south of us, Ben?"

"They're already crippled; sections have been knocked out so they can't be used as footbridges."

"I'm not criticizing, Ben."

"I know. It's part of your job to follow up, make damn sure I haven't missed anything. And I appreciate the good work that you've done." He smiled at her. "Have you seen Emil?"

That got a laugh out of her. "I feel sorry for him. I think he's really in love with that girl."

"He probably is. He's screwed around all his life, chasing every skirt he could find without getting emotionally involved. Now that the real thing has reared up and slapped him in the face, or shot him in the butt, whatever, he doesn't know what to do."

"You speak from experience, Ben?"

"Yes." Damned if Ben was going to pursue this subject. "How's your sandwich?"

"Very good."

"How are your quarters?"

"Nice. Almost like home."

"And where has home been in the last few years?"

"Up in the northwest. Then out on the Plains. I've never stayed long in one spot. Pretty much just been moving around."

"Looking for what?"

"I don't know, Ben. And that is an honest answer."

"I believe you. If you'll recall, that's what I started out to do, years back."

"I remember. You were going to write a journal about what happened and how the survivors responded to the Great War. How far did you get in doing that?"

He shook his head. "I really didn't even get started. The Tri-States were born; I was busy running that . . . not that I wanted to," he added. "I just got stuck with the job. Then the war came."

"Then you were president."

"Again, against my will. And for the past few years seems like all we've been doing is fighting one war after another."

"No special woman in your life, Ben?"

He met her blues. "Yes, Jerre. There will always be a special woman in my life."

"Whether I like it or not?"

"Whether you like it or not."

"And there is nothing I can do to change your mind?"

"How do you stop loving someone?" He finally spoke the words to her. He had spoken them silently for years.

She dropped her gaze and finished her sandwich. Neither of them spoke during the rest of the meal. She rose and dropped the paper plate into the trash. "Guess I'll be getting back to work, Ben. Thank you for the sandwich."

"You're certainly welcome." He waited until he was certain she had made it back to her office and then picked up his Thompson and went outside to stand for a time. The weather was still abnormally warm for the middle of winter.

The stench of death still clung faintly, sickly sweet over the city. Ben knew some of his people had taken this time to tow the barges full of dead creepies out to sea and dump them. It was not a job that anyone relished, but one that had to be done to keep down disease.

No one had reported any contact with what was left of the shattered army of Night People this day. Ben suspected they had given up and pulled back into what hidey-holes they had left and were waiting for death to take them.

Gene Savie and his survivors entered his head. Ben just could not make up his mind about that bunch.

He agreed with the leader of the Underground People, Paul, that it was highly unlikely that Savie and his group could have survived in the city without making some sort of deal with the Night People.

But the Judges were gone, and the back had been broken of those creepies remaining in the city. Knowing that, why, then, would they be so seemingly unwilling to help in the fight against Khamsin? It just didn't make any sense to Ben.

He shrugged it off and went back inside his CP. He'd turn in early this night. There was that old guerrilla fighter's adage: eat when you can, drink when you can, and sleep when you can. For you never knew when you might get the chance to do any of the three again.

Ben was up several hours before dawn, drinking coffee and once more going over maps of the city. The question paramount in his mind: *Have I missed anything?*

He could not think of a thing.

Now it was in the hands of God and the guns in the hands of Rebels.

Beth walked in, yawning. "I saw your light, General. Anything I can get you?"

"How about a miracle?" Ben grinned at her.

"'Fraid I'm fresh out of those, General. But"—she returned the grin—"we found a food warehouse late yesterday. Lots of it in good shape. How about some cinnamon toast for breakfast?"

"Cinnamon toast. I haven't had that in years."

"Then you better come on. Thermopolis is down in the kitchen and he's already eaten half a loaf of bread and a pound of butter."

THREE

After having to practically arm-wrestle Thermopolis for the cinnamon can, Ben ate the rest of the fresh-baked bread, covered liberally with butter and sugar and cinnamon.

Jerre entered the kitchen and said, "Doctor Chase would disapprove of all that sugar."

"You want some?" Ben asked, his mouth full.

"Naturally." She sat down and took what was left on Ben's plate and grinned at him as she chomped away.

"I'm not fixin' any more of this damn bread!" Jersey bitched.

"I've had plenty," Thermopolis said.

"Yeah. Me, too," Ben echoed, then looked at Thermopolis. "Where is your wife?"

"I left her sleeping. I got up when I heard Emil pacing the floor and muttering to himself about tiny arrows piercing his heart."

"He certainly has been smitten, that's for sure." Ben looked up as Beth entered the room.

"Khamsin's started his offensive, General. And he's hitting hard."

"Let's go to work, gang. If our people can keep on sucking them in, at dawn tomorrow, we blow the bridges." He stood up and sighed. "And God have mercy on our souls if I've made a mistake."

"We voted to stay, General," Jersey reminded him.

"We're all in this together."

Ben nodded, smiled, and stepped outside into the abnormally warm morning. He looked up at the sky. "Hold on for just one more morning," he muttered. "Then You can send the damnedest blizzard this city has ever known."

Khamsin was a bit more adventurous that day, moving a little faster and taking a few more chances. The Rebels held on for what they hoped was a respectable length of time, then pulled back, drawing the Libyan ever deeper into the city.

"All his troops across?" Ben asked a spotter pilot.

"Ten-four, General. They're in."

Ben's smile was tight. "It won't be long now. Any more movement over in New Jersey?"

"Those that didn't accompany Khamsin are staying put, General."

"Ten-four. Do a couple of flybys a day and keep me posted." Ben turned to Cooper. "Pull the Blazer around. We're going to take a ride."

In the Blazer, Cooper asked, "Where to, General?"

"North."

Beth radioed the instructions to the lead vehicles as Ben was studying a city map. She didn't have to tell them where they were going; they all knew. Right up to the front lines.

"We'll let him advance down to Hillside today," Ben said. "He's going to slow up and be very goosy clearing the area around the Cloisters, suspecting ambushes. Come the night, he'll probably spread his troops out just north of One Hundred Ninety-third Street. Tomorrow morning, we'll give him One Hundred Ninety-second and One Hundred Ninety-first. As soon as he passes One Hundred Ninety-first, we'll blow the bridges. That will stop him cold for a few hours while he assesses the situation." He looked up. "Get this convoy moving, Beth. You know where we're going."

"Yes, sir." She lifted her mike.

The convoy drove over to Fifth Avenue and turned north. At the edge of Central Park, Ben ordered a halt and got out.

"You people stay in the truck," he told them, just as Ike came walking up.

"You monitoring the front?" Ben asked him.

"Yeah. Khamsin's got some confidence back this morning. Our people have given him a two blocks already. They say he's really punching hard."

"We don't want him to think it's a cakewalk. Get on the horn and tell our people to draw some blood and then pull back. I don't want Khamsin past One Hundred Ninety-third Street this day."

"You figurin' on bringin' the bridges down by about this time tomorrow, Ben?"

"Right. So get your explosives people in position. I'm heading on up the line."

"Watch your ass up there, partner." Ike grinned.

Ben leaned to one side and took a look at Ike's more than ample south gate. "You should talk!"

Rolling north on Fifth Avenue, those in the small convoy had the time to study the seemingly dead city.

"Used to be millions of people in these streets," Ben said aloud, looking at the empty shops and office buildings. "The greatest city in the world. All it needs now is for someone to kick a little dirt over it."

"And that's what we're going to do, General?" Jersey asked.

"That's what we're going to do. In a manner of speaking."

They rolled on in silence for a few blocks. "What happened to the Night People, Ben?" Jerre asked.

"I think they gave up once they discovered the Judges had abandoned them. I think they burrowed deep and intend to keep their heads down for the duration. They don't know it, but they just voluntarily crawled into their own graves."

As they approached Frawley Circle, Ben said, "Tell

the lead vehicles to hang a left here, Beth. Then pick up Nicholas Avenue. We'll stay with that all the way up to our lines."

As they passed Lennox, Ben caught a glimpse of black movement as the figure scurried back into the gloom of a building. "They're not all in their holes," he said, pointing out the furtive movement. "But they don't want to mix it up with us, either."

A gunner in a Duster swung his twin-mount .50s and gave the inside of the ground floor a hard burst in passing. The big slugs chopped away at the murky interior, kicking up dust and knocking down plaster and paneling.

The column rolled on, swinging onto Nicholas. They saw no more Night People as they made their way through the littered streets of the city.

Ben reached over and opened the front air vents, allowing some ventilation to circulate through the Blazer. He guessed the outside temperature was in the 60s. Far too warm for this time of year. Except for spots in the alleys where the sun never touched, the city was almost entirely free of snow.

"Much too warm," he muttered. "The storm is going to be a bad one, and it could hit anytime."

"Sir?" Cooper asked.

"You have the chains with you, Cooper?"

"Yes, sir."

"Beth, tell the lead vehicles to angle off at One Hundred and Twenty-fifth Street. Go on over to the waterfront. I want to take a full look at the sky. I think this storm is just about on us."

"Done, sir."

Ben twisted in the seat, looking at the cargo space behind the rear seat. All their arctic gear was there, along with cases of ammo, food, camp stoves, grenades, and water. Cooper was a natural-born clown, but when it came to survival, he was all business, keeping the Blazer stocked with everything he felt they might need to stay alive.

"Did you remember toilet paper, Cooper?" Ben asked him with a smile.

"I got a box full of hundred-dollar bills, General. About a million dollars' worth, I reckon."

"That should do it," Ben said, looking out the window, trying to get a glimpse of the sky. He finally gave up on that.

At the waterfront, Ben stood by the Blazer, waiting until his teams had secured the area; then he walked up to the parkway and took a look around. He had mixed emotions about what he was seeing.

The sky held a very flat, almost ominous look, stretching from north to west. This weather system was coming straight out of Canada and was coming at them with a vengeance.

"It'll hit us this afternoon," Ben predicted. "And it's going to be a bitch-kitty."

"Do we head back for the CP, General?" Jersey asked, a hopeful note in her voice.

"What do you think, Jersey?" Ben grinned at her.

"Somehow I knew you'd say that."

Ben waved the Rebels around him. "All you people have arctic gear with you?"

Most did, stored in the trunks and tanks.

"Those that don't, double up in a vehicle and head on back," Ben ordered. He knew his forward teams were supplied with foul-weather gear; he had personally seen to that. "Let's head on up the line, gang."

They backtracked, picked up Broadway, and headed north.

"Are we going to get stuck up here, Ben?" Jerre asked.

"I hope not. But there is always that possibility. Doesn't make any difference. We've got the supplies so we can sit it out. I've got to see firsthand what Khamsin has to throw at us."

But his eyes kept sliding toward the sky as they drove toward his Rebels' northernmost positions.

At the front, Ben joined one group of Rebels, startling them by his presence, and viewed the battleground through binoculars. A tank leaped into view through the powerful lenses. Ben lowered the glasses and again looked up at the sky.

"Is it getting colder or is it just my imagination?"

"It's dropped a few degrees, General. The sky sure has a funky look to it."

Ben made up his mind. "Fall back, people. Give them some territory and see if they'll take the new bait. Beth, get me Ike on the horn. Scramble and translator, please."

"General Ike, sir," Beth said.

"Ask him if his explosives people have left yet?"

"He says ten-four, sir."

"Tell him to get them into position to blow the bridges as soon as possible. Wait for my orders to do so."

"Message acknowledged, sir. General Ike wants to know what's up."

"One hell of a fast-moving winter storm, of the major type. That's what's up. Now I have to come up with some way of getting the Hot Fart and his turds down a few more blocks. Bump me when your people are in position. Eagle out. Let's back up, people."

The Rebels fell back a full two blocks, leaving it wide open for Khamsin. And this time the troops of Khamsin poured across, moving fast and with very little resistance from the Rebels.

At 191st Street, Ben ordered a line thrown up and told his people to hold for a few minutes and draw some blood. To Beth: "Get me the forward units east and west of our position." With them on the horn, he asked, "This is Eagle. Any signs of infiltrators?"

"Negative, sir. We have them in sight, but they're maintaining east and west positions in line with the central force."

"Ten-four. Get ready to fall back further with Sonny." He turned to the forward team leader. "Drop some mortar rounds in on them, Sonny. Just as many HEs as you drop in a couple of minutes and then grab your ass and make a run for it."

"Yes, sir!"

"Get me Ike, Beth."

"On the horn, General."

"Ike. When I give the word, blow them all, all the way down to the footbridge. You ten-four that?"

"I copy it, Eagle. Man, it's gettin' *cold!*"

"I can ten-four that, Shark. I look for snow in about an hour. Must have dropped twenty degrees in that many minutes. That's why I've got to keep Khamsin on the move, so he won't notice it so much. Eagle out."

The flutter and crash of mortars put an end to any conversation level below a shout.

"Let's go!" Ben shouted at his team. "Get to your vehicles. Move, move! Sonny! One more minute and you get your asses out of here. All the way down to a Hundred Eighty-first Street. That's an order!"

"Yes, sir."

In the Blazer, Ben said, "Beth, tell Dan and Buddy and Tina to get up here. Meet us at the High Bridge Park. We'll link up at the swimming pool. That's on One Seventy-third. Tell them to bring five days' rations, full arctic gear, and all the ammo they can stagger with. I want plenty of fifties and Big Thumpers. Tell them to shake a leg."

To Cooper, "Get us down to a Hundred Eighty-first Street, Coop. Then over to the Harlem River Drive. I'm the cause of it, so I want to witness history being shattered. Move. Beth, stay in contact with Sonny and his forward teams."

"Yes, sir."

As they drove, all could tell it was turning colder very quickly. "Mind if I turn the heater on, sir?" Cooper asked.

"Be my guest, Coop."

"General?" Beth spoke from the backseat. "Our spotters in the skyscrapers have reported in. They've been investigating as much of the buildings as possible, and each team has found dozens of creepie bodies. The creepies killed themselves en masse."

Ben nodded his head. "Tell them to bust some windows and toss the bodies out. Then have some teams shovel up what's left and truck it to the barges."

"Yes, sir."

"Probably in every building in the city," Ben said,

gazing out the window and seeing the streets grow darker as the massive storm approached, the winds churning and howling high above the earth, the clouds beginning to block the sunlight.

"It's going to be a bad one, Ben," Jerre said. "I've seen them out on the plains. It won't be as bad here because of the buildings, but if you get caught in one out there, you're dead."

"Yes. I'm sure that Khamsin and his people have winter gear, but not like ours." He suddenly smiled, and Jersey caught it.

"Oh, hell! I've seen that smile before. What are you thinking, General?"

"Head-hunting, Short Stuff. Cutting some throats in the night."

"Coming up on the bridges, sir," Cooper said, pulling onto Harlem Drive.

At the High Bridge, Cooper stopped and Ben and the others got out. Ben had left his Thompson in the Blazer, electing to carry the M14, with longer range and just as much punch. He squatted down, staring at the three bridges.

"What are you thinking, Ben?" Jerre asked.

"What I'm about to destroy, and I don't think history is going to treat me very kindly for doing it."

FOUR

"Sonny reporting the fighting is very heavy, General," Beth related. "He's steadily falling back, and Khamsin is right on his heels."

"When he gets to One Hundred Eighty-first Street, let me know. Once there, Khamsin is going to find the going will not be so easy."

"Trucks coming, Ben," Jerre said.

Ben nodded, again making a battlefront decision. "Beth, tell my tank commanders to get the monsters cranked and up here."

"Yes, sir."

"Looks like Colonel Gray brought an extra company up with him, sir."

"I'd have been disappointed if he hadn't." He turned to face Dan and Buddy and Tina. He quickly explained what was happening. "Buddy, you and your team unpack your snow gear. Emergency food packets and fuel tabs; the whole nine yards. If it snows this afternoon, you're going head-hunting tonight."

"Sonny and his people have formed a line at a Hundred Eighty-first Street, General," Beth reported. "They have linked up with the other companies and are holding."

Ben held out his hand as he leaned up against a concrete barrier. "Give me the mike, Beth. This is Eagle to Shark . . ." He sighed heavily, almost painfully. "Shark, blow the bridges." He slowly handed the mike back to Beth.

It really wasn't a spectacular sight—just a dull crumping sort of sound as sections of the bridges collapsed and fell into the river. The tons of debris sent up cascades of water from the Harlem River.

All up and down the line, from the northernmost tip of the island down to the footbridge on FDR Drive, the bridges that once were vital links to Manhattan were crippled. It took less than one minute to destroy thirteen bridges.

"General," Beth said, "Sonny says all fighting from Khamsin's side has stopped."

"I'll just bet it has," Ben said grimly. "Khamsin probably went into a state of shock when his recon teams gave him the news about the bridges. Give me the mike, Beth. This is Eagle. Hit them, Sonny. Hit them hard. Tanks, mortars, rockets, everything you've got, use it!"

The thundering boom of 105s and 90mm cannon rolled toward the men and women standing in the now downright cold winds alongside the river.

Something very soft touched Ben's face. He brushed it away.

"Ben?" Jerre touched his arm. "It's starting to snow."

In less than an hour, the snow was coming down so thick and so hard it had dropped visibility to near zero. Ben had led the new companies north to beef up the three companies stretched out west to east along 181st Street, from Lafayette Plaza over to the now impassable Washington Bridge.

But the near-blizzardlike conditions had brought Khamsin and his people to a dead halt; they had never seen anything like this in South Carolina, and while they had winter clothing, it was not enough to cope with what was yet to come at them from Mother Nature.

And Mother Nature wasn't going to be alone in sending surprises at the Libyan.

* * *

"All the bridges have been blown in our sector, General," Khamsin was told. "And we suspect that all the bridges on the east side have also been destroyed, or at least crippled."

"Not all the bridges," Khamsin found his voice. "Ben Raines has left himself a hole. Wager on that."

The field commander did not think this to be a proper time to remind the Hot Wind that Sister Voleta had warned him not to cross over into Manhattan. Not a good time at all.

The field commander waited for orders.

"We cannot fight a war in this miserable weather," Khamsin said after a long sigh. "And as skillful as Ben Raines is . . ." And it pained the terrorist to compliment Ben Raines in any manner. ". . . I doubt that he can, either. Make certain our loyal troops are well fed and housed adequately. We'll wait out the storm."

"Yes, sir." The man waited, knowing that his general was not yet finished.

"Ben Raines is worse than any filthy dog who ever wandered the earth!" Khamsin spat out the words. "He must be destroyed, Akim. Whatever the cost, we must kill Ben Raines."

I would much prefer to get my ass clear of this miserable island, Akim thought. *Preferably without getting it shot off.* But he did not speak those words aloud.

"Ben Raines will do nothing in this damnable blizzard," the Hot Wind prophesied. "You may leave now, Akim."

"Are all our forward units pulled back?"

"Yes, sir. They've used the storm to pull back to our sector."

A solid line had been formed at 173rd Street, stretching from the Hudson to the Harlem rivers.

"Tell our Long Toms to start lobbing them in, Beth. They have the coordinates. HE, Willie Peter, and incendiary. Let's make it a very long and totally miserable night for the Hot Fart. I want nothing but rubble between us and Khamsin. Commence firing and keep it up."

"All Long Toms commence firing," Beth gave the orders.

A few seconds later, the men and women on the line at 173rd heard the first rounds sing over their heads.

Ben smiled. "I hope Khamsin is sitting on the pot when the first rounds fall."

"Do you want my team to stand down, Father?" Buddy asked.

"Yes. Let's let artillery have the first dance, Buddy. You'll have plenty of other chances before all this is over."

The first rounds of high-explosive shells hit the tops of buildings in Khamsin's sector and sent tons of rubble crashing down into the streets. Khamsin was not sitting on the pot, but he was changing clothes in his CP when the first rounds came tearing into his sector. He had one leg in his fresh field pants when a round landed just across the street. The concussion of the HE blowing knocked out all the windows and outside-facing doors in his CP and sent Khamsin rolling on the floor. The two guards who had been posted outside the CP's main entrance were splattered all over the street when the second round dropped in.

Khamsin managed to get his other leg in his pants and jam his feet into boots as other rounds came in, singing their deadly songs. One round set a building on fire, another round tore the top off another building, and the third round of white phosphorus peppered troops of the Hot Wind as they scrambled for cover, running out in the open. They lay screaming in the streets as the Willie Peter burned through flesh and bone.

"Khamsin will return the shelling," Ben said. "Have our spotters in the tall buildings coordinate the returning fire."

Ben waited until Beth had relayed those orders.

"Khamsin doesn't have the range to reach our Long Toms south of us, so he'll be trying to drop some mail directly in on us from his tanks and eighty-ones. He's got the range, if his crews are worth a damn, so get ready for it.

It isn't going to be pleasant. Order the people in bunkers."

"All personnel into bunkers," Beth relayed the orders. "Deep and keep it tight."

Ben grinned at her and she blushed.

It was an afternoon and evening of artillery as the big guns roared and spat out death and destruction, the flames leaping out from the muzzles as the rounds were hurled into the air.

The Rebels on the front line took some wounded, but no deaths, since they were dug in and heavily sandbagged against shrapnel.

Khamsin and his people were not so lucky. They had not had time to adequately fortify their positions and were forced to take to the basements. In many cases, the heavy shelling from Ben's Long Toms brought the buildings crashing down on them, burying them under tons and tons of rubble.

"All right," Ben ordered a few hours after dark, with the snow still coming down with blinding thickness. "Have our gunners start demolishing the area between Khamsin and us, Beth."

Those orders relayed, Beth said, "General Ike on the horn, sir." She handed the mike to him.

"Go, Shark."

"What's up, Ben? We're sitting down here with our thumbs stuck up our butts wondering what's going on. What is goin' on, Ben?"

"A defined battlefront, Ike. A no-man's land. We might make several of them before this is all over. When Khamsin advances, I don't want his people to have any type of adequate shelter. I want them to be just as cold and hungry and miserable as I can make them. Ten-four?"

"Ten-four, Ben. Holler when you need some more personnel up there."

"Be ready to come up quickly, Ike. And pass the word to the others. Eagle out."

Ben turned to Beth. "Have the shelling continue until midnight. The crews can stand down then." When those orders had been sent and received, Ben took the mike.

"This is Eagle to Tall Eyes. What's it looking like?"

The spotters in the skyscrapers reported back. "A lot of fires, Eagle. You've got about a four- or five-block area that is burning. Night glasses are picking up a lot of destruction. Khamsin and his people are going to have a rough time of it picking through all that mess."

"That's the plan. Eagle out."

The deadly song of the shells as they passed overhead continued unabated. Jerre and Jersey and a few of the others of Ben's personal team tried to sleep, or at best, rest, during the late hours of the first night of open warfare between the men and women of the Rebels and the troops of the Hot Wind.

At midnight, Ben ordered all shelling stopped and Khamsin followed shortly afterward. A silence fell over the northernmost section of the island of Manhattan. Ben stepped out of his hastily bunkered CP and looked to the north. The snow was still coming down hard, in thick wet flakes, but the flames from the fires caused by the heavy shelling, leaping high into the night sky, could still be seen very clearly.

Buddy walked over to join his father. "I have a good feeling about all this," the young man said. "I know we have a lot of hard fighting ahead of us, and Rebels will be hurt and killed, but I think I can taste victory."

"It's there," his father acknowledged. "Just as long as we don't become too overconfident. And don't forget, we've still got your mother and Monte and Ashley to deal with."

"How do you plan on dealing with them?"

"I don't know," Ben admitted. "I'm just taking it one step at a time."

One round from Khamsin's gunner had hit the building across the street from Ben's forward CP, knocking a huge hole in the front of the structure and littering the street with bricks and mortar and twisted bits of steel reenforcing rod.

And the snow continued to fall; the streets were already buried under a thick blanket of white.

"Let's get some sleep, boy," Ben said. "Come the dawn, we're going to be busy."

Ben was on the line before dawn; this close up, he was making a lot of his Rebels nervous.

"Relax, people," Ben told them, squatting beside a Duster. "Before this is over, we'll all be fighting shoulder to shoulder."

Ben looked up the wide snow-covered expanse of St. Nicholas Street as far as the night would allow. "Any of you see anything moving last night?"

"Nothing, General," a young Rebel said. "After that hammering we gave them last night, I would imagine they're going to keep their heads down."

"Don't count on it, son. Khamsin is going to hit us and hit us hard. He wants to kill me so badly he'll expend every man he's got to do it."

"How many troops you figure he's got, sir?"

"Between six and seven thousand. Another two-three thousand of Monte's and Ashley's and Sister Voleta's people sitting over there in New Jersey, waiting to see what happens before they commit. But I don't think they'll try any type of boat crossing. They'll wait and strike from ambush when we get on the road."

"Dammit, Ben!" Jerre yelled at him from behind, finally finding him. "You had us all worried." She walked to his side.

The Rebels on either side of him seemed to melt back into the graying light, giving the general and the lady plenty of room.

Ben smiled at her. "You could have brought some coffee, Jerre."

She smiled thinly and held up a thermos of coffee. "You want me to pour, too?"

"If you like."

Tin cups filled with the hot black brew, they sipped in the dim new light of fresh morning and stared at each other, their breath as steamy in the cold air as the vapors coming off the brew.

"When do you think Khamsin will hit us, Ben?"

"Within the hour. He'll probably start with some artillery to soften us up."

"Then don't you think it would be wise to seek some shelter?"

"Only if there's some breakfast waiting. Besides, we'll be able to hear the rounds coming about ten seconds before they hit."

"That's so comforting to know." She looked at the strange expression on his face. "What's the matter, Ben?"

"Incoming mail, Jerre." He grabbed her around the waist and literally tossed her behind a sandbagged enclosure, coming in right behind just as the artillery shells started dropping all around them.

FIVE

They huddled close as the ground trembled around them. The street was showered with falling debris as rounds smashed into buildings and exploded. Ben protected her with his body as best he could, both of them shivering as they lay on a blanket of snow that had gathered inside the topless sandbag enclosure.

Ben fumbled for his walkie-talkie and yelled for Beth.

"Here, sir!"

"Order all units to commence firing, Beth," he yelled over the crash and boom of the incoming rounds. "Give them everything we've got in return."

He could not hear her reply, but within seconds, friendly mail was singing and whining overhead, heading for impact with Khamsin's lines.

The incoming slackened as Ben's gunners laid down a lethal wall of flying steel and Willie Peter; then the incoming faded out entirely.

"Let's go!" Ben yelled, his hearing temporarily impaired from the recent explosions.

Together, they ran for the safety of his bunkered CP. Behind them, Khamsin's people had resumed their shelling. The concussion of an incoming round literally blew them inside the CP. The door had been knocked off its hinges the night before.

"You all right?" Ben asked, sitting up on the dirty floor.

"Oh, just dandy! But I dropped the thermos back there."

Ben started laughing at the expression on her face, and the laughter was infectious. It was almost like old times, years past. Almost.

"General?" Beth said. She was holding out the mike. Her voice sounded as if it came from the bottom of a well. "General Ike on the horn."

"Go ahead, Ike. But talk loud. My hearing is shot for a moment. I'm still hearing booming in my ears. What's up?"

"Hell, you tell me! Are you all right up there?"

"Oh, yeah. I haven't received any casualty reports yet, but I don't think we suffered any major injuries. We're pretty well dug in. . . ."

A runner stepped into the CP. "Khamsin's people advancing, General. Comin' at us hard."

"Gotta go, Ike. Work to do. Talk to you later." Ben picked up his M14 and moved to the door. There were no sounds of any incoming, so he concluded that Khamsin was letting his infantry carry the load on this one. He turned to the runner. "Pass the word up and down the line and the word is Hold! Hold until you receive orders from me. Go, son!"

He looked at Beth. "Tanks in position on our flanks, Beth. Mortars and heavy machine guns in the middle." He looked at Buddy. "You ready, boy?"

"After you, Father."

Ben and Buddy, with the remainder of Ben's personal team right behind them, ran from the CP and took up positions behind what was left of a wall, facing north. Ben repositioned some concrete blocks and bipodded the M14 just as the first of Khamsin's troops came darting into view.

"Hold fire," Ben ordered, and Beth relayed the orders. "Let them get on top of us and then give them everything you've got. Everybody keep their heads down; absolutely no movement."

The troops of Khamsin's army moved closer, slower now that they were closing. The snowing had abated somewhat, after dumping several feet of snow on the city, and with the full dawning, Ben felt sure the temperature would be dropping. Soon it would be too cold to snow. Soon it would be just miserable.

But not as miserable as Ben intended to make it for the Hot Wind.

"Steady, steady," Ben said, and Beth whispered the words into the mike. "I'll open the dance. Wait for me, people."

The enemy was a block away, then half a block and closing rapidly, the footing treacherous in the deep snow. Nothing moved before their eyes. The last reported lines of the Rebels seemed deserted.

"Now!" Ben said, and pulled the trigger, the old Thunder Lizard set on full auto.

The cold air was split with hot lead; the fluttering of mortar rounds sang as they floated in. Tanks cut loose their cannon; 40mm, 90mm, and 105 rounds blasted the white-covered calmness of the city.

Still the troops of the Hot Wind pressed on, using their dead comrades for cover as they sprawled on the snowy ground.

"We're too light!" Ben yelled in Beth's ear, his voice just carrying over the rattle and crash of weapons. "Order all Rebels to begin falling back. Regroup at a Hundred Sixty-eighth Street. Order West and his people up. Tell them to stretch out east of Broadway to the river. We'll take everything west of Broadway."

Beth nodded her head and gave the orders calmly. Ben was going to hate to lose her; but he had a hunch that when this was over, she was going back to Lev and the cows.

"Make it appear to be a rout," he heard her say, and Ben smiled at the words. She was one tough lady who knew the way his mind worked. "Pull them after us. Let's go!"

She looked at Ben. "Cooper and the others are in the Blazer, waiting for us, sir." Her gaze lingered on his face. "Jerre's there."

"Let's go! We'll set up around the old Columbia-Presbyterian Medical Center for a time."

They ran for the Blazer, parked a block away. Cooper had put chains on the tires, and the engine was ticking over when they reached it.

"Go, Coop," Ben said, as the women piled into the backseat.

"West reporting his men are on the way, General," Beth told him, listening through a headset. "Generals Ike and Jefferys have moved several companies north just in case."

"Good. Bump Dan." He turned up the volume of the radio under the dash.

"Dan here, sir."

"Buddy with you?"

"Ten-four, sir. We're spearheading."

An artillery round exploded against a building, showering them with fragments of brick and mortar before they could pass through it.

"Close," Ben muttered.

Several creepies ran out of a building and pointed AKs at the Blazer. Cooper cut the wheel and ran over them, their bones crunching and flesh tearing as the chain-covered tires spun the life out of them. Their screaming faded as their blood stained the snow of the street.

"Saves ammo," Coop said with a tight smile.

"The man can think about something other than women," Jersey said from the backseat.

"I lust for your body, baby!" Cooper fired back. "I dream about you at night."

"I retract that statement. Drive, Cooper, and shut your mouth. Don't think. It's too much a strain on your brain."

"Creepies in the medical center," Dan's voice came through the speaker. "I would guess several hundred of them."

"Just about the time we think we're rid of them, they pop up again," Ben said, reaching for the mike. "Dan, we can't fight two fronts. Order tanks up and destroy the complex. Willie Peter and HE plastic rounds. Use flamethrowers to torch the ground floors. Set up behind the complex."

"Ten-four, General."

"I'm not going to lose any more people to those bastards," Ben growled. "I'm tired of jacking around with them. Coop, take us around behind the center on a Hundred Sixty-fourth Street. Khamsin's men won't try to punch through a blazing fire."

Coop slid around a snowy corner and came out on 164th Street. Tanks were already blasting away at the huge old complex, and flames and smoke were pouring out of the building's top floors. Rebels with flamethrowers were working on the ground floors while others were tossing homemade Molotov cocktails through the shattered windows, the firebombs catching and spreading flames.

"Mortar the roof," Ben spoke into the mike. "Cave it in on them. You ten-four that, West?"

"Ten-four, General. Setting up mortar teams now. You going to call in coordinates?"

"Affirmative. Drop them in when ready. I'll correct if need be."

"Back us up a few hundred meters, Coop," Ben told him.

From their position a few blocks east of the medical complex, West's men began lobbing in mortar rounds, the first ones falling short. Ben corrected and the rounds began striking their target.

"Dead on, West," Ben said. "Keep it up."

The mortar crews began dropping in incendiaries, and within moments, the medical center was engulfed in flames. Black-robed crawlers were hurling themselves out of windows, trying to escape the raging flames. The Rebels shot any who survived the fall to the ground.

Standing outside the Blazer, Ben lifted the mike. "Buddy, take your teams and set up along the Henry Hudson Parkway just in case Khamsin's people might try some flanking moves."

"Ten-four, Father."

"Tina, you and your teams join me."

"On the way, Pops."

"Cease firing, West. Good job. That place will continue burning for hours. Khamsin won't try to punch through all that. They'll be hitting your sector hard any moment."

"I see them, Ben. We'll hold until you tell us to fall back," he added calmly. It was not a brag; the mercenary knew his men and knew what they could do.

"Wogs advancing across a Hundred Seventieth Street, General," Beth told him.

Ben looked at her, a smile on his lips. *"Wogs,* Beth?"

"Slip of the tongue, General. That's what my father used to call them. When the Palestinians declared open war on Israel, my father lost nearly all of his family over there. My mother was there visiting. They killed her. I just don't like those people, General. Not one damn bit."

What could he say to her? He remembered as a teenager talking with World War II veterans who until their dying day hated the Germans or the Japanese.

Ben also noticed that Beth had taken her M16 from the back of the Blazer and was carrying filled clip pouches around her waist.

"Whatever, Beth." Ben motioned a young Rebel over to him. "Take the radio, son. Give Beth a break."

"Yes, sir."

Beth looked at Ben for a moment, then slipped out of the radio and handed it to the young man. She took up her M16 and wriggled around behind a pile of debris until she had staked out as comfortable a position as possible.

"What's your name, son?" Ben asked.

"Chuck, sir."

"All right, Chuck. You stay with us. If a translator is needed, hand the mike to Beth."

"Yes, sir."

"Stay out of the line of fire and don't let the radio take a hit if you can help it."

"Yes, sir!"

Ben knelt down beside Beth. "Back on the line, Beth?"

"Yes, sir. I have a really personal interest in this fight."

Ben nodded and waved his team down just as Tina and her people were pulling up. Ben spread them out between Fort Washington Avenue and Broadway then returned to kneel down beside Beth and Jerre and Jersey. Cooper had taken up position in a building behind a 5.56-caliber machine gun called the Minimi. Each prepacked and belted ammo box contained 250 rounds, and the Minimi could spit out the lead with a vengeance.

"Where'd you get that thing, Cooper?" Ben called.

"I stole it from the Canadians!" He grinned with his reply.

"Armies never change," Ben muttered.

"Here they come, sir," Jersey called.

Ben found him a spot and lifted the M14, set on full rock and roll and bipodded. "Chuck, tell the people to fire whenever they get a target."

Ben sighted in, pulled the trigger, and began to make life awfully uncomfortable for some of Khamsin's troops.

All up and down the line, the Rebels found targets and sent Khamsin's people either diving for cover or sprawled on the snow. Cooper's Minimi was rattling out 5.56-caliber slugs. Beth was very carefully picking her shots, and her aim was true. Between shots, she was muttering some highly uncomplimentary remarks about the enemy. Like she'd said, she had a personal interest in this fight.

"Spotters report Khamsin is moving up tanks, General!" Chuck called.

"Send our Abramses out, Chuck. All Dusters and other light tanks hold in position." Ben knew that his Abramses were much more heavily armored and better gunned than Khamsin's lighter tanks. It would not be much of a fight.

Ben, watching through binoculars, saw one Abrams round a corner, lower its main cannon, and blow one of the Hot Wind's tanks clear off one track and then turn it into a fiery death trap with armor-piercing rounds.

Another Abrams clanked up the street, looking for trouble. It soon found it in the form of Khamsin's heaviest tank. Khamsin lost another tank to Ben when the gunner fired an antitank round called a HEAT, and the enemy tank exploded from the inside out, frying its crew.

With two of his tanks out and two more crippled, Khamsin recalled them. They just were no match for Ben's heavier tanks.

"All tanks return," Ben ordered Chuck. "No pursuit."

Chuck relayed the orders, then said, "Khamsin's people are dropping back, sir. They're crossing a Hundred Seventy-first and formed a line."

"All right, people," Ben called. "Get ready for mortars and artillery. Get yourselves bunkered in as best you can and grab your asses. Khamsin is going to give us all he's got!"

SIX

Khamsin spent the early hours of the afternoon dropping artillery rounds on where he thought Ben and his Rebels were hunkered. But when the first shells started falling, Ben had shifted his people several blocks to the south.

Khamsin was shelling an empty sector.

Over on the east side of the island, West chuckled, then said to one of his men, "Smooth move. Like silk. Khamsin is detroying the exact sector Ben had proposed destroying. The silly bastard is doing our work. We have found a home, Monroe. I always said if I ever found a better tactician than myself, I'd follow him up to and through the gates of Hell. I've found him."

The shelling stopped. Within seconds, Ben ordered, "Back on the line, people. Move, move, move." He grabbed up the mike. "West! Move your people back to our original lines. Let's have a surprise waiting for Khamsin."

Laughing at Ben's downright sneakiness, the mercenary yelled his men forward through the snow, and they took their hidden positions in deserted buildings.

Khamsin's men came running through the cold snowy streets, racing toward the smoking desolation left by their gunners.

They ran straight into the guns of Ben Raines's Rebels and died by the dozens—died wondering what had happened and why their great religious leader, the Hot Wind, had been so wrong.

Ben occasionally watched as Beth coolly and calmly picked her shots, rarely missing. There was a grim expression on her face, and her eyes were flint hard with long-overdue satisfaction.

"Enjoying yourself, Beth?" he asked during a short lull in the fighting.

"Retribution, General. Pure and simple." She lifted her M16 and knocked another of Khamsin's terrorists sprawling to the snow—then shot him again to put an end to his squalling.

"I'm going to miss you when you go back to Lev and his cows, Beth."

She cut her eyes. "I ain't gone yet, General."

As night fell over that shattered portion of the city, Khamsin sat in his drafty CP and did not savor the copper taste of defeat that had formed on his tongue.

He sent his tanks into battle, and Ben Raines had bigger and better tanks. He sent his troops into battle, and Ben Raines's Rebels slaughtered them. He poured hundreds of rounds of artillery into a sector, and Ben Raines and his Rebels were not there. Then the Rebels materialized like ghosts, and more of his troops were dead.

The man was a devil!

Ben sat in his warm CP and enjoyed a spot of bourbon from a cache his people had found. He had ordered whiskey for all his Rebels who wanted a couple of drinks. The whiskey sort of killed the taste of the goop that Doctor Chase called field rations. Highly nutritious, but with all the flavor of a horseshoe. Some Rebels even went so far as to say it tasted like something that dropped from a horse.

Jerre looked into her opened field-ration packet. "What is this crap?"

"I do not have the vaguest idea. And to tell you the truth, I'm afraid to ask Chase. He might tell me."

It was at times like these that Ben felt a closeness to Jerre. More on his part than hers, he knew. But a feeling that he enjoyed; more than this was something that he knew could never be and would never be.

Then why wouldn't he accept that? *I have,* the other side of his brain countered. *I have for years, and gone right on living, so what's the problem, brain?*

A simple yet complex emotion called Love, you dummy! the other side fired back.

Ben stilled the arguing sides of his brain when he became conscious of Jerre staring at him through the dim lantern light in the CP.

The others of his personal team were resting, after having endured the blandness of their field rations. Except for Beth, who was sitting far across the room, cleaning her M16, making ready for tomorrow's fight. She was certainly doing her part to right what she felt was a two-thousand-year-old wrong against her people.

"Thinking up more brilliant tactical moves to use against Khamsin, Ben?" Jerre asked in a soft voice.

"'Fraid not, kid. I'm about tacticaled out for this day."

"Tacticaled? Is there such a word?"

"I don't think so. Call it poetic license."

"What would you be doing right now, Ben, if the Great War had not occurred?"

Ben was thoughtful for a few seconds. "Probably getting drunk, listening to classical music."

"Did you drink a lot back then, Ben?"

"I wasn't an alcoholic, but I probably drank more than I should."

"Why?"

"A question I often asked myself, Jerre. Back then."

"And the answer, Ben . . . ?"

"I never came up with one that satisfied me."

"There was no special lady in your life that day the bombs came?"

Ben shook his head. "No. I guess I spent a lot of years just waiting for the right one to come along, instead of going out and looking for her."

"And she never did come along."

"Not back then, Jerre. Maybe we just better drop the subject before you think I'm leading you into or up to something."

"I don't think that. What were you looking for in a woman, Ben?"

"I'm not even sure. After I got snakebit—in a manner of speaking—more than a few times, I think I just resigned myself to the fact that I would live alone; that that would probably be best all the way around."

"That's a pretty dismal thought, Ben."

"Yes, it is. But have you fared any better, Jerre?"

"You shoot from the hip, don't you, Ben?" It was her turn to be thoughtful for a few seconds. "I guess I haven't, Ben. But at least I can say I've been trying."

"And have you succeeded in finding your ideal soulmate?"

"Obviously not." A touch of ice in her reply.

"Whatever happened to . . . what was his name? Matt."

She shrugged her shoulders.

"I heard he was killed."

No reply.

"How many more after that?"

"And you've been chaste, I suppose?" she came back at him, a surprising amount of heat in her voice.

"Oh, hell, no! There have probably been more women in my life during the past five years than in all the time before Tri-States."

"Which is symptomatic of . . . ?"

"Symptomatic? Hell, I don't know. You tell me."

"You're lying, Ben."

"That make you feel proud?"

"I didn't do anything, Ben."

"I never said you did."

"This conversation is going around in circles."

"As always."

"Good night, Ben." She stood up and walked over to

her bedroll.

Ben picked up his M14 and walked outside. As usual, they were so close, yet worlds apart. He rolled a cigarette and blew smoke to the cold breeze.

"Everything all right, General?" a sentry asked, passing by.

Ben smiled despite his tangled inner feelings. "Better than nothing, I suppose."

Ben, very quietly and with prior notice, moved his troops up three blocks several hours before dawn, knowing it was a risky move that could well backfire on them all. Just before dawn, Khamsin ordered the Rebel lines shelled.

Khamsin's light artillery hammered away for over an hour, and then he ordered his troops to advance.

The Libyan troops walked a half a block and came face-to-face with hard-eyed Rebels, who turned the cold morning into a steamy bloodbath. The slaughter took less than ten minutes; then the Rebels were fading back toward the south, moving like white-shrouded ghosts, leaving behind them an area bloodstained and littered with the bodies of the Hot Wind's troops.

Sister Voleta, Monte, and Ashley sat over in New Jersey and monitored radio traffic. Ben was not using translators except for the most important communications.

"Brilliant," Ashley said. "I hate the bastard, but I have to concede his daring in warfare."

Monte didn't know what in the hell Ashley was talking about.

Sister Voleta remained, for the most part, silent. She still had not been able to figure out where Ben Raines was going once he got off the island of Manhattan. But she knew one thing: Ben Raines was slaughtering the Libyan's troops, almost as if he were playing with them.

She thought of something, rejecting it almost as soon as it popped into her head. Not even Ben Raines would try something that stupid.

Or would he?

No, she concluded, throwing the idea onto her mental junkpile.

"I hate to bring this up," Ashley said. "But we only have food for about two more weeks. After that, we're going to have to start rationing or do a lot of hunting. We have a lot of mouths to feed."

"It will be over on the island in about a week," Sister Voleta predicted. "There is no way that Khamsin can hold out any longer than that."

"I agree with that," Monte said. "He must have lost a full quarter of his people in the last twenty-four, thirty-six hours."

"I disagree," Ashley objected. "The battles will go on much longer than a week."

Sister Voleta looked at him. "Why do you say that?"

"Khamsin has learned a hard lesson. From now on, there will be no more head-to-head confrontations. At least not from Khamsin's side. I think Khamsin will be forced to resort to guerrilla tactics. If he can pull it off. He knows, now, that Ben outguns him. He'll have sense enough to see—I hope—that Ben has deliberately set up clearly defined fronts, and that if Khamsin continues his present method of fighting, Ben will slowly but surely pound him into the concrete."

Sister Voleta grunted.

"You pretty brilliant yourself," Monte said. "I knew I done right in makin' you second in command."

Ashley glowed under the warm light of verbal praise. Even coming from a near-cretin like Monte.

"But Khamsin cannot hope to defeat Ben Raines using guerrilla warfare," Voleta said. "The Rebels are masters at that."

"He knows it," Ashley replied. "But he's willing to die in order to kill Ben."

Siter Voleta rose and walked out of the room.

Ashley's eyes followed the woman. "And so is she,

Monte. Remember that. She's a fanatic. We must be careful not to let ourselves be sucked into a death trap."

"Whatever you say, Ashley. You're runnin' the show, partner."

Khamsin looked at the reports from his commanders and winced at the totals.

A full twenty-five percent of his army had been destroyed. Estimates were that less than twenty of the Rebels had died; maybe that many more were wounded.

And they were trapped on this miserable island. Trapped, except for the bridges at the south end, which, Khamsin concluded, Ben Raines intended to use as his escape route.

He studied a map of the city and felt hopelessness settle in the pit of his stomach. There was no way he could get sappers down that far without being detected. And what was the point of blowing those bridges? That would seal his own fate as well as Raines's.

But wasn't that what he wanted? Hadn't he made his boast that Ben Raines would die even if he had to die along with him?

Yes, if that was the only way. Yes. He would willingly die. "If Allah wills it," he muttered. "Allah be praised."

"What's the word from Khamsin's lines?" Ben asked Chuck.

"Forward teams report nothing, sir. No movement of any kind."

"He's probably had it for today. Now I have to put myself in his boots and try to figure out what I'd do."

Ben had shifted his battle lines once again, moving them all down to 155th Street. For the remainder of that day, he had his people booby-trapping the ground floors of buildings and laying claymores in alleys. Ben was giving Khamsin a half a dozen blocks, but they would be very dangerous blocks, and with each explosion, the morale of the Hot Wind's troops would sag.

And after that? Ben thought. What would Khamsin do? *I have him outgunned with artillery; I have heavier tanks. So putting myself in his boots, what would I do?*

Hit and run. Guerrilla warfare. Sure. The man was trained as a terrorist.

"Chuck?" Ben called across the room. The young man looked up. "Alert all units to be heads up for sneak attacks; hit-and-run guerrilla warfare."

"Yes, sir." He glanced up at the door, then took his radio and went outside; he could always say it was for better reception.

Ben noticed and turned his head, meeting the level gaze of Jerre. "So it's getting down to your type of warfare, huh, Ben?"

"That's what the Rebels are famous for, Jerre. If that's what Khamsin wants, we'll sure oblige him."

"The others might not realize it, Ben, but I know you've been taking a lot of chances. Not just you personally, but with the others. Why?"

"I want this over with, Jerre. I want to get the hell off this island and back to Base Camp One and just rest for a time. I'm not a young buck anymore."

"You're not that old, Ben."

"Thanks. But calendars don't lie."

"Mind if I tag along back to Louisiana with you?"

"What would be the point? It wouldn't change anything. Nothing at all."

"Giving up on me, Ben?"

"Yes. I am."

"That's not like you."

"Comes a time, Jerre, when a man, or woman, has to say it's over. With us, it never got started. And it never will."

"And we can't be friends?"

"You know the answer to that."

"This sounds an awful lot like goodbye."

"I guess it is, Jerre. I've got a war to run, and we took a lot more wounded than I've let on. Chase needs some help—desperately. You can either volunteer, or I'll order you down."

"At least I can get a hot bath down there. When do you want me to leave?"

"I can have Cooper run you down there now."

"Suits the shit out of me, Ben." There was enough ice in her tone to freeze a side of beef.

"See you around, kid."

She turned her back to him and left without another word.

SEVEN

Beth and Jersey and Cooper gave him the cold shoulder the rest of that day. Chuck didn't know what the hell was going on, so he was bewildered by it all.

"It's not you, Chuck," Ben assured him. "Relax. My team is a little miffed at me."

"About Miss Hunter?"

"Yes. You're very astute."

"I know what that means, General. And I'm not. Hell, sir, the whole camp knows about you and Jerre. But you got to do what you think is right for the both of you. And I reckon you done it."

Ben smiled, then laughed. "Yes, Chuck, I reckon I did."

Ben went to bed early that night. There were no booming explosions during the night to awaken him, so he reasoned that Khamsin had not yet begun his move south.

He dressed and stepped out of the CP long before dawn, walking across the snow-covered street to Dan's billet. There had been no more snowfall, but it was bitterly cold, his boots crunching on the frozen snow.

He saw faint candlelight in Dan's quarters and knocked on the door. "Up, Dan?"

"Come on in, General. I was just brewing some tea. Would you like some?"

"Yes, I would." Ben sat down. "I gather there were no surprises last night."

"Not a peep out of them. And our Tall Eyes reports nothing is moving over in New Jersey."

"They're waiting for the outcome of this. Then they'll move." Ben accepted a cup of tea and sipped. "Have you opened your breakfast packet yet?"

"I'm afraid to."

"Well," Ben sighed, digging in his pocket. "No time like the present, I suppose."

Dan grimaced as Ben opened the packet. "What in the world is that stuff?"

"It's guaranteed to be highly nutritious and as good for you as mother's milk."

Dan opened his food packet, took a small bite of whatever the inert lump was, and grimaced. "I have a small bottle of hot sauce I would be happy to share."

"Thank you. Where is it?"

After breakfast, Dan asked, "What's up for today, General?"

"We pull back. Khamsin will think we're closing with our people south of us."

Dan looked at the man in the dim, flickering candlelight. He saw the smile on Ben's face and knew there was more to come.

"I'm going to order Ike's unit to start the pull-out to Brooklyn."

Dan waited.

"And not to be furtive about it. I want Khamsin to come busting down here after us. I want to see what those over in New Jersey will do, and I want to end this damn war and get off the island. It's like a big, ugly, festering boil, Dan. Let's bring it to a head."

Dan looked at his crumpled-up food packet. "The sooner we do, the sooner we can stop dining on this totally unpalatable goop."

"That in itself is a good enough reason."

Before the grayness of dawn touched the eastern skies, Ben was on the radio to Ike. Until Ike could pack it up and get moving, the transmissions would be scrambled.

"You know the drill, Ike. Get moving and get things

ready to receive on the docks."

"Ten-four, Ben. Shark out."

Ben stood up. "Let's take a ride, people."

They drove through the predawn light to Chase's hospital without seeing a single living thing or having a shot fired at them.

"Eerie," Jersey muttered. "It's like we're on another planet."

"Two more generations would have had to seek life on another planet if the Great War had not come when it did," Ben said.

Cooper cut his eyes. "Why, sir?"

"The Greenhouse Effect, Coop. This planet was in serious trouble. We were deliberately destroying it because of man's greed and stupidity. Some scientists predicted that by the year Twenty-one Hundred, the Earth would have been almost uninhabitable. So the war did some good after all."

"Smoke and other crap from cars and trucks and factories was causing it, right, General?" Jersey asked from the backseat.

"That's right. That's why in a few years, Base Camp One will be a model town, using solar energy to heat—among other things—and very nearly pollution-free. If the government had thrown its time and money toward solar power instead of wasting billions of dollars on nuclear power . . . well, hell, it's a moot point now. But we'll do it, people. We'll rebuild out of the ashes; hell, we are rebuilding! We just have to keep plugging . . . and fighting."

In the hospital, Ben located Chase and dropped the news on him.

"Get everyone ready to ride, Lamar. You'll be going across with Ike; probably late this afternoon. I'm ordering flybys of JFK Airport to check for creepies. But I'm pretty well convinced they've bugged out. I'll have people clearing a few thousand feet; just enough for our birds to get in and out so you and the badly wounded can be flown back to Base Camp One."

"The wounded can go," the doctor told him. "I'm staying."

"I won't argue with you, Lamar. You want to stay, fine. Just start packing up and get ready to move out quickly." He smiled at the man. "I'll see you over in Brooklyn, Lamar."

"Watch your butt, Ben. I'm tired of picking lead out of you."

"Oh, yeah. I'll do that."

Ben saw Jerre in the hall as he was leaving. They stared at each other for a moment; then she turned her back to him without speaking.

"When this is over," Ben muttered, "I think I'll look up Emil and we'll get drunk. We do have at least one thing in common."

"Sir?" Jersey asked.

"Nothing, Jersey. Just muttering to myself. Let's go see Ike."

Ike wasn't wasting any time. His sector was packing up and clearing out fast. As Ike's people left, Cecil and his bunch were swinging over from the park to link up with Striganov's team, who were also spreading out to cover the gap left by Ike's leaving.

"Put the wounded in the middle of your column, Ike. They'll meet you at the Manhattan Bridge this afternoon. Assign part of your people to clearing a runway at JFK so the wounded can be flown back to Base Camp One. You know what else has to be done. You're going to run into a few creepies over there. But predictions are not many of them are left. Of course," Ben added dryly, "we've all said that before—about two dozen times."

"Who goes next, Ben?"

"Cecil, probably. Although he'll bitch and fuss about that."

The two old friends shook hands. "I'll have everything set up for you, Ben." He looked hard at the man. "Who is gonna be the last to leave the island?"

"Me, Ike. You knew that without asking."

"I was hopin' you'd change your mind. Any further

intell on Gene Savie and his bunch?"

"Dribs and drabs. None of it good. I still haven't made up my mind about that bunch. Probably won't until the last minute. Hell, I might go see them now. Luck to you, Ike."

Ben turned and walked away. He paused and looked back. "Keep an eye on Jerre for me, Ike."

Ike nodded. "Will do, Ben."

"Where to, General?" Cooper asked.

"To see Gene Savie and his bunch. Might as well bring it all to a head."

Buddy and his team and Tina and her team followed the Blazer. Ben stared down a pasty-faced member of Savie's survivors. "Get Gene out here. Now."

The Rebels had spread out in a half circle around Ben as Gene crunched through the snow, walking up to Ben.

"You wanted to see me, General Raines."

"Not really. But it's time for some truth, Savie. How deep in cahoots were you with the Night People?"

"Why . . . not at all, General."

"You're a goddamned liar, Savie! There is no way you could have survived as long as you did without striking some kind of deal with them."

Savie tried to meet Ben's steady gaze, but his eyes kept sliding to one side or the other. "They forced us to work with them," he finally said, his tone about as believable as a dentist who says that this isn't going to hurt a bit.

"You're slime, Savie. Pure slime. You and the rest of your scum turned your backs to the horror, for years. You're just as bad as the creepies." Ben's hand lashed out and slapped the man across the face. "Look at me when I talk to you, you son of a bitch!"

A thin trickle of blood leaked out of Savie's mouth. He made no effort to raise the weapon he carried in his hand.

"Stay out of my way until this is over, Savie," Ben warned him. "As a matter of fact, stay out of everybody's way. Some Rebel just might take it into his or her head to kill you!"

Ben turned around and walked off, leaving a badly

shaken Gene Savie staring at his back. Savie slowly looked around him, looking at the hard eyes of the Rebels. "They forced us to do it," he repeated. "You don't know what it was like here. You don't!"

One of the Rebels moved the muzzle of his M16. "You better carry your ass, Savie. 'Cause there isn't a one of us that wouldn't have rather died than work with the creepies. They'd have had to hunt us down like a wounded animal and kill us, one by one. Now get on out of here, you slimy bastard! Just lookin' at you makes me want to puke. Move!"

When Savie had walked away, toward his apartment building, a Rebel asked, "Do you reckon General Raines is gonna take them with us?"

He got a quick glance and a hard smile. "Don't bet on it. I got me a hunch the general is gonna leave them on the island."

Ben drove over to Colonel West's position and briefed the man on his encounter with Savie.

West spat on the snow. "We don't need them out there," he said, jerking his head to indicate anywhere outside the confines of Manhattan Island.

"I don't intend to take them with us."

West's smile was very thin. "I didn't think you would."

"You and your people and Tina and her teams follow Cecil and Buddy out of here when the time comes. Rebet and Danjou will go next, then Striganov, with Emil and Thermopolis. I'll come out last with Dan."

"When do you figure the total bug-out will take place?"

"Another three-four days. Maybe five. It all depends on how well Khamsin takes the bait. I want him in the center of the city before we push the button."

"And Savie and his people?"

"After we take the kids from them, I don't care where they'll be."

"Ahh! Not only have I discovered that you are a hopeless romantic, but that you also have a soft spot in your heart for kids and animals, Ben."

"Guilty on all counts, West. Dan will round them up

just before we bug out."

Ben drove over to speak to Cecil. "You go after Ike, Cec. . . ."

"Now, goddammit, Ben!"

"No arguments, Cec. I've got to have my second-in-command free and clear should anything happen to me. If I get caught up in the firestorm, you know what to do. Have you spoken with the Underground People?"

"Yes. They're ready to leave. They say they plan to make their way to Colorado. I understand they have others like them living in caves out there."

"To each his own," Ben said. "They're good people. All right, Cec. The fighting isn't over yet. I'll see you before the bug-out."

Ben briefed the others on their role in the bug-out and then returned to his CP.

"Dan, you take a team and hit Savie's apartment complex the morning of the bug-out. Grab the kids and take them over to Striganov's sector. Buddy, you'll leave with Cecil's battalion. Dan and I will be the last to leave the city."

"Yes, sir."

"Any word as yet on whether Khamsin has taken the bait we offered?"

"Tall Eyes report a few patrols have made their way into that sector," Dan told him. "It's a good thing we didn't booby-trap the first few blocks."

"What now, Father?" Buddy asked, the youth in him impatient.

Ben smiled. "We wait."

EIGHT

Khamsin halted his recon teams a block before they would hit the booby-trapped buildings and alleyways. Then he began slowly moving up his main force, still several thousand strong, to join his forward patrols.

They spread out west to east, from river to river, and settled in for the night.

Tall Eyes reported this to Ben.

"Do we hit them, Father?" Buddy asked.

"Be patient, son. Why should we risk our lives when we have a hundred or so booby traps to do the killing for us? What's the matter, boy? You got a girl back at Base Camp One?"

"I have girls wherever I go, Father," the son replied, trying to look stern and very worldly.

Ben laughed at him and ruffled the young man's hair.

"Typical Raines," Dan remarked, saluting the pair with an uplifted empty teacup.

"General Ike pulling out, sir," Chuck said. "And he's got his tanks snorting and clanking, going around in circles."

"That's what I wanted him to do. Surely Khamsin had sense enough to send some spotters up to the top floors of tall buildings."

"I think the man's hatred for you, and us, has clouded his mind," Dan said. He lifted the lid on his teapot and inhaled the fragrance of the steeping tea. "Nothing finer in all the world," he said with a smile. "Now if I just had some decent biscuits to go with it."

"We had biscuits for lunch," Buddy told him.

"He means cookies," Ben said.

"But he said biscuits."

"Trust me."

"Tea, gentlemen?" Dan smiled.

"I'll pass," Ben said. "Give me the radio, Chuck. Go have yourself a cup of tea."

"I hate tea, sir."

Dan looked offended. "The tastes of Americans never cease to amaze me."

Ben lifted the mike. "Eagle to Shark on scramble."

"Go, Eagle."

"Any indications that Khamsin is watching or listening to all that racket?"

"I got to believe he is, Eagle. The man may be a little bit nuts, but I don't believe he's a fool."

"All right, Ike. Safe journey."

"Ten-four, Eagle. Shark out."

Ben looked at Buddy. "Take a recon team up north, Buddy. Don't mix it up with any of Khamsin's people. I want reports, not blood. Take off."

"On my way."

"You sure you won't have a spot of tea?" Dan asked.

"I hate tea!" Chuck said. "Yuck!"

"A large contingent of Rebels leaving their sector, General," a runner told Khamsin.

"Heading where?"

"East."

"Brooklyn. It has to be. They're heading across the river." Khamsin was thoughtful for a moment. "But why? Why now? What is that filthy dog Raines pulling? He gave us half a dozen blocks. Why? We've encountered no traps. So why did he do it and what is he doing now?"

"Perhaps he is running away?" one of the general's

gofers suggested.

Khamsin frosted him silent with one long dark look. "Running away from what? Us? If he is running away, he's doing it laughing, and not from fear. Admit it, people. I have. He's done nothing but toy with us. He has manipulated us with the ease of a puppet-master. We advance in the morning—very slowly, very carefully. Let's see what Ben Raines is giving us . . . and why he gave us those blocks."

Buddy was back at ten o'clock, reporting to Dan. "Nothing moving up there. The streets are deserted. But the troops of the Hot Wind are on an unusually high level of alert."

"Which probably indicates they will make some sort of move come the dawn. Thanks, Buddy. Go get some rest. I'll advise your father."

Ben listened and said, "We'll roll out an hour earlier, Dan, and move everybody south ten blocks, to a Hundred Forty-fifth Street. Let's give Khamsin all the room he needs. Once he hits that booby-trapped area, he'll slow down, probably for a day. That will give Ike more time to wrap things up in Brooklyn. I want Khamsin in the Central Park area before we make our final bug-out. There isn't much in the way of lethal doses north of the park. Let him come on."

"Going to be interesting when his men hit the booby-trapped areas."

"Very interesting."

Ben started pulling his people back several hours before dawn, moving them down to 145th Street. But even with this move, Khamsin was still fifty blocks away from the northernmost edge of Central Park.

By dawn, only Ben and Dan and one company of Rebels were still on the line, and they were all ready to bug out.

A shattering roar split the white calmness of early dawn, the explosion setting off half a dozen other booby traps nearby. Buildings collapsed, sending walls tumbling down onto the troops of the Hot Wind. Entire storefronts were blown out into the snow-covered streets, the bricks and tangled steel rods becoming as lethal as a hail of bullets, breaking bones, ripping flesh and smashing skulls.

"I do believe Khamsin's men have reached the scene," Dan observed, munching on a cracker.

"Right-o," Ben said, with a smile, lifting his binoculars.

The powerful lenses brought the street of destruction leaping into his eyes. Huge clouds of dust were lifting into the air; small fires had been set by incendiary bombs. The flames began reaching out and igniting the dry wood of other buildings. Black smoke soon joined the dust clouds, spiraling up into the sky, to linger around the top floors of tall buildings.

"Stay out of the buildings!" Khamsin screamed his orders, understanding then why Ben Raines had so willingly given up so many blocks; but also knowing that the Rebels could not have booby-trapped all the buildings down to their lines.

Wherever the hell Ben Raines's lines might be, Khamsin thought bitterly.

"Stay in the streets and out of the buildings and alleys," Khamsin ordered, calming himself. "Move through the next five blocks swiftly but carefully."

"He's put it together," Ben said, lowering his field glasses. "All right, gang, let's split and leave the field wide open for the bastards."

Ben felt something wet touch and slide down his cheek. He looked up at the sky. Snowing again. Marvelous. Anything to help make life miserable for the Blowhole and his mini-farts.

"What do you find so amusing, Father?" Buddy asked, looking at the smile on Ben's face.

"The end to this damn war, son. It's within our grasp."

"Khamsin's men moving closer, sir," Dan pointed out. "I suggest we depart as hastily as possible."

"In other words, Dan, you want us to carry our asses out of here?"

"Crudely put, but that sums it all up rather well, yes."

"You're deep in thought, General," Beth said, breaking the silence in the makeshift office just off 145th Street.

"I'm about to make one of those semi-famous, so-called 'command decisions,' Beth," he said with a smile. "And if I'm wrong, I'll be putting us in a bad spot."

"If it'll get us off this frozen isalnd, General," Jersey said, "I'm for it."

"It'll put us one step closer, that's for sure. Chuck, get me General Jefferys on scramble."

"Go, Eagle," Cecil's voice came through the speaker.

"Bug-out time, Cec. Right now. And make it noisy. I want Khamsin to regain some confidence."

"Ben . . ."

"No bitching, Cec. Has to be. Pack it up and clear the island today. Eagle out." He glanced up at Buddy. "Take off, boy. You're leaving with him."

"If that is your wish, Father."

"It is." He stood up and shook hands with his son. "I'll see you in a few days. Go say goodbye to your sister."

Buddy quickly gathered his gear and was gone out the door, yelling for his team to pack it up.

"Chuck, advise the others of General Jefferys's leaving. And tell Colonel West to be ready to bug out at a moment's notice."

"Yes, sir."

Ben picked up his M14 and walked outside, to stand for a moment on the sidewalk, the snow gently and silently falling around him.

Beth stepped outside to join him.

"We can't wait much longer, Beth," Ben told her. "We can't let the bridges get to the point where they become impassable due to snow. Chuck!" he yelled over his shoulder.

The young man appeared in the broken doorway.

"Advise the other commanders to fall back to Central Park as soon as Cecil has left his sector. We'll give Khamsin the upper part of Manhattan. Maybe that will get the lead out of his ass and put some steel into his backbone."

"Yes, sir."

"I'll tell Coop to bring the Blazer around," Beth said.

The Rebels began falling back just as Cecil and his battalion were leaving their sector, heading for the bridge and Brooklyn. And they made no effort to hide their withdrawal from any unfriendly eyes that might be watching.

By dusk, all the Rebels had pulled back to Central Park and were bunkering themselves.

To the north, a thoroughly confused Khamsin was conferring with his field commanders.

"We've encountered no more booby-trapped buildings?"

"No, General. None."

"No snipers, nothing?"

"No, General. Nothing to stand in our way."

"Except this damnable snow," Khamsin muttered. "By all that is holy I do not know what Ben Raines is doing. That is not true. I know *what* he is doing. I do not know *why* he is doing it."

"For sure he is making preparations to leave the island, General."

"I know that! But why? Don't delude yourselves, gentlemen: Ben Raines and his Rebels could easily defeat us in this dreadful place. Surely by now you have all admitted that to yourselves. You may say it aloud. I know it is true."

The field commanders all exchanged glances, but they would not speak those words aloud. They had never been defeated. In all their years of roaming the world, they had always been victorious.

Except for the few times they had butted heads with Ben Raines.

"We advance first thing in the morning," Khamsin said wearily. "I must pray for guidance."

"I can't bear to be parted from my precious flower!" Emil wailed, standing in front of Ben in his CP. He threw his arms wide, and his helmet slipped down over his eyes.

"Emil . . . !"

"Her voice is like a gentle fragrance. Her lips two rose petals." He pushed the helmet back up so he could see. "Assign me to Danjou's battalion, General. Please!"

"Hell, no! Major Danjou would never forgive me. Look, Emil . . ."

"Michelle is the true love of my life. She is the wind beneath my combat boots. . . ."

Ben poured a glass of whiskey and drank it down. Neat. He did his best to tune Emil out. It was no use. Emil blithered and blathered and ranted and raved. Ben was afraid he might start speaking in tongues any moment.

"Emil . . . !"

"She is my treasure at the end of the rainbow. The light at the end of a long dismal day . . ."

Ben poured another drink.

Emil started singing "Bridge over Troubled Water."

"That does it," Ben muttered, and started to rise.

"Don't stop me now!" Emil said. "I'm gettin' to the good part."

Ben sat down and rolled a cigarette and smoked and listened. He didn't want to listen, but short of shooting Emil, he didn't know what else to do.

Emil finally finished and sat down. "Help me, General Raines!" he pleaded.

Ben poured Emil a glass of booze and pushed it toward him. "Have a drink, Emil. I'll have one with you. Believe me, after that performance, I need one."

Emil knocked back the drink and held out his glass for a refill. "That's good hooch."

"Thank you. Now, Emil, listen to me. I know, personally, what you're going through."

"You!"

"Sure. Don't you think I've ever been rejected?"

"Did you love her?"

"I still do, Emil. Just as much as I did yesterday but not as much as I will tomorrow."

Emil burst into tears.

"Now what's wrong, Emil?"

Emil honked his nose and wiped his eyes. "What you just said."

"What about it?"

"It was so fucking beautiful I couldn't hardly stand it!"

"Thank you." Ben thought about that for a second. "I think."

"But how do you cope with it, Ben? How do you stand it?"

Ben gave each empty glass another splash. "Emil, let me tell you something. Memories. That's how I cope with it. I remember all the laughs we had. All the good times. And we did have some good times. A lot of good times. Memories can be beautiful, Emil. I have in my mind a picture of her standing in front of some windows, with the sunlight hitting her. I thought then, and do now, that she is the most beautiful woman in the world.

"But she and I can never be, Emil. So I've learned to accept that and live with it. She will always hold a special place in my heart. But I'm not going to stop living because we can never be . . . or rather, be the way I want us to be."

Emil met Ben's eyes. "Jerre Hunter."

"That's right, Emil. But this is just between us. Man to man."

"On my word of honor, Ben. I'll never breathe a word of it. I got an idea, Ben Raines."

"Lay it on me, Emil."

"Let's us, you and me, two men of the world who now find ourselves with broken hearts . . . let's get shit-faced drunk!"

NINE

Ben carried Emil out into the anteroom, slung over his shoulder like a sack of feed.

"That didn't take long," Jersey said.

"Emil passed out during the second verse of 'Ruby, Don't Take Your Love to Town.'"

With Cooper taking his shoulders and Chuck taking his legs, they carried Emil out to the Blazer.

"Take him to his quarters, boys. And handle him gently. His heart is broken."

"So is his voice," Chuck remarked. "I believe that's the worst singing I ever heard."

Shaking his head and laughing, Ben walked back inside. He went to the radio, fiddled with it until he figured out how to work it—conscious of Beth watching him with a smile on her face—and tried to reach Ike. No responses.

"You got to turn it on, General," Beth called from across the room. "The black plastic switch on the right. Right there."

Muttering, Ben turned the equipment on and waited for it to warm up.

"It's ready to go, General. It stays hot from a backup battery. If you want it on scramble, flip that silver toggle switch on the left side. Right there."

"Thank you, Beth. Eagle to Shark." He waited while a runner located Ike.

"Go, Eagle."

"How's it going over there, Ike?"

"Better than we expected, Ben. We got the engines in these old rust buckets ticking over like perpetual motion machines. We got the winches and cranes working to lift most of our gear on board."

"That's good news, Ike. We've moved down to the park and are waiting for Khamsin to follow. Did Cec get over?"

"That's ten-four, Ben. We cleared one section of a runway. The wounded will be flying back to Base Camp One in the morning. We have not seen one sign of any creepies."

"That's ten-four, Ike. Talk to you next day. Eagle out."

Ben walked outside to stand in the snow and cold for a time. It was coming down to the wire, and it all depended on Khamsin pushing hard and how Sister Voleta and Monte and Ashley would react once the plan went into effect.

Ben tried to put himself in the place of those over in New Jersey. Ben felt he could figure what Ashley would do. He did not know enough about Monte to reach any firm conclusions, and Ben knew he should not even attempt to plumb the depths of the mind of Sister Voleta. She was totally but brilliantly insane. So there was no way of knowing what she might do.

And Sister Voleta was also a fanatic, her sole purpose for being to destroy Ben Raines. Like Khamsin, she would willingly die if in doing so she could be assured of Ben's death.

Ben returned to the warmth of the building and sat down on his cot, pulling off his boots and stretching out. He expected Khamsin to start his advance in the morning. If the Libyan did as Ben thought, his Rebels would have to hold their current positions for at least one full day, and then begin falling back, sucking Khamsin deeper and deeper into lower Manhattan. Anywhere past 86th Street would be ideal. They had enough fuel oil and gasoline to ensure a big bang and a steady burn in lower Manhattan.

The chemicals would take care of any who survived the

initial blast and burn. Ike and Dan had planted explosives at stress points of many buildings, guaranteed to bring them down.

Ben went to sleep thinking of the bug-out and the devastation that would follow. He went to sleep wondering if he and his Rebels could pull it off.

And he went to sleep thinking of Jerre.

Since he went to sleep so early in the evening, he was up long before any of the others. He dressed quietly and picked up his M14, slipping through the darkened anteroom and stepping outside.

"Ben Raines," he whispered to the sentry who had whirled around as Ben exited the building.

"Yes, sir. You startled me, sir. Christ, it isn't even three o'clock yet."

"I'll stand your watch, girl. You go get us a couple cups of coffee."

"Yes, sir!" She grinned at him, glad for a chance to get out of the cold.

Ben squatted down on the sidewalk and looked up at the sky. Not a star in sight. And the air was not only cold, it was wet. More snow on the way.

And that was not good news.

Two more days of snow, and bridge traffic during the bug-out would be slowed to a snail's pace. That was both good and bad for a couple of reasons. The bug-out would have to be executed very quickly, but if it was snowing, the dispersion of the chemical agents in the wet air would be greatly reduced and would thus place the Rebels in less danger should there be a wind shift. Ben's weather people had given him the green light for the day after tomorrow. But it might have to be sooner.

"Damn!" Ben said. He also felt that the snow would slow Khamsin's troops in their advance. And they needed to be at the northernmost section of Central Park in thirty-six hours. Then, one more day of the Rebels falling back, and Ben could cut the tiger loose.

And when to order West to bug out? No later than tomorrow evening, for sure. Khamsin's spotters would know that at least three battalions had left the city. That just might prompt the man to make a full frontal attack against the weakened lines at the park.

Maybe.

The sentry returned with two cups of coffee and some hot bread. "I conned the cook out of the bread, General."

"Smells good. Thanks. Everything quiet during the night?"

"Like a grave, sir." She squatted down beside him and they ate the bread and sipped the coffee.

Ben knew her face but not her name. "What's your name?" he asked.

"Penny."

"Got a family, Penny?"

"No, sir. Maybe when all the fighting is over I can think about that. I been fighting with the Rebels for three years. I kind of envy those who do have kids, but it's not for me, not just yet."

"You'd miss the action?"

"For sure. It gets in your blood. Here it doesn't make any difference if you're a man or woman. Everybody is equal. I had me a man down in Texas—back when I was just a kid, fifteen years old. The day he told me he was the boss and I do what he tells me to do, that's the day I told him to shove it and left. I joined up with Ramos and his people and then was transferred to a base camp over in North Carolina."

"Equality is the way I planned it, Penny. How old were you when the Great War came?"

"I think I was eight, General. Some folks took me in for a few years, then the man raped me. I was about twelve, I guess. I split and stayed with some other kids for a couple more years."

She didn't elaborate on what took place between ages twelve and fifteen and Ben didn't push it. Over the years he had spoken with hundreds of kids who had been caught up in those years directly after the Great War. Theirs had been a mean, miserable and scary existence. Many had drifted to the Tri-States. Most had stayed and become part of the Rebels.

"They going to hit us today, General?"

"I would, if I were in Khamsin's boots."

"We really going to sail out of the harbor in those big ships over yonder in Brooklyn?" She pronounced it "Brookering."

"That's the plan, Penny."

"That'll be fun. I never been on a ship. I never even seen one up close."

"It won't be long now."

Ben rolled his people out at four o'clock and after breakfast, told them to get into position.

Chuck got the field commanders on the horn and Ben took the mike, telling Chuck to take it off scramble. He knew his words would be monitored up in Khamsin's CP. "This is Eagle. We don't use artillery unless they open up with it first. Let's see if the Hot Fart and his assholes have the courage to face cold nerve and hot lead. They've got us outnumbered three or four to one, but I don't think any of them have what it takes in the guts department. Dawn will tell the story, I suppose. Eagle out."

When Khamsin was told of the challenge, he took it calmly, and then reached exactly the conclusion that Ben had hoped for.

"A challenge between generals," Khamsin spoke softly. "I see now why he fought without honor at first."

"Why, General?"

"To bring our forces closer to his number, naturally. Very well, I accept his challenge. No tanks, no artillery." He held up a finger. "Do not fear. The forces of Allah will prevail."

"Recon teams report Khamsin and men are on the way, General," Chuck related. "Looks like he took the bait. No tanks and no artillery."

Ben smiled. "Very good. This time tomorrow, we can

start moving our heavy tanks across the bridges."

"We gonna load them on the ships, General?"

"Some of them. I guess we'll have to leave the rest." He again allowed himself a strange smile and picked up a map, studying it, seemingly unconcerned that approximately four thousand decidedly hostile troops were rapidly moving toward his position.

Ben walked over to Chuck. "Take a break, Chuck. I need to use the radio for a minute."

"Ah . . . yes, sir! You want it on scramble?"

"Please."

Ben sat alone in the CP for several minutes, alternately looking at a map and speaking into the mike. Then, again with that strange smile on his face, he hung up the mike and stepped outside.

"Let's go fight a war, gang."

Neither side gave up an inch of ground all through that long and bloody day. Toward evening, it began to snow again, and Ben had to make a decision and make it fast.

He drove over to Colonel West's position. "Bug out tonight, Colonel. Take Tina and her teams and head for New Jersey. We can't wait any longer. Another twenty-four hours of snow, those bridges will be impassable even with chains."

"All right, Ben. But you're damn sure going to be short."

"Even shorter come noon tomorrow, West."

"That's the final bug-out?"

"That's it."

The two professional soldiers stood looking at each other for a moment, both of them smiling. West broke the silence.

"I always said if I ever found a better tactician than myself, I'd follow him through Hell and back again. I found him."

"Let's see if it'll work before you start heaping accolades on my head."

"Oh, it'll work." He gripped Ben's arm. "See you, Ben."

"Take care of my kid."

"Will do."

Ben waited and watched as West began grouping his people. Tina came to his side.

"Why do I get this feeling, Pops, that you're about to pull something damned sneaky again?"

"Me? Girl, you know I would never do anything like that."

"Right, Pops. Sure. Now then, what about Jerre?"

Ben stiffened just a bit, and it wasn't from the cold. "What about her?"

"She told me she wanted to return to Louisiana with us."

"So I can bump into her every goddamn time I turn around? So I can see her with other men? Get real, girl! No way."

"She's assigned to us, Dad. You know how shitty that's going to look when you deliberately send her off to the boondocks?"

Ben was silent for a moment. Then he sighed. "Maybe it's time for me to open up the plains states, girl. Yeah. I've been thinking about that. Just taking a battalion and striking out, looking for trouble."

"Running away is a better name for it." When he did not acknowledge her comment, she said, "Are you going to run from her all your life?"

"I do not wish to continue this discussion any longer, Tina. It's bug-out time, girl. Join your team."

"Yes, *sir,* General!" Then the expression on her face softened and she kissed Ben's cheek. "You have to do what you think is best, Dad. I'm with you whatever you do."

"Thanks. You take care. I'll see you tomorrow afternoon."

"I still think you're going to pull something sneaky."

"Never! You know I am as straightforward as a bullet. As honest as Abe Lincoln. As truthful as George Washington. As pure as the driven snow. As honorable as a minister. As . . ."

"Full of crap as you have always been," she finished it

for him.

Ben gave her a swat on the rear and she ran away, over the snow, laughing. "I'll tell Jerre you said hello," she called over her shoulder.

"Yeah, you probably will," Ben muttered. "And when you do, she'll probably spit in your eye or hang a cussing on you."

TEN

"How is Ben?" Jerre asked.

"Ben is Ben," Tina told her. "He's never going to change."

West's column had made it over the bridges without difficulty and were bivouacked in New Jersey. Tina and Jerre were having a very welcome cup of coffee and talking.

"I'm tired of drifting, Tina. I want a home, some permanency in my life."

"Dad isn't going to kick up a fuss if you come to Base Camp One with us. Just stay out of his way and don't flaunt your boyfriends in his face. Dad's going to pull out anyway, probably within a couple of weeks of our returning."

"If I come back with you?"

"Whether you do or not. Cecil will be running the show at the base camp because he's better at administration than Dad. Cecil has him a lady friend and would rather stay home. Oh, Dad will bitch and moan about his getting old and all that type of crap, and about how he's too old for the field and this, that, and the other thing. But he's never going to leave combat to others. He's always going to be right in the thick of it. Just make plans to come on back with us. Like I said, just stay away from Dad when he's in camp."

Jerre nodded her head. "What's going on around here,

Tina? Something is very strange. The docks are off-limits except for a few people."

"I don't know, Jerre. But I have this feeling that Dad is pulling something very sneaky and keeping it close to the vest."

"General Jefferys said he wanted everybody in their sleeping bags by nine o'clock tonight. He also said that everybody was going to have a very busy day facing us tomorrow. But what the hell are we going to be doing?"

"Beats me, girl. You know Ben, he's full of surprises."

"Yes, I know that only too well. And he can spring them on you right out of the blue."

Ben stepped out and looked up into a dark but snowy predawn morning. "Now or never," he muttered. He walked back into the CP and located the radio, taking it outside. "Eagle to Hawk."

Cecil was on the horn within a moment. "Go, Eagle."

"Get them up and moving, Cec. We'll be bugging out at noon."

"Ten-four, Ben. We'll cross at the easternmost point, well out of range of any of their spotters, and then angle toward rendezvous."

"Affirmative. Eagle out." He got Rebet and Danjou and gave the orders. "Bug out, gentlemen. And don't be quiet about it. I'll see you across."

Dan had joined him. "Get the kids, Dan."

"Right, sir." Dan waved his team to vehicles.

Gene Savie awakened to a cold muzzle pressing against his face.

"I do hate to be so abrupt this early in the morning, don't you know?" Dan spoke softly. "It isn't a bit civil. But we're going to relieve you all of a burden."

"What are you talking about?" his wife asked.

"Your children, Madame. I do hope you will not kick up too much of a fuss abot it. I hate unpleasantness before I have had my morning cup."

"You son of a bitch!" Gene cursed him.

Dan's smile was thin. "I wouldn't want you to get in the habit of calling me that. I might take umbrage at the slur against my mother and become quite hostile. Like bashing your teeth out with the butt of this weapon."

Gene slumped back onto the pillows.

"Take all the art you can gather, people," Dan reminded his Scouts. "They won't be needing it."

Gene and his wife lay in the dark bedroom and glared at Dan.

A few moments passed in silence.

"We've got them, Colonel!" a Scout called.

"Very good." He smiled at Gene and wife. "Ta-ta, now, folks. Do enjoy yourselves . . . in the time you have left. Oh, and don't attempt to leave your apartments. I'll have sharpshooters posted here and there. Good day!" he called cheerfully.

"What's happening?" his wife cried.

"Ben Raines is leaving us on the island, that's what is happening. Just relax. We can strike a deal with the Libyan just like we did with the Night People."

"But the children!"

"Less mouths to feed."

Dan took the very quiet and scared kids to Striganov.

"What do you plan to do with them once we are clear of the island?" the Russian asked.

"Spread them around our various outposts, I suppose," Dan told him.

"Do you suppose Ben would object if some of them went to Canada?"

Dan smiled. "I don't think he would mind at all, General." He was watching as some of the Russian troops were busy making friends with the children.

"Good, good!" Georgi said, then began assigning personnel to get the kids off the island. They would leave immediately.

Dawn began streaking the eastern sky as Khamsin's troops began firing at the Rebel-held lines.

"Fall back," Ben ordered. "Down to Ninety-sixth Street. Let's go, people. Fall back as if you're running in fear from the Hot Fart."

The Rebels pulled back, giving the Libyan troops twelve more blocks of the city.

"Throw up a line here," Ben ordered. "We've got to hold until noon."

The Rebels stopped the fast advance of the Libyan troops and held firm. There were few casualties on either side that morning. The snow already on the ground and more coming down made visibility poor and any type of movement very dangerous.

"Get any vehicles that we don't need out of here," Ben instructed Dan. "Get them across the bridges. Have the drivers of the vehicles that are staying with us turn them around and keep them ready to go."

Dan was back at Ben's side in a moment.

"The bridges wired and ready to blow, Dan?"

"All set, General."

Ben checked his watch then opened a map case. "When we bug out, Dan, we'll take Amsterdam all the way down until it intersects with Broadway. We'll follow Broadway down to Fourteenth Street and then I'll angle off to Fourth. We'll head down to the two lower bridges, then across to Brooklyn. As soon as we're on the bridges, blow the Williamsburg Bridge."

"Ten-four, General."

"All the Tall Eyes down and clear?"

"Yes, sir."

"All recon patrols back to our lines?"

"All back home, sir."

"What am I forgetting, Dan?"

"I can't think of a thing, sir. I believe we are ready to put the stopper in the bottle."

"Just a few more hours," Ben muttered, his voice barely audible over the crash of combat.

"Rebet and Danjou are across," Chuck relayed the message to Ben.

Emil walked up, looking like the original Sad Sack.

"Did my sweet poopsie arrive in Brooklyn safely?" he asked.

"Yes, Emil," Ben replied, fighting to hide his smile. "Your rose of no-man's-land is safe."

"I feel like the sun has gone forever out of my life," Emil moaned, looking as if he might tune up and start bawling any second. Or singing, and one was just as bad as the other.

"Hang on, Emil," Ben told him. "You'll be together again." He silently groaned as soon as the words left his mouth, for he knew Emil was old enough to remember that song.

Emil burst out in song.

Dan looked on and listened, his face a study in emotions as Emil bellowed out the words, his voice carrying over the rattle of gunfire.

Ben turned to a Rebel. "Go find Thermopolis. Tell him to get his people—and Emil and his group—across the river. As quickly as possible." He grabbed Emil by the shoulders. "Emil! Get ready to head for Brooklyn. Your sweet baboo is waiting."

"Oh, thank you from the bottom of my heart!" Emil shouted. He ran off, slipping and sliding in the snow, to join his group.

"Thermopolis is not going to be happy about this," Dan said.

"Would you like to escort Emil across the bridge?"

"God forbid!"

"Let's go to work."

The men and women walked toward the sounds of battle.

Ben was leaning up against a truck when Thermopolis and his group drove past in their VWs. Emil was sitting in the backseat of Thermopolis's Bug. He looked very happy, and he was singing.

Thermopolis looked long at Ben, an extremely disgusted expression on his face, then raised his hand and gave Ben the finger.

Ben was still laughing and Dan was losing the struggle

to maintain a straight face as the short column faded out of sight, the chains on the tires clanking and clicking and rattling as they gripped the snowy street.

"We can't have any amateurs on this last run, Dan. Get the Underground People out. Tell them to move out now."

Within minutes, the trucks carrying the strange and pale men and women and children of the underground moved past.

"Gettin' down to the nut-cuttin' now," Jersey commented.

Dan glanced at her. "What a quaint expression. You certainly have a way with words."

"Thanks," Jersey said with a straight face.

"Wind is beginning to shift around," Coop said. "Another hour or so and it'll be coming straight out of the east."

"That's when we'll make our move, people. Blazer all packed, Coop?"

"Ten-four, General. Sittin' on go."

Ben stuck out his hand and Dan shook it. "Return to your unit, Dan. Get ready to bug out. I'll advise General Striganov and his people they'll be leaving within the hour."

"I shall see you on Broadway, General. Naturally, you will be leading the parade?"

"Wrong. My team will be the last ones off this island, Dan."

"I had to try."

"I was waiting for it."

"Good luck, sir."

"Same to you, Dan."

The Englishman wheeled around and began the short walk back to his unit of Scouts.

Ben stood in the cold winds and blowing snow and rolled a cigarette, his mind racing back and forth like a restless panther in a cage. He began to pace up and down the sidewalk.

Had he remembered everything?

He thought so.

His personal team stood around him in silence, watching him pace the snow.

Ben sighed and stopped his restless walking. He looked at his team. "Take a look around you, gang. Take a look at the Big Apple. We're about to tear the core out of it. It's a good thing Hizzoner isn't around to see this."

"Who, sir?" Coop asked.

"The mayor. He would have been very unhappy with me." Ben lifted the map and for the tenth time in an hour studied the route to freedom. "Miles to go," he muttered. "And we're leaving so many treasures behind us."

"Sir," Jersey said. "We got a hundred *tons* of books and paintings and stuff being loaded over in Brooklyn. More than I ever dreamed we'd manage to salvage. If history hangs a lot of blame on you, then the historians can just go kiss ass!"

Ben was startled for a moment; then he burst out laughing. "You're right, Jersey. Thanks for taking a load off me."

"You're welcome," the little lady said.

"Let's go cross some bridges, gang. Chuck, tell General Striganov to bug out!"

ELEVEN

As soon as Khamsin's troops realized what was happening, they radioed the news back to his CP.

"Pursue them!" Khamsin screamed. "Don't let them reach the bridges. Cut them off."

Easy to say. But Ben had prepared for that move, as well.

What Khamsin did not know, but was about to discover, was that East 65th Street, from the park all the way over to the East River, was blocked by as many junked vehicles as the Rebels had been able to drag in from all over that part of the city.

Khamsin split his forces, one group pushing down from the recently abandoned battle lines on the east side of the park, the other group chasing after Ben on the west side of the park.

Some of Gene Savie's group, seeing what was taking place, ran out of their apartments and tried to wave down the troops of the Hot Wind.

"We're friends!" they screamed at the trucks. "We're on your side. We're glad to see you."

"Please stop!" Gene shouted. "Please. We're your friends."

The Libyans laughed at them.

"Leave them be," a field commander ordered. "When we get back we'll shoot the men and have our way with the women."

The race went on through the slick snowy streets of

the city.

In the Blazer, Ben took a page from Emil's book and began humming "Homeward Bound."

With chains on all four wheels, Cooper could maneuver the four-wheel-drive vehicle almost as well as if he were driving on dry pavement. Since they were the last vehicle in the column, Ben decided to have some fun by tossing grenades out of his open window.

That action kept Khamsin's men back a good two blocks, for the Rebel grenades were almost twice as powerful as the old conventional type.

Ben picked up his mike and keyed it. "Dan? When we reach Columbus Circle, spread a couple hundred pounds of HE around the area and put a two-minute timer on it. That ought to catch Khamsin's column just right. Keep the east lane, east side clear."

"Ten-four, sir."

Cooper glanced at a battered old sign. West 72nd Street. It was going to be close. He picked up his mike. "You guys up front wanna kick it in the ass some? I sure would appreciate it."

The column picked up speed.

"What's the matter, Coop?" Ben said with a smile. "You getting nervous?"

"Oh, no! Not me, sir."

"He doesn't lie any better than he drives," Jersey remarked.

Coop slid through Columbus Circle, his face shiny with sweat. "Shit!" he yelled, relief very evident in his voice as they cleared the hidden explosives.

The high explosives blew just as the third truck in Khamsin's column passed over it. The truck and its occupants were splattered all over the area. The huge explosion blew the gas tanks on several more trucks and created a massive, burning traffic jam. The twisted and mangled and bloody bodies of the Hot Wind's soldiers littered the snow.

The Rebel column sped past 57th Street and continued south, toward Times Square.

"We're blocked!" Akim screamed into his mike. "Completely blocked at Sixty-fifth Street."

"Backtrack!" Khamsin squalled into his mike. "Backtrack and cut over through the park." He was frantically eyeing an old city map. "Just past the zoo there is a road that cuts south, it will bring you out on Central Park South. Move, Akim, move!"

"Times Square." Ben pointed it out, much like a tour director. "I almost got mugged in this area one night."

They passed the Times Building.

"Macy's is just a few blocks down, ladies. I wish we had the time to stop and browse, but I'm afraid our schedule just won't permit it. Pressing business and all that, you know?"

"Comedian," Jersey muttered. "A grenade-tossing comedian."

"Yeah, you could say he bombed out," Beth said.

Ben groaned as the others laughed.

They were through Herald Square and then passing the Flatiron Building on 23rd Street.

Ben keyed his mike. "Dan, everything is still Go. You cross on the Brooklyn Bridge. I'll take the Manhattan Bridge."

"Ten-four, General."

"Lead Scout," Ben radioed, "when you get down here to Union Square Park, just past it, hang a left and you'll pick up Fourth Avenue, turn right on Fourth. That changes to Bowery later on. Stay with it. We might even see a bum or two."

"Sir?"

"Never mind. We'll pick up the bridge just off Confucius Plaza."

"Yes, sir."

"Where the hell did our pursuit go?" Beth asked, twisting around in the backseat.

"They probably got all tangled up," Ben said with a smile as the others groaned.

Coop followed the column as they turned onto Fourth.

"Cooper Square right down there a few blocks," Ben

told him.

"All right! Probably named after one of my famous relatives."

"Probably where they *hung* one of your relatives," Jersey fired back.

"Speaking of being hung . . ." Cooper laughed as he was booed and hissed quiet from Beth and Jersey.

"General Striganov is across," the speaker spewed the words. "What is your twenty, General?" Dan asked.

"Coming up on Houston."

"I'm crossing Canal. I'll wait for you, General."

"Ten-fifty on that, Dan. You get across the bridge."

"Yes, sir."

"Khamsin's people in sight, General," Beth told him.

Ben rolled down his window and began tossing grenades out as fast as his people could hand them to him and he could pull the pins.

Khamsin's column fell back several blocks. Bullets began slamming into the back of the Blazer.

"That's very annoying," Ben remarked, as they sped past Delancey Street. He read the old street sign. "Just a couple of minutes more, gang." He picked up his mike.

"Eagle to Shark?"

"Go, Eagle."

"I think we just might have a few vehicles on our tail when we cross. Have some reception waiting for them, please."

"Ten-four, Eagle."

Ben flipped the radio to scramble. "To all units crossing over. Do not go to the docks. Repeat, do not go to the docks. You will rendezvous with me just off the Brooklyn-Queens Expressway on Navy Street. Shark, shove off."

"Aye, aye, Captain." Ike's voice contained a lot of high humor.

"What the hell . . . ?" Cooper muttered.

They were on the bridge and staying in the ruts made by previous vehicles.

The sound of a ship's horn drifted to them.

Jersey looked at Beth and Beth looked at Chuck.

"Don't ask me," he said. "I just work here."

"Eagle to West."

"Go, Eagle."

"You may have the honors, sir."

"That's a big ten-four, General. But it is with a mixture of sadness and satisfaction."

"I understand the emotions, West. Peel the Apple."

Behind them, in several hundred spots throughout the city, massive charges blew, bringing buildings down and sending deadly gas wafting through the cold air. Electronically opened valves sent gasoline flooding into the subway system and the sewer tunnels under the city. The fumes ignited and exploded. Entire sections of streets were lifted high into the air. The methane was ignited and flames leaped hundreds of feet into the air as the methane mixed with gasoline.

And the poisonous chemicals reached human lungs and flesh.

"You across, Dan?" Ben radioed.

"Ten-four, sir."

"So are we. Blow the bridges."

Those who had chased Ben and his columns through the city were caught on the bridge as sections of both spans were blown. The fast-moving trucks could not stop in time. They plunged off the bridge, falling through the blown sections to the icy waters below, carrying their screaming human cargo to a watery death.

Ben did not immediately look back on the death of a city. Had he looked, he would have seen huge columns of smoke rising into the snowy air, flames dancing and twisting from the gasoline and methane as they touched and torched dusty old buildings.

On both sides of Central Park, and from 86th Street down to Battery Park, a fiery maelstrom had enveloped the city, one fire feeding another as the flames spread unchecked.

Only one battalion of Khamsin's troops was above the deadly line of fire and poison chemicals. Khamsin ordered them into protective gear and began moving them back toward the north, the taste of defeat bitter in his mouth.

Gene and Kay Savie and their collaborators made it away from the chemicals and flames with the clothes on their backs, their weapons, and damn little else. They got into their once-expensive cars and station wagons and raced toward the north.

John Savie sat in the backseat of his son's car and muttered, "I always knew that Ben Raines was a no-good, no-talent son of a bitch!"

He looked back at the city and cursed.

Flames were rapidly moving up the dusty interiors of the tall towers of the city, building with a hideous fury as the tons of papers within the offices exploded in flames, the force blowing out windows and pocking the snow-covered streets with shards of glass.

As the water in the sewers and tunnels began to boil, steam began to build, producing pressure with no adequate release valve. The working energy finally reached the exploding point and blew, the collected masses blowing great holes in the streets of lower Manhattan and in the basements and lower levels of buildings. That action proved too much for structures already weakened by age and neglect. Steel twisted and concrete buckled, bringing hundreds of thousands of tons of ragged debris down into the streets.

Khamsin looked back at the holocaust and cursed Ben Raines, damning him forever to the pits of Hell and the demons therein.

In the department stores of the city, mannequins melted as the fires reached near-impossible temperatures; silk and satin and cotton burst into flames; expensive jewelry melted; and five-hundred-dollar bottles of perfume and cologne exploded, one last and very brief touch of extravagance splashing an aroma-salute to a dying city.

Those troops of the Hot Wind who had been caught in lower Manhattan now lay choking on the snow, the deadly gases ending their lives just as the flames touched them, or they lay buried and forever forgotten beneath tons of rubble as buildings collapsed.

Those Night People who dared challenge Ben Raines and his Rebels, those who remained in the city, went up in a puff of fire and smoke, for they had no place left to run.

Ben ordered the Blazer stopped on an overpass of the Brooklyn-Queens Expressway. He stood by the railing, facing west, a hard wind blowing at his back. Lower Manhattan was completely enveloped in smoke and fire and explosions. Below him, on the streets under the overpass, Rebels waited in silence, all of them looking at the destruction across the cold and silent river.

One Rebel in the crowd of men and women standing in the cold and snow turned to face Ben, standing above him. He raised his M16 high in the air and let a Rebel yell rip the air. Ben cut his eyes and looked at the man.

Others in the crowd turned, raised their weapons and cut the cold winds with wild Rebel yells of victory. Behind them, the black smoke roiled angrily and darkly into the air.

Soon all the Rebels on the streets and expressway were yelling, pumping their weapons up and down in a victory salute.

Ben let them work off weeks of collected steam, their cries of victory filling the snowy air.

Then he lifted his M14 into the air and joined in the celebration.

Far in the distance, the sounds of ships' horns joined the victory yells as Ike led the three-ship, nearly empty convoy out into Lower New York Bay, past Fort Hancock, and then assumed a southerly heading.

Buddy stood by Ike's side on the bridge of the lead ship, both of them looking back at New York City.

"This was a deliberate move by my father, wasn't it, Ike?" the young man asked. "My being here with you, I mean."

"Yes."

"So I would not have to be a part of fighting against my mother."

"Yes."

"He had this in mind all along, didn't he? This ruse,

I mean?"

"Just about from the git-go, boy."

"Where will we land these monsters?"

Ike laughed at him. "We'll find us some docks down south with the equipment to offload our vehicles, and then we'll head on back to Base Camp One."

Buddy stared at the smoke that was once lower Manhattan. "My mother is going to be highly displeased with this action," he commented.

"That's the general idea, boy."

TWELVE

Spotters posted along the New Jersey shore had seen the ships leave, steaming stately along and then cutting out into the Atlantic. They had radioed back to Sister Voleta.

"Damn him!" she exploded. "This idea came to me but I rejected it as unworkable. Goddamn Ben Raines! Somehow he pulled it off."

Ashley had been stunned as he watched the beginning of the destruction of New York City, and then he shook himself out of it and ordered everybody to move south, quickly, all the way down to Middlesex County.

"Why?" Monte demanded.

"Because I don't trust Ben Raines," Ashley told him.

They waited at the rendezvous point for the last men to arrive. They did not arrive.

"That's about what I thought," Ashley said.

"What the hell are you talkin' about?" Monte challenged him. "Them boys was good soldiers. They wouldn't run off. They'll be along."

"They will never be along," Ashley told him. "Ben used some sort of chemicals; poisonous gases. I wondered why he was waiting to cut and run. He was waiting for the wind to change, to blow straight out of the east."

Even Sister Voleta was shaken. "If we had stayed, we

would all be dead."

"Yes. I think that, too, was his plan."

Monte shook his head. "This guy ain't human. He's cruel! But . . . with him and his people all gone on them ships, what are we gonna do?"

Ashley squatted down and warmed his hands over an open fire. *"If* Ben Raines and his Rebels are indeed on those ships."

"Now what the hell do you mean by that?"

Sister Voleta listened in silence.

"You have to understand how Ben's mind works. He is such a sneaky son of a bitch. I'll wager that not one percent of his people knew what he was going to do until it was actually taking place."

"You mean he don't even trust his own people?"

"Oh, he trusts them. Of course he does. That's not why he does it. If one of them were captured and tortured, they might break and talk. Be quiet and let me think for a moment. Your silence would be most gratifying."

Monte closed his mouth and pouted.

Ashley was thoughtful for a moment and then said, "We know that Ben has spotter planes. Probably based down at this old military complex." He punched at a worn map. "McGuire, Dix, the Naval Air Station. Somewhere in there. What if, just for argument's sake, Ben was not on those ships, but instead headed north out of Brooklyn . . . say, crossing into the Bronx here," he pointed, "on either Six-seventy-eight or Two-ninety-five. He would then proceed up into Westchester County and cross the Hudson using the Tappan Zee bridge, then cut south and come down behind us."

"So what's with this spotter plane business?" Monte asked.

"If spotter planes go up more than just a couple of times," Sister Voleta said, "that would mean that they weren't just doing reconnaissance of the city. They would be searching for us."

"Precisely!" Ashley beamed.

"It would be just like that son of a bitch to pull something of this nature," Voleta said.

"We'll rendezvous with Cecil at this point," Ben said, putting his finger on Gypsy Sprain Reservoir. "East side. He's taken command of the units Ike left behind." Ben turned to Chuck. "Advise the spotters to do no flybys of any area until I order them up. Tell them to keep the birds on the ground. Do it now."

Chuck nodded and walked to the Blazer.

"Now I'll answer the question I know you all have in your minds: What in the hell is going on? I've already briefed Ike and Cecil; now it's your turn.

"We're going to finish Monte and Ashley and Sister Voleta once and for all. If we have to chase them all the way to California, then that's what we'll do. Georgi and Danjou and Rebet say they're in this fight for the duration. That's good—I welcome their assistance.

"What we're going to try is swinging north and then coming down on them. I'm sure you've all noticed that none of our heavy stuff was loaded on ship. Ike took just enough to get him through to Base Camp One . . . if he should run into trouble."

Ben paused for a moment, turning to look at the smoke pouring into the sky from the hundreds of unchecked fires in the city. He shook his head and turned back to his people.

"Once we rendezvous with Cecil, we'll continue north and cross over the Hudson here." Again he punched the map. "North of the Tappan Zee Bridge. It's out of our way, but Ashley may have figured this move out—give him credit, he's a jerk, but plenty smart—and have it ready to blow when we cross. Then we'll head south, slowly, giving Dan's Scouts plenty of time to range far out in front of us.

"When Monte and the others are located, we'll hit them and hit them hard, and get this nasty business over with—

at last.

"All right, people. Let's mount up and head north."

It was slow going picking their way through the rubble-strewn and snowy streets of the Bronx. It was a ghost town, with not one living thing seen by any of the Rebels.

"Eerie." Even Ben said it aloud.

"Will the fires spread over this far, General?" Jersey asked.

"I doubt it. The city will burn for several weeks, in spots, and then the fires will burn out when all the wood and other flammable materials have been used up. But for any left alive over there, it's going to be damned uncomfortable."

The column finally picked its way through the mess and rolled north into Westchester County. It was well after dark when they reached the rendezvous point and linked up with Cecil's command.

They were all tired and cold and hungry.

Cecil moved them on a few miles north to a deserted town where his people had cleaned out a high school and adjoining buildings, including the gym. There, the Rebels had set up a kitchen and placed stoves all around the complex. Huge containers of water were being heated, providing the Rebels with a very quick but very welcome warm bath. To a person they were dirty and smelling of stale sweat and death.

"Hell of a fire," Cecil commented, after Ben had bathed and shaved and had a bite to eat. "Any way of knowing whether we got Khamsin personally?"

"No. But knowing that thug's luck, I doubt it. But we destroyed probably ninety-five percent of his army. And the five percent remaining are going to be a long time recouping from this beating. If he's alive, and I feel that he is, he'll get off the island and set up someplace—on a much smaller scale, but we'll see him again, somewhere down the road."

"Monte and Ashley and Sister Voleta?"

"A thorn in our sides. And don't count them short. They're still a force to be reckoned with. For a time I toyed with the idea of just going on back home, bypassing them. But all that would do is delay matters and give them time to recruit more people, and we won't have the time to deal with them later. So it's now."

"You want to explain that 'we won't have the time' bit?"

"Trouble out west. Not even Ike knows of this, Cecil, so keep it between us for a time. Dan advised me a few days ago that two of his long-range recon patrols have been wiped out. When the first failed to report as usual, another was sent down from Washington State. They reported, through Katzman, that a very large force has set up in Wyoming, ranging in all directions. Then no more was heard from them. We can only assume they're dead."

"What type of force?"

"I don't know. Whatever or whoever it is, it's big and mean and nasty. Ramos dispatched planes up from the southwest base. They never returned and never reported one damn word."

"Shit!"

"At least."

"Who are you sending, Ben?"

Ben stared at him for a moment and then smiled his reply.

Cec got the message. "Oh, come on, Ben!" he raged. "We've got the makings of a model city down in Louisiana. You've got it to run."

"Correction, old friend. *You* have it to run. And you've got Patrice to think about. You two are talking marriage, aren't you?"

"Well, yes, but . . ."

"No buts. It's settled. I'm going to do some shaking up on this run. Pure volunteer all the way. After we return to Base Camp One, I'll ask for volunteers and re-form the units. I'll take one full battalion and support units. But that's tomorrow, we've still got a lot of fighting facing us today."

"You're letting yourself in for trouble with this volunteer business, Ben."

"How do you mean?"

"Jerre conducted herself well on the island, didn't she?"

"After her initial freeze-up, yes, very well. Why do you ask?"

"What are you going to do should she volunteer?"

"Reject her."

"On what basis, Ben? You know the way we operate. You made the rules."

"I have discussed matters with Jerre. She knows how I feel. She won't volunteer." *I hope,* he silently added.

The Rebels got a good eight hours' sleep that night, and upon awakening, each took another short, warm bath; they were beginning to feel human once again as they lined up for their first full breakfast in days.

Striganov sat down at Ben's table, a worried look on his face.

"What's the matter, Georgi?"

"I just got word from back home. Trouble. Gangs have resurfaced, stronger than before. Our home guard is holding them at bay, but . . ." He let that trail off.

"You need to split off and head back?"

"Maybe. But let's see if we can't wrap up this nasty business first. What's happening, Ben? We destroy one gang of thugs and three more pop up."

"Everything has broken down, Georgi. There are no rules to follow, no guidelines for the young, no heroes to look up to. Kids who were three and four years old when the Great War came are now seventeen and eighteen years old. And they've known nothing except savagery. It was to be expected. I, too, have trouble." He told the Russian about his teams being killed in the west.

Georgi was thoughtful for a moment. Then he smiled a grim soldier's smile. "I think we shall be working together again, Ben Raines."

"Very soon."

"Yes."

"When I get back to Base Camp One, I'm outfitting one battalion with support."

"All volunteer?"

"To the last person. There is no telling how long we'll remain in the field."

"Ben," the Russian said softly, for Ben's ears only. "While we are far from being old men, we are no longer young bucks. The juices still run hot within us, and, God willing, shall continue to do so for many more years. Is that part of the reason you are once more taking to the field?"

Ben smiled. "You sure chose a roundabout way of asking a simple question. Yeah, Georgi, it is."

"So you will take to the grind of the field in order that she may live in peace and comfort?"

"It isn't an entirely selfless act, Georgi. I'm doing what I think is best for both of us. Besides, I like the field."

"And you think she will never know?"

"Oh, no. She'll know. Whether she'll give a damn is up for grabs."

Georgi refilled their coffee mugs. "I have been blessed in my middle age, Ben. I have found a woman who loves me." He shrugged philosophically, and then smiled, a twinkle in his eyes. "But I, too, love the field. So I can both sympathize and empathize with you." He sighed. "Well, now that we have discussed matters of the heart—to not much avail—how about your children's part in this talked-about sojourn into the Wild West?"

"Oh, I'm sure they'll both go. Dan will be the first to volunteer. I'd hate to think of him not being there. I couldn't keep West and his men out of it if I tried. But I think I'll send them off in a different direction, with a rendezvous point to be determined later."

"Have you given any thought to this being the same gang of thugs working both countries? Although borders don't matter much anymore."

"It might be. If that's the case, it's one hell of a big force. And not one that we should take lightly. Georgi, go ahead and take your people back home. We can handle this. Besides, I need some firsthand intelligence as to what's happening out West. Stay in radio contact with me, please."

"You're sure about this?"

"Yes. I would imagine your men are worried about their families."

"To be sure. Ben? With so many women in the Rebels, how do you keep down camp romances? That's something that's puzzled me for some time."

"I don't try to keep them down. I'm sure there are a lot of them going on. But they know to keep it discreet, and if they marry, one of them is leaving the field for a noncombat job at some outpost or base camp. So far it's worked."

Georgi nodded his head and sighed. "Well, it's a long way back home, Ben Raines. Almost three thousand miles. And sitting here isn't getting us any closer." He smiled and stuck out his hand. "I'll keep in radio contact with you and I'm looking forward to seeing you again, this spring or summer."

Ben took the offered hand. "Take it easy, friend. And thanks for all your help."

Georgi Striganov smiled and left the table, stopping at the table where Rebet and Danjou were having breakfast, and telling them the news. Both of them turned with a smile and tossed Ben a salute.

Ben returned the smile and the salute and watched the three men leave the gym. He mulled over the final casualty reports from the fight in New York. Seventy dead and more than two hundred wounded. A hundred and fifty of those wounded had been flown back to Base Camp One.

Doctor Holly Allardt had flown back with the last planeload.

He looked up as Tina and Jerre came walking into the large gym for breakfast. Already Ben was experiencing a sense of loss just looking at Jerre.

Emil abruptly took his mind off Jerre when the little man came running into the gym and threw his arms wide. "My poopsie-whoopsie is leaving!" he wailed. "The light in my life has been forever dimmed. Oh, woe is me!"

"Oh, shit!" Ben muttered.

THIRTEEN

Ben had found Thermopolis's eye and motioned for him to please do something with Emil. With a disgusted look on his face, the hippie and several of his friends carried the squalling Emil out of the gym. Ben waggled his finger for Dan to join him.

"As soon as Tina finishes breakfast, Dan, get her and her team on the road north. I want her a full ten miles ahead of us checking things out, all the way up to the bridge."

"Right, General. Jerre?"

"What about her?"

"She's rejoined Tina's team."

"Always has something to prove." Ben shook his head. "Well, it's her ass. Sure, send her with Tina."

"I'll have them gone within the hour."

"Tell our people we're leaving at ten o'clock, Dan."

"Ten-four, General."

Ben watched as Dan stopped at a table to inform some of his Scouts. The whole group of them burst out singing the old Willie Nelson song "On the Road Again."

As was his custom before beginning any new campaign, Ben walked the length of the convoy, chatting briefly with each driver and as many of his Rebels as time would allow. The snowing had stopped, the day bright and sunny, the temperature right around the thirty-degree mark, according to an old thermometer Ben had found still nailed to the side of a building.

"Tina reports the roads are slick as owl crap," Ben told one driver. "Even with chains it's going to be slow going. We won't make the bridge today. We're not going to try."

To another: "Going to be home before spring, Davy. You can get that garden in."

Back up the other side of the convoy he walked, his waterproof arctic boots crunching the snow and his breath steaming the air as he spoke to the men and women of the Rebels.

Back in his Blazer, Ben spoke to Cooper. "Let's go, Coop. We have miles ahead of us."

The long column snaked ahead and began to stretch out. Striganov's columns had pulled out almost two hours before, and the Rebel drivers were following their ruts. Striganov would drive all the way up to the Canadian border, crossing over the St. Lawrence at Montreal.

It was a beautiful day, and the beauty, although barren and void of human life, was not lost on the Rebels, who had been locked between the tall buildings of New York City for week after drab and bleak and dangerous week.

The Rebels saw no signs of human life, but the wildlife had returned: bear and deer were making a dramatic return to their rightful place in the scheme of things. Ben also suspected that behind the deep timber and brush that had overtaken the earth, mutants were watching the long convoy pass. Ben had pretty much left the beastlike creatures alone over the past few years.

Possessing some sort of native intelligence, the huge mutants seemed to understand that Ben would not harm them if they left the humans alone.

So far, it had worked out.

At one time, Rebel scientists had theorized that disease had wiped out the misshapen and grotesque creatures. That had proved to be a false assumption. The mutants were very much a part of the rural landscape. But they stayed well away from humans.

And, Ben thought with a smile, the wolves had returned

over the years, the elusive and magnificent animals once more roaming the timber, doing their part in maintaining the balance within the animal world.

No Rebel shot a wolf. Those orders came from Ben Raines. Only if a person found himself or herself in a life-threatening situation with a wolf was deadly force to be used. And since that never happened, and would never happen if one possessed even the most basic knowledge of and respect for wolves—which all Rebels did, thanks to Ben—the wolf was back, running wild and free, safe from ignorant rednecks and other assorted fools with guns.

Ben knew, from extensive research on the subject, that in the United States, over a hundred-year period, there had never been a documented account of a human ever being attacked by a healthy, full-grown wolf—without the human provoking the attack. Ben had always believed that if Little Red Riding Hood was eaten by a wolf, she probably started the incident by poking the wolf in the eye with a stick.

There had been many changes in the treatment of wildlife since Ben started ramrodding the show. Animals were still hunted for food, but only if absolutely necessary, and never for sport. Kids were taught in school—from the earliest grades—to respect wildlife. Theirs was a natural place in the scheme of things. Given enough land to roam and hunt, animals would take care of animals without human interference.

And as long as Ben was alive, humans would not interfere.

The Rebels spent the night in the deserted town of Croton-on-Hudson. Tina and her team had made a fast but thorough inspection of the town.

"It doesn't appear that human life has existed in this place for years, Dad," she told him. "It's just like every town we've inspected on this run—nothing. No dogs, no cats, nothing."

"They've gone back to the wild, Tina. They're seeing us, but we're not seeing them. And only the toughest of dog breeds have survived. The working breeds probably made it by feeding on the smaller, pampered breeds. It isn't cruel, it's just the way it is. Animals don't kill for sport, girl. Only man kills for sport. How about the bridge up ahead?"

"It's okay, structurally. But it's going to be tough to cross unless we can find some snow blades to hook onto our trucks and plow a lane open."

"We'll get on that in the morning; find a state highway department building and start rigging the trucks. You find us a place for the night?"

"Several of them. School, gym, motels—the whole town is ours."

Ben squatted in the snow and watched as several trucks, now equipped with snow blades, carved a lane down the center of the bridge. Slowly the convoy made their way across the Hudson River and once more began their trek. By nightfall, they had only traveled twenty-five miles. The roads were several feet deep in snow. Tina's team had been forced to rejoin the main column and let the snowplows forge ahead, plowing a path for the vehicles. In many cases, had it not been for the old, for the most part wireless power poles, they would not have been able even to find the road as it twisted and turned through the deep snow.

The column had to travel many miles before they could turn back south, since sections of the New York State Thruway had been destroyed. When they did finally cut south, using state and county roads, the traveling was even slower.

"At this pace," Dan said, "we just might lose our quarry. They might get tired of waiting and start to wonder if perhaps we all were on those ships."

"Possibly," Ben acknowledged. "If so, we'll meet them another day. But I think they're still just about where we left them. South of the city, probably."

The men turned as the last of the vehicles began pulling into camp for that night. Thermopolis and his people had been forced to find big tractor-trailer rigs with flatbeds and chain down and transport their VWs that way; the snow was just too deep for the Bugs and many of the vans. The hippies were not about to give up their VWs. That would be as unthinkable as cutting their hair or shaving.

"Enjoying the sightseeing?" Ben asked, as Thermopolis and some of his group walked up.

"Actually, yes. The scenery is breathtaking. And the air is so clean. Ben Raines, what do you people do with your garbage?"

"We bury it so the earth can once more claim it."

"Goddamn walking contradiction," Thermopolis muttered as he went his way. "Shoots every human being in sight and worries about the environment. Blows up entire cities and protects the wolves. Jesus Christ!"

"How's Emil?" Ben called.

Thermopolis turned around, a bleak look on his face. "In mourning. He says if he could find some sackcloth he'd wear it. He's already sprinkled ashes on his head. I don't think he realizes that sackcloth was originally made of goats' hair. Come to think of it, I might mention that to him."

"Please don't. He'll go out hunting goats and get lost."

"Yes. There is that to consider. Both pro and con." He turned to leave.

"Look after him, Therm. Remember, his heart has been broken."

"Thank you so very much, Ben Raines. Your faith in me is very nearly overwhelming."

Dan lifted a map. "We should reach Highway Seventeen sometime tomorrow. That will take us to the New York Thruway, then on into New Jersey. Each day the sun shines, the going becomes a bit easier. I would predict three days to confrontation."

"On the morning of the third day, I'll order spotter planes up to make one pass over the city. Two people to a plane. They should be able to pinpoint the bogie camp. But when they do, we're going to have to drive as fast as possible and hit them hard."

"With General Striganov and his people gone, we're too short to try to box them in."

"I know. We're going to have to hit them so hard and so fast, we put them into a rout. Voleta's forces are made up mostly of thugs and punks and remnants of various motorcycle gangs. Their bikes are absolutely useless in this weather, and besides, they don't know jack shit about tactics anyways. Monte probably has the larger force, but they are going to be cold and miserable and surly and have never had to rely on anything except brute force to get their way. Ashley and his men will be the ones we'll have to destroy and do it totally—if we can. Of course, none of us have any idea, really, how many people we'll be going up against until the spotters give us some kind of a report; even then it's going to be pure guesswork."

"Let's get us a bite to eat," Dan suggested. "Chase has promised faithfully that this evening's meal will be something to remember."

"That's what I'm afraid of."

The convoy pulled out the next morning, just at dawn. And it promised to be another bright and sunny day, the sunshine continuing to melt the snow and turn the roads slushy, especially for the vehicles rolling along at the rear of the long column.

At noon they reached Highway 17 and turned southeast, angling toward the New York State Thruway. Ben sent a team in to check out Middletown. When they reported back it was the same as always on this trip: nothing. Absolutely no signs of life.

"The Night People ranged out far, didn't they?" Ben said, sticking his arm out the window and motioning the column to move on.

"We'll fight them again, won't we, General?" Jersey asked.

"I'm sure. But after the lesson we handed them in New York City, you can bet the Judges will contact their kind around the country and warn them to fight shy of us. I'm thinking they'll also try to adopt a more normal type of outward lifestyle."

"You mean dress like us or other civilians?" Beth asked.

"Yes. And perhaps even bathe occasionally. But that might be asking too much."

"If I never smell one of those creeps again, it'll be too soon," Chuck said. "I don't think I ever smelled anything like that in my life."

"Killed the taste of the field rations," Cooper offered.

All agreed that was about the only good thing to be said for the creepies.

They spent the night at a small town not far from the West Point Military Reservation.

"No desire to go inspect the place, Ben?" Cecil asked, over dinner.

"None whatsoever. I always figured all that crap the cadets had to go through to be a lot of bullshit. And it must have been," he said with a small smile. "I'm running the biggest army known to exist anywhere in the world, and they're all dead."

The sun continued to shine, and the column was moving much faster; they would be well inside New Jersey before noon.

Ben ordered the convoy halted and two spotter planes up.

"They were practically sitting in our laps, General," a spotter reported. "They're all strung out between Twin Rivers and what appears to be . . . ah, Kingston, I guess it is. If I had to take a guess, I'd say about fifteen hundred to two thousand of them. They must have been joined by some other outlaws."

"Probably. Did they appear to be nervous at seeing you?"

"Ten-fifty, General. Some of them waved at us."

"All right. Thanks. Return to base and pack it up. Get out of there. There are little airports south of your position. Try the Camden-Burlington airport. That's just off the New Jersey Turnpike. Check it out and give me a bump one way or the other. Eagle out."

Ben looked at Dan and Cecil and West. "Ashley's got something up his sleeve. Dan, get your Scouts out. Let's find out what the hell is going on."

FOURTEEN

Ben had skirted the area around New York City, and the column had wound their way through the countryside. Ben halted the convoy in Somerset County and told his people to eat and rest. It might be the last chance to do so for several days.

Late that night, the Scouts reported back. "They seem to be strung out in a line running southeast from Kingston over to Twin Rivers. They're in private homes all up and down the line."

"You saw them in the homes?" Ben questioned.

"We observed a few of them through long lenses, yes, sir."

"And that is all that's there, too," Ben said, leaning back and sipping at his coffee. "All they were waiting for is the spotters to note their positions and then the bulk of them took off, leaving fires burning and a few behind to throw us off."

"Where'd they go?" Tina asked.

"That, my dear, is a damn good question." He glanced at the Scout. "You saw people moving around in those houses?"

"Ah . . . no, sir. Not moving around. Sitting in chairs . . ." The Scout trailed it off, frowning. "I think, sir, that we've been had."

"Right. I think so, too. Heads up, people. Full alert.

Everybody spread their people up and down the line from . . ." Ben studied the map. He had no idea where the enemy was and no clue as to where they might strike. "Shit!" he spat out the word. "Spread out all over the town and I want a total blackout. No smoking, no fires, no light whatsoever. Get everybody in full arctic gear for warmth. Move!"

The town of Sommerville went black as the orders spread. One minute there were lights all over the place from portable generators and cook fires; the next minute it was as if someone had flipped a giant switch.

Ashley was smiling with thoughts of total victory dancing in his head, when all of a sudden the sugarplum pudding turned rancid.

"Hey!" Monte yelled. "The damn place done went dark on us!"

"There is nothing wrong with my vision," Ashley told him. "That bastard figured it out. That has got to be the luckiest man on the face of the earth."

"Let's charge!" Monte yelled. "Hell, we got 'em outnumbered!"

"Let's don't." Ashley nixed that. "I prefer to go on living for quite a few more years. Be quiet, let me think."

"How many lights is that?" Ben asked Chuck, who was monitoring through a headset as Rebels with night lenses began reporting flashes of lights from matches, probably from lighting cigarettes.

"Eight, sir. Fifteen hundred meters out in a rough line running east and west."

"Uh-huh. Ashley swung his people around as we moved up into town." Ben lifted his own mike. "Gunners, you have the coordinates?"

"Ten-four, sir."

"Commence firing."

The quiet starry night was shattered as every piece of artillery Ben had at his disposal began booming out its lethal loads.

"Willie Peter," Ben ordered. "Let's start some fires. It's a cold night."

Grinning at Ben's deadly humor, Chuck relayed the orders.

Showers of white phosphorus began lashing the night, the burning shards setting homes and buildings burning. The flames, burning unchecked, soon began ravishing the area, leaping from building to building and putting the enemy's troops into a rout, running wildly in all directions in an effort to escape the flames.

"Cease firing," Ben ordered. "And stand down to a low alert. I don't think they'll be back this night."

At dawn, Ben ordered the spotter planes up while the Rebels began a body count. While not many of the thugs had been killed during the short shelling, it had obviously knocked a large hole in their morale, for the eyes in the skies could not locate any sign of the outlaws.

"Both good and bad," Ben said. "They've gone, but where?"

"Spotters report the roads are almost entirely free of snow," Ben was told. "So they can't track the retreat that way."

"Dan, get your Scouts out. The rest of us will be moving down the New Jersey Turnpike. We'll cross the river between Trenton and Philly and set up camp on the outskirts of Philly. Might as well see what the city holds."

"More Night People, General?" Chuck asked.

"Probably."

"If we find them there, are we going to destroy the city?"

"We don't have enough explosives left, Chuck. We're running low on everything except bullets and grenades.

If we come face-to-face with any major battles, it's going to be damn near hand-to-hand from here on in. Let's pack it up, gang."

Dan sent his Scouts out, ranging all the way down to Philadelphia. They reported back that they could find no sign of Monte or Ashley or Sister Voleta's people, but that Philadelphia contained some life. What type of life, unclear.

"Do not enter the city," Ben ordered. "Hold what you've got. Make no moves until we get there."

It was not that long a run down to Philly, and with the roads nearly clear, the convoy made good time, arriving at the outskirts a couple of hours before dark.

Ben approached his daughter. And Jerre. He ignored Jerre. "What's it look like in there, Tina?"

"I didn't go in. She went in with Ham and a team." Tina jerked a thumb toward Jerre.

Ben turned to face her. "So what did you find?"

"A lot of people without much organization. It looks like a huge hobo camp. I felt sorry for them."

"You would. How far in did you penetrate and using what route?"

"We went as far as Pennypack Park, using highway one. It ran right past the North Philadelphia Airport. The airport appears to be intact, but littered."

"Tina, at first light, take a team in and clear a runway for our planes. We've got to be resupplied from Base Camp One." He cut his eyes to Jerre. "That was a good report. Thank you."

"You are certainly welcome, sir," Jerre said, her words very crisp.

The snow had melted on the roads, but Ben didn't have to look far to find plenty of ice.

"We'll set up for the night in this area. We'll enter Philly in the morning." He wheeled around and exited that spot before he came down with a bad case of frostbite.

"I thought for a time we were in for a warming trend,"

Dan spoke to Colonel West. "It appears I was badly mistaken."

"I think I have bits of ice on my nose," West agreed.

The men cut their eyes to Tina and Jerre, both of whom were glaring at them, not appreciating their stabs at humor one little bit.

"Shall we take our leave, Colonel West?" Dan suggested.

"By all means, Colonel Gray." He looked at Tina. "Shall we have our evening meal together as usual?"

"I'll be busy," she frosted him. "Thank you."

"I'm available," Dan told the mercenary. "Just don't try to kiss me."

After dinner, Ben went over the list of remaining supplies and shook his head. "We'll make the airport our CP," he told his team. "As soon as a runway is clear, our birds from down south can start resupplying us. We'll enter the city in the morning. But I got a hunch that, from what Jerre said, all we're going to find is a bunch of goddamn losers waiting for someone else to do for them."

"And we do what with them?" Chuck asked.

"We help the elderly and the young—probably ship them back to a base camp. The rest can go to hell."

"We see this a lot," Jersey explained to Chuck. "We'll find a group of people really putting things back together again. Schools, collective gardens, farms, the whole nine yards. But we see more of people just doing nothing. The way we feel is this: If these people won't do anything here, for instance, they're not going to do anything after we leave . . . no matter what we do to help them."

"We've tried it the other way, Chuck," Ben told the young man. "It just doesn't work. These people you'll see tomorrow—most of them—were a pretty sorry bunch before the Great War. Whiners and complainers. Always looking for the easy way. No matter what an employer paid them, it was never enough to their way of thinking. These are the people who eagerly supported any wealth redistribution programs dreamed up by politicians. These people are narrow-minded, lazy, ignorant, and for the most part, good for nothing. You'll see. I promise you."

"Are you here to help us?" a man asked Ben. A group of people had been waiting at the airport for the arrival of the Rebels.

"Why in the hell didn't you help yourselves?" Ben asked him.

The question seemed to confuse the man. He blinked a couple of times. "We have defended our city, General."

"Your city? The goddamn city is dead, man! How in the hell are you going to grow crops on concrete? Have you restored any type of power? Running water? Sewage? I can answer the last question. No. The place stinks like a cesspool. What do you do with your waste, just dump it in the gutters? I believe you do. I've seen this a hundred times. When you've fouled one neighborhood beyond belief, you simply move to another. Have you set up schools for the young? Do you have a system of government? I doubt it."

Ben pushed the man away with a gloved hand. "Get out of our way. We've got work to do."

The man was astonished. "But we need help! We need food and clothing."

Ben withered him silent with a look. Something was all wrong here; but Ben couldn't pinpoint it. "Then grow your food and sew your clothing. And stop bothering me." He turned his back on the small crowd and walked away. The crowd started to follow. They stopped when a squad of hard-eyed and heavily armed Rebels blocked their way.

Ben walked up to Dan. "Get your teams out, Dan. Round up the kids and take them to the old state hospital building we passed coming in. That's where Chase is setting up. As soon as our birds come in and unload, we'll start flying the kids out."

"Hard man," Rosebud whispered to her husband.

"Hard times," Thermopolis replied, and was astonished to hear those words coming out of his mouth.

Rosebud stared at him.

"I gotta get out of this army," he said. "It's beginning to cloud my ability to reason."

Cecil walked up to Ben. "Some of the . . . citizens say you're being unreasonable, and that they want to become part of the Rebel army."

Ben leaned against a vehicle and rolled a smoke, licking the tube tight and lighting up. "And you told them . . . ?" He couldn't shake the feeling that something was terribly wrong.

"I told them we would take their request under advisement and would give them our reply sometime in the near future."

"Cec, you certainly have a way with words. You're going to love running things when we get back to Base Camp One."

"I'd be lying if I said I wasn't looking forward to it, Ben."

"You and Patrice going to tie the knot?"

"It's a distinct possibility."

"I'm glad, and you know I mean that, Cec."

"I know. You're really going to stay in the field, Ben?"

"Yes, I am, Cec. I figure it'll take four or five weeks back at the base to reorganize and get reequipped for the field. I'm handing all the administrative duties over to you the instant we get back."

"And you'll be gone . . . ?"

"I don't know, Cec. When I do get back, it won't be for any lengthy stay." He smiled at his friend. "So I expect many great and monumental tasks to be accomplished while I'm gone."

Cecil grunted. "Well, if your mind is made up, I won't try to talk you out of it."

"And I appreciate that. Now then, what do you think about exploring Philadelphia?"

"Well, as my daddy used to say, it sure beats the hell out of a lick upside the head!"

"Bullshit!" Ben said with a laugh. "Your father was a

psychiatrist and your mother was a college professor, and I happen to know that you hold a Ph.D. from what was once a very prestigious Eastern university. So don't pull your cotton-patch coon business on me!"

"Cotton-patch coon? Good God!" Cecil roared with laughter, and Ben joined him, while other Rebels stood and stared at the men, thinking that one of them must have told a hell of a funny joke.

FIFTEEN

"Care to come along with us?" Ben asked Thermopolis. "It'll get you away from Emil for a few hours."

That did it. "I'll ride with General Jefferys," Thermopolis said. "Let me tell Rosebud where I'll be."

"Bring her along if she wants to come."

She did. Sitting in the backseat of Cecil's Blazer with her husband, she said, "If someone had told me years back that someday I would be a part of a Rebel army, armed to the teeth and fighting all over the United States—or what's left of it—I would have laughed at them."

Cecil smiled. "Both my wife and I were college professors back before the Great War, Rosebud. Believe me, I know what you mean."

"Your wife was killed during the fighting of the Tri-States, was she not?"

"Yes."

"And you've been with Ben Raines . . . ?"

"Since the beginning. And I can tell you that no man ever fought harder to avoid being placed in charge of the Rebels than Ben."

"And Ben's wife . . . ?"

"Salina. She was about ready to give birth to their son when she was killed during the fighting. The baby was born as she lay dying."

"Did Ben love her?"

"No. He told her he did. But she always knew that he

was in love with Jerre; had been for years and would always be in love with her. But he was never unfaithful to Salina. Ben has a very rigid moral code about marriage. Ike's wife was also killed during the fighting. Ben was very badly wounded. We got creamed and Ben rebuilt the Rebels, practically from the ground up. The rest is, as they say—whoever they might be—history."

"Pulling over just up ahead," Ben's voice came through the speaker.

They all got out and stood staring at the littered and filthy streets.

"Christ, what a mess!" Ben was the first to speak. "And those sorry bastards want to join us? To do what, do you suppose?" That feeling of something being very wrong continued to nag at his mind.

"To get a free ride," Jersey answered him. "Look at this place. New York City was a paradise compared to this hog pen."

"Let's go see the rest of it," Ben said. "But I think it's going to be a short tour. This is making me sick."

He was to be a lot sicker at heart before the morning was over.

They toured the downtown area, inspecting a few of the once fine hotels for a few floors up. The citizens had fouled every room. It appeared that when one room became too filthy—and that took some doing—they would just move to another and start all over.

Most of the historical old homes had been ravaged by looters and vandals. The Betsy Ross House had filth and profanity spray-painted all over it and on the inside walls. The Christ Church Burial Ground had been desecrated with shovels and sledgehammers. St. George's Methodist Church had been burned.

"I've seen enough," Ben said.

"For once, I agree with you," Thermopolis told him, pointing. "Look over there."

Ben's eyes narrowed and his face hardened as he read what was spray-painted on the side of a building. Someone, or a group of people, had tried to remove it, but the letters were still readable. And that nagging feeling opened wide to the light.

THE JUDGES RULE

"Just like Gene Savie and his bunch." Cecil put it together for them all. "Only these people fit right in with them—with the possible exception of being cannibals, and I'm not so sure I'd rule that out."

"Chuck, tell our people to go on middle alert. Warn them that the city might be filled with creepies." Ben stood for a moment, mentally sorting out some facts. "Cecil, didn't you tell me that the group of people you talked with seemed upset when they learned that we were going to tour the city?"

"Seemed that way to me, Ben."

"What was that spokesman's name?"

"Allen."

"Let's go see this Allen person."

Ben walked up to Allen and pointed his .45 at the man's head. Allen paled under the dirt on his face and his hands began to tremble.

"The Night People, Allen, where are they?"

"General Raines . . . I don't have no idea what you're talking about. I ain't never seen no Night People."

Ben eared the hammer back, the metallic cocking sound loud in the silence.

"If you think I won't blow your goddamned head off, Allen, then you don't know much about me," Ben warned the man.

"They all pulled out!" Allen screamed. "They done left."

"That's better. Why did they leave and when?"

"Nearabouts a week ago. They got some sort of message from New York City. I don't know where they went."

"How long have they been in the city?"

"Forever, I reckon! Don't kill me, I don't want to die."

"You and your scummy-assed bunch worked with them, right? And don't lie to me, you bastard!"

Allen bobbed his head up and down.

"You filth! You and your bunch procured people for them to eat, right?"

"Yes, sir! But we was forced to do it."

"You're a liar. You could have left anytime you wanted to leave. There are no blockades around this city. You weren't chained or imprisoned. Everything you and your scumbags did you all did willingly. Now, isn't that the truth?"

"We had to live!" the man shouted.

"I hope you enjoyed it, because you haven't got much longer."

Allen looked around him, searching for any sign of compassion in the eyes of the Rebels.

He found none.

"They'll get you, Raines," Allen hissed. "They're everywhere. In every city still left standing in the world. They been here for a couple of centuries, growin', and growin', and growin'. They's a couple hundred thousand of them in the States alone. Maybe as many as half a million. You'll never defeat them, Raines. They'll cut your heart out and eat it!" He screamed the last.

"How many left in the city?"

Allen just grinned at him, and to Ben's thinking, the grin of a Nazi SS man must have looked the same way.

Ben pulled the trigger. The force of the big .45-caliber slug, fired at almost point-blank range, knocked Allen off his feet. The man was dead before he bounced on the dirty street.

Ben walked up to a woman and placed the muzzle of the .45 between her eyes, the muzzle touching the dirty flesh of her forehead.

"You want to die?"

"No, sir! I'll tell you anything you want to know. I promise I will."

Not one of the filth-encrusted citizens made a move. They were all looking down the muzzles of Rebel weapons.

"How many Night People left in the city?"

"I don't know, sir! Maybe a couple of thousand. When it was learned that you and your troops were winning in New York City, the message come that they was to scatter; to split up and fan out, seek new places to live. I swear to God that's the truth!"

"God!" Ben's voice was harsh. "You profane His name by speaking it from that cesspool you call a mouth!"

"We had nothin'," the woman said, her words shaky with fear. "Not 'til they surfaced and we struck a deal with them . . ."

"I get it. Now I know. You were instructed, or you volunteered to join us to infiltrate our ranks. Where do you live?"

She said nothing.

"Speak, goddamn you!" Ben shouted.

"When did you put it together?" she finally spoke.

"About fifteen minutes ago. Dan? Are the kids all clear?"

"Ten-four, sir. They're at the hospital."

"Order security at the hospital to go to full alert, Chuck."

"What's up, Ben Raines?" Thermopolis asked.

"They're all Night People, Therm. Every one of them."

The woman tried to grab for Ben's pistol. The .45 roared, the slug striking her on the jaw and angling up to exit out the top of her head.

The crowd of men and women grabbed for weapons concealed under their ragged-appearing clothing.

It was no contest.

The Rebels opened fire, most firing from a distance of no more than thirty meters.

"Death before defeat!" a man shouted.

Ben shot him in the head.

"The Judges rule!" a woman screamed, leveling an Uzi at Thermopolis.

Rosebud stitched her with her Mini-14. Rosebud loved most living things. She loved her man more.

The battle was very intense, and very short. Within seconds the street was littered with bodies, the gutters running with blood.

Silence crept over the battleground, broken only by an occasional moan from a dying creepie. A shot from a Rebel hastened the process.

"Jesus God!" West shouted, driving up in a Hummer and viewing the carnage. "What the hell happened, Ben?"

Ben very quickly briefed the mercenary.

West's driver, Curly, arched one eyebrow. "Looks like we got a long war ahead of us, Colonel."

"To be sure, Curly. But that is our chosen destiny, is it not?"

"From Africa to Central America to the States," another of his men said. "I never would have thought it."

"What now, Ben?" West asked.

"We've got to be here for at least several more days, getting resupplied for the run back home. West, you and your men take everything north of Market Street. Cecil and his battalion will take everything south of it. That's up to the Schuylkill River. I'll take everything west of the river. Hunt them down and kill them!"

Ben set up his CP just across the river, in an old Post Office building—after first clearing the building of creepies. Then the gruesome task the Rebels thought they'd left behind them in the ruined rubble of New York City began anew. Although not on such a huge scale.

There were no defined battle lines; this was deadly house-to-house search and destroy, with no one knowing what lay behind a closed door or at the darkened end of basement steps.

Sister Voleta, Monte, Ashley, and their forces had seemingly dropped out of sight; however, Ben knew he had not seen the last of them, and when they did resurface, he felt they would be much stronger and more difficult to deal with. But for now, another deadly hunt was on.

Ben's teams spread out all over the city, looking for any elderly people. There were none. Only bones.

"Ghastly business, what?" Dan commented, over a cup

of tea during a break in the S&D.

"Looks like the creepies disposed of the elderly first," Ben said. "I guess they were fattening up the kids, not of their persuasion, for later dining." Ben spat his disgust on the sidewalk.

"Speaking of the kids . . ."

"The doctors say the younger ones will be all right. But the ones thirteen and over, for the most part, are hardcore crawlers, so thoroughly brainwashed they will never come around."

And you plan to do what with them?" Thermopolis inquired.

"Leave them here when we pull out. What'd you think I was going to do, shoot them?"

"I hoped not. But let me play devil's advocate for a moment."

"Go ahead."

"When you turn them loose, they'll just return to their cannibalistic ways."

"That is true, sadly."

"And they and their kids and all their kind will grow up despising you, Ben Raines."

"That is also true. But I still can't kill a thirteen- or fourteen-year-old, Therm. Not unless he or she is pointing some type of weapon at me."

"They'll be a threat to me and to others as well as to you and yours, Ben."

"That is certainly true. Do you want to be the one to kill them, Therm?"

He shook his head. "No. No. I could not do that, and there is no one in my group who could." He was silent for a few seconds. "And I wouldn't have anyone around me who could. I think," he added.

"It's like I keep telling you, Therm. You and me, we're not all that different. We both want a cool shade tree in the summer and a fire to keep the chill away during the winter. We want to be able to sit on our front porch and watch the squirrels play and the hummingbirds feed. We like to have friends around us for companionship and conversation. We both want peace, Thermopolis. The only real difference between us is how we were going about attaining it."

"How we *were* going about attaining it?"

Ben smiled. "You're here, aren't you? That's a weapon in your hand, and another one belted around your waist. There isn't fifteen cents' worth of difference between us. Really, there never was. See you, Therm." Ben walked away.

Thermopolis stood with a frown on his face. Rosebud walked to him. "What's the matter with you?" she asked.

He pointed toward Ben. "I just hate it when he's right!"

SIXTEEN

With two runways cleared for landings and takeoffs, birds from Base Camp One began bringing in badly needed artillery rounds for the tanks and mortars. They also brought in hundreds of cases of home-canned vegetables and meats just slaughtered and boxed in dry ice. The cargo planes brought in fresh BDUs to replace the torn and frayed battle dress the Rebels now wore. The planes brought in soap and socks, boots and berets and bras and underwear, bombs and bullets and belts. Planes were landing every hour around the clock, the runways lighted by flares at night. They offloaded their cargo, grabbed a bite to eat and cup of coffee—sometimes a few hours' rest—and were back in the air.

During the daylight hours, the Rebels continued their deadly search-and-destroy missions throughout the city. And destroy they did, sometimes burning entire blocks of the old city to flush out the night crawlers, shooting them as the flesh-eaters ran from the burning buildings.

It was New York City all over again, and while on a much smaller scale, just as deadly, just as dangerous, and just as nerve-racking.

The Rebels' eyes smarted from the smoke of the torched buildings; their clothes stank of sweat and soot and blood and death. They worked slowly but relentlessly, clearing block by block. Finally, after working a five-block area, from Market all the way over to the Spring Garden Street

Bridge, without finding a single creepie, Ben called a halt to it.

"I don't think there's two hundred creepies left in the city," Ben told his commanders, from company level down to squad leaders. "So let's knock it off. Tell your people to stand down and relax for twenty-four hours. We'll shove off day after tomorrow."

Dan and West and Cecil stayed behind. "Gentlemen," Ben looked at them.

"What are you going to do with the kids, Ben?" Cecil asked.

"They've already been flown back to base camp."

"You know what I mean, Ben."

"Nothing. I don't plan on doing anything with them. I plan on leaving them right here when we leave."

West breathed a very audible sigh.

"Something on your mind, Colonel?" Ben asked.

"I must be getting old—turning into some sort of sentimental fool!"

"And that means . . . ?"

"Ben, some of those kids are just in their teens."

"I'm aware of that. Say what's on your mind, West."

"Well, some of my men have agreed, if it's all right with you, to take a few of the kids with us. We think we can shape them up."

"It'll be your responsibility. Solely," Ben cautioned him.

"I'm aware of that."

"Fine with me. I just hope you don't wake up some evening with one of them carving off part of your leg for a late-night snack."

The convoy pulled out of the Philadelphia area just as the weather was once more turning foul after days of pleasant weather. A cold, bone-chilling rain was falling as the Rebels pulled away from the still-smoking city, heading west.

Ben had traveled the straight westerly route before, and

wanted to see some new country this run, so he ordered the foward teams to plot them a southwesterly route. The city faded behind them. On the morning of the second day out, the recon teams reported smoke coming from chimneys; it looked like some sort of small community, set well back from the highway.

Ben pulled the convoy over and told the recon teams, "Check it out. Carefully." He sat in the Blazer and waited, the hard rain drumming on the roof.

"They're not friendly, Eagle," the team leader's voice came through the speaker. "They ordered us off the land."

"Did you tell them who we were, recon, and that we mean them no harm?"

"Ten-four, Eagle. They said they didn't like you and didn't want to have anything to do with you."

"Whether they like me or not is their business," Ben radioed. "Do they have children?"

"Ten-four, Eagle. A whole bunch of kids all gathered around us."

"Ask one of the kids if they can read and write."

Ben waited for a few moments. Thermopolis walked up to the Blazer and Ben rolled down his window. Thermopolis had been listening to the exchange over a walkie-talkie.

"And if the kids cannot read or write, Ben Raines?" he asked, rain lashing at his face.

"We'll take the kids with us."

"Just about the time I get where I like you, you pull something like this. Goddammit, Ben, what gives you the right to take someone's kids from them?"

"Thermopolis, we cannot have a nation of illiterates, not if this battered country is ever going to pull out of the ashes of war. Education is right up there with survival."

"They can't read or write, Eagle," the voice came out of the speaker.

Ben lifted his mike. "How many people in the community?"

"I'd say a hundred, tops."

"Stay put. Tanks, forward. Circle the community. West,

your men in position behind the tanks."

Ben waited.

"You're really going to take the kids, aren't you, Ben?" Thermopolis asked.

"We've been doing it for years, Therm."

"In position, Eagle."

"Tell the leaders of that redneck community I want to talk to them—right now!" Ben got out of the Blazer and faced Thermopolis. "You want to come along?"

"I wouldn't miss it for the world."

It was a miserable day all the way around, and Ben was in no mood for a lot of lip from near-cretins. He faced the group of men and came right to the point.

"Why can't your children read and write?"

"'Tain't none of your goddamn concern whether they can or cain't, General."

Thermopolis then noticed that Ben Raines was awfully quick. The man with the smart—and now bloody—mouth also noticed it, from his position flat on his back in the muddy front yard.

"Oh, but it is my concern," Ben said. "It is the concern of every person in this shattered nation who possesses a forward-looking mentality. Now get your ass up off the ground and face me!"

The man crawled to his hands and knees and stood up, with the help of a couple of his buddies.

Ben said, "I will repeat the question again. And if you do not give me an answer that holds some degree of civility, I will take the butt of this M14 and knock your goddamn teeth down your throat. Why can't your children read and write?"

"Never seen no use for it, General." The man wiped his bloody mouth with the back of his hand.

Ben glanced at the ramshackle buildings of the community. In western vernacular it would have been called a rawhide outfit: not built to last for any length of time.

"Can you read and write?" Ben asked.

"Some. I never cared much for it. Readin' makes my

head hurt. I'd ruther watch the TV."

"What do you do now?"

"Huh?"

"There is no television, you idiot. What do you do now?"

"Nothin'."

"How do you feed yourselves? Do you have gardens?"

"Shore. The wimmin work 'em. The men does what men is 'posed to do. Hunt and fish. Beat the wimmin ever' now and then to keep 'em in line."

Several female Rebels stirred at that remark, and the man's eyes flicked to them for a second. Somewhere amid the rot of his brain, he realized he had erred—badly.

"Tina," Ben called.

"Here, Dad."

"Take a team and go house to house. Explain our philosophy to the women of this . . . community of ignorance. Ask them if they'd like to join us. And you might explain to them that we are taking the children."

The man did not stir at that.

"That doesn't bother you?" Ben asked.

"Naw. Not really. Snot-noses is a bunch of bother anyways."

"Jesus Christ!" Thermopolis muttered.

"But you ain't takin' Jenny," the man stated flatly.

"Who is Jenny?"

"My oldest girl. She tends to my needs when the old woman don't feel up to it."

The man looked to be about thirty-five . . . rotting teeth and all. So Ben figured the 'old woman' bit was nothing more than a colloquialism.

And Ben did not have to be told what the man meant by Jenny "tending to his needs."

"How old is Jenny?"

"Twelve, I reckon."

"And how long has she been tending to your needs?"

"Three-four years."

"Having sex, you mean?"

"She enjoys it. Says she don't, but a man can tell.

Wimmin was put here with a hole. Ain't no point in lettin' it go to waste."

Ben noticed that Rosebud had joined them, and that the muzzle of her rifle was pointed a few inches below the man's belt buckle. If she shot him there, he would not have to worry about anyone ever again tending to his needs.

"Dan, find this Jenny. Take her to Chase and tell him what's going on. We'll wait for his report. It won't take long. As a matter of fact, tell the medical team to inspect all the kids for signs of sexual abuse. Male and female. I think we've lifted the cover off of a snake pit here."

"I said you ain't takin' my Jenny," the man spoke, his breath very foul.

"We're goin', Hoyt," the voice came from Ben's left. He cut his eyes.

A very pretty woman, perhaps in her late twenties, stood with several children. One boy, two girls.

"I'll whup your ass, woman!" Hoyt warned.

"No, you won't," Ben corrected. "Just stand still and shut that flapping mouth." He looked at the woman. "Take your kids and go with this lady." He nodded at Beth. "You don't have to stay here against your will. Has this man, Hoyt, been having sexual relations with his daughter?"

"Jenny. Yes. And he just started with Abby." She placed a hand on the wet, uncovered head of a girl no more than seven or eight.

"Beth, take them to the medical teams."

Hoyt stood and cussed Ben, his breath steamy in the cold rainy air.

A dozen women and perhaps thirty or forty kids came trooping out of the shacks. Several of the women had black eyes and bruises on their faces. The kids looked malnourished and frightened.

"This ain't constitutional!" another man stuck his mouth into it.

Ben laughed at him.

Beth returned after only a few minutes and whispered in Ben's ear. Ben nodded his understanding.

Tina walked up. "That's it, Dad. All the women and kids are out."

Beth whispered to Tina. Tina drew back, a grim look on her wet face. "All of them?"

"Yes," Hoyt and the other men heard Beth say. "And several of the boys have been sodomized."

"Colonel West, you and your men will stay here with me. The rest of you return to your units and prepare to pull out."

"Does that include me?" Thermopolis asked.

"That depends entirely upon how strong your stomach is, Therm. And, of course, your interpretation of law and order."

Rosebud touched his arm. "Come on. Let's get back to the van."

"Tanks out," Ben told Chuck. Then conversation was impossible for a few moments, while the tanks roared and spun around in the earth, moving back to the road.

"Chuck, you and Cooper return to the Blazer."

"Yes, sir."

"Beth, you and Jersey going to stay for this?"

Their reply was to click their weapons off safety.

Behind the wheel of his VW van, Thermopolis was not startled when the rattle of gunfire cut the cold wet air. He watched as Ben and West and the others walked slowly down the muddy hillside to their vehicles.

"This has got to be the most barbaric time since man stuck his head out of the caves," he said.

Rosebud gave him a cold but not unloving look. "Either that, or justice was just served."

SEVENTEEN

Ben ordered the convoy on a straight westerly route and instructed Dan's Scouts to check out the York airport, but to stay out of the city itself until the main force had caught up with them.

"That was a town of about forty-five thousand at one time. Big enough for a lot of night crawlers to hide in. If they're in here, we clean them out. We're going to be waiting a couple of days for the birds to come get these new people. There should be enough motels and private homes close by for us to use. Check them out."

And it was as Ben had suspected. The place contained the flesh-eaters.

"How's the airport look?"

"It's going to take some cleaning up, but it's usable. Gong to take us a day or more to pick up all the litter and shove these old cars and trucks out of the way and patch some holes in a runway."

"Throw up a line of defense against possible attack from the creepies. They're sure to know about what went down in Philadelphia. We're about two hours behind you. Hold what you've got."

"No sweat, General."

Dan was standing outside Ben's Blazer, wearing a poncho and hood against the still-falling rain. "No sweat?" he muttered. "I shall certainly give him a lesson in military courtesy. And promptly."

Ben smiled at the Englishman. But he did not interfere. Each commander ran his or her own unit, and Ben seldom interfered.

Ben looked around. "Chuck isn't back yet? Where'd he go?"

"Back to see Doctor Chase," Beth told him. "He was sweating and running a fever. I think he's coming down with pneumonia. I've treated it before, General."

"I'll take your word for it, Beth. You want some help with the radio?"

"I asked for a replacement, sir."

"Good," Ben said absently, his mind on other matters.

"By your leave, sir," Dan abruptly said, and went walking off, quick-stepping through the rain.

"What was all that about?" Ben asked, not expecting a reply and receiving none. Had he turned around, he would have seen Beth and Jersey winking at each other.

Cooper was looking in the rearview mirror. "Oh, shit," he muttered.

Ben cut his yes. "What's that, Coop?"

"Nothing, sir."

"Well, here I am," the voice spoke through the open window, Ben's side.

Ben looked into very familiar blues. "I can see that. What are you doing here, Jerre?"

"You sent for me!"

"I didn't send for you!"

"Well, dammit, I was told you needed someone on the radio. I'm radio trained. By the way, Chuck will have to be flown back to Base Camp One. He has pneumonia."

"I'm sorry to hear that. Oh, hell, get in out of the rain."

With everybody settled, Ben said to Cooper, "Get this circus on the road, Coop. I swear to God, I sometimes think we ought to charge admission."

"Is something the matter, *General?*" Jerre asked very sweetly.

Ben ground his teeth together and broke off an old filling.

* * *

"Oww! Goddammit!" Ben roared.

"General, I have to clean out the old cavity before I can fill it. It'll only take a few more seconds."

"Hurry it up!"

"Yes, sir." The dentist did not like to work on the general. Made him nervous.

What he didn't know was that Ben had been scared to death of dentists all his life. But he sure as hell wasn't going to admit it. Not to a soul.

After a few more minutes of trying not to hurt Ben—which he didn't—the dentist stepped back. "There you are, General. Good as new."

"Thank you. Can I go?"

"Oh, yes, sir."

"Thank you." Ben got the hell out of the converted truck. Quickly. He never could stand the smell of dentists' offices or hospitals.

Tina caught up with him. "I'm so happy to see that you survived your terrible ordeal, Pops."

"Your concern is touching."

"Why are you talking funny?"

"Because my damn mouth is numb!"

"You'll probably need an interpreter for a few hours. You want me to call Jerre?"

Ben shook his head and had to smile. It was rough humor, no disrespect was meant by it, and he knew it. And Ben also knew that those involved really wanted him and Jerre to make up. This was their way of showing concern for the both of them.

"Well, the damn rain has stopped," Ben said, looking up at a few rays of sun trying to cut through the clouds. "Something good is coming out of this lash-up."

"You want me to reassign Jerre, Dad?"

"No. In a few more weeks we'll be out of each other's hair for good."

"How do you know that's what she wants, Dad? Has she told you so herself?"

"It's going to be totally volunteer, Tina," Ben said, hedging her question. "And we're going to be in the field for a long time. Maybe as long as a year before returning to base. Talk it over with Ham and the rest of your team, Okay?"

"Okay, Pop. But you know that I'm going. So is Buddy. What are you going to do if Jerre volunteers?"

"She won't."

"How do you know that?"

"Because you're going to see to it, daughter."

The Rebels began a house-to-house, building-to-building search of York, flushing out the creepies and destroying them.

With the rain gone, the weather turned mild once more, and the Rebels shed their heavy winter gear. But all knew that the winter was far from over, and this warm weather might roll over onto a nasty side at any time.

The birds flew in, picked up their passengers, and were gone, heading back south. They carried with them twelve wounded Rebels from the operations in Philly and York.

Two dead were buried far from York, so they could not be dug up and eaten by the creeps.

"Let's wrap it up and get the hell gone from here," Ben told his commanders. "Tina, you and your team cut us a path southwest. Wait a minute." He looked at Jerre. "You want to go through Cumberland, Jerre?"

"Why?"

"Because it was your home, kid."

She was silent for a moment. Met Ben's eyes. "Might as well, I guess." As usual, keeping a tight lid on her true inner feelings.

Ben nodded and turned to Tina. "We'll cut south and pick up Interstate Seventy at Hagerstown, follow that all the way over to Cumberland." He looked at the atlas's index. "Hagerstown was about thirty-five thousand and Cumberland was about twenty-five thousand. Could be creepie-time again, people. So heads up."

The column rolled out at midday, meandering around on state and county roads, heading more west than south. They saw no signs of human life. Southeast of their position, and fading fast, lay the devastation that was once Baltimore and Washington.

The weather was holding in the Rebels' favor, with the skies blue and the temperature in the low fifties during the day, dropping down to near freezing at night.

"Scout to Eagle," Tina's voice came through the speaker.

"Go, Scout."

"We'll hold here at Waynesboro, Eagle. Something you need to see."

"Ten-four, Scout. We're about an hour behind you. We'll approach on Sixteen."

As he approached the town, Ben began to suspect what Tina and her Scouts had found. It was very clear that a battle had recently taken place on both sides of the winding old country road.

Ben halted the column and got out to inspect what was left of a small town just a few miles east of Hagerstown. Carrion birds had feasted on the naked bodies that lay outside the homes—after flesh had been cut from the bodies. The brass of shell casings lay twinkling on the ground.

"They put up a fight," Jersey observed. "They weren't taken easy."

All the bodies had been carved on, with great hunks of flesh cut away.

And Ben noticed something else, too: those children of the Night People that West and the others had brought with them, in hopes of salvaging, were staring intently at the mutilated bodies, a savage gleam in their cold, murderous eyes.

"I see it," West spoke the words softly.

"Watch them very carefully, West," Ben cautioned. "I have a strong suspicion they'll revert back faster than you can blink."

The mercenary nodded, his face grim.

Ben ordered the bodies placed in a house and the house burned.

They could find no bodies of creepies. But all knew that

with the recent victory of the Rebels, the crawlers had probably discarded their robes for a traditional form of dress. And the creepies, if they did not carry off their dead, would probably have no compunction about carving up or eating their own.

Ben waved the column on and linked up with Tina on the outskirts of Waynesboro.

"Hell of a fight here, Dad. You saw what went down at that little town just east of here?"

"Right. We burned the bodies. Jerre, order tanks into the town, everything buttoned down."

The tanks rumbled and clanked past and disappeared into the silent town. Silent, but with the smell of death hanging unseen over it.

With the column halted, West had positioned some of his men around the vehicles containing the children of the creepies.

Tina watched the move and met her dad's eyes.

"The little bastards were licking their chops back in that town. West has realized that he made a terrible mistake in bringing them, but neither he nor I know what to do to rectify it—not at this stage of the game." He sighed. "Well, we know *what* to do, we just don't want to do it."

Tina cut her eyes to the teenagers. They stared back at her, the hatred cutting like sharp invisible knives in the sunny afternoon. "It's coming down to no prisoners at all, isn't it, Dad?"

"No. I won't permit that. I'm not going to kill children. If we find them, we take them alive and then leave them."

"So we can fight them again another day." It was not a question; more a statement of fact.

"I guess so, girl."

The roaring of cannon fire from the tanks tore the afternoon. The rattle of machine guns immediately followed.

"Back to work," Ben said, a grim note in the statement.

It was grim, but it was short, as the Rebels smashed the small stronghold of Night People.

During the mopping-up, a small pocket of prisoners

was found in a basement. Naked, abused, and very nearly out of their minds from fear and the ravages of day after long day of degradation at the hands of their captors.

"See if you can get some of these old vehicles running," Ben told his people. "We can't leave these people here. We're going to have to open up a runway at Cumberland and call for more birds from the base. Dan, start getting statements from the survivors. We've got to know what we're up against in the next town."

"How goddamn many of these creatures are we facing?" Dan asked, using rare profanity.

"Several hundred thousand, if we can believe what those crud back in Philly told us."

"Are you thinking that this force out west is aligned with the creepies?"

"I don't know. But it wouldn't surprise me. I think we're going to be—we *are*—facing the greatest threat we've ever encountered. And we'd damn well better win it."

EIGHTEEN

Ben led the convoy over to the Interstate, using a badly rutted country road, and halted them at Greencastle. That town, unlike the others, showed no signs of any battle. No shell casings, no blood, no bodies.

"This place was abandoned years ago," West said. "The survivors probably decided that living beside any well-traveled road, like this Interstate, meant trouble and grouped out in the country. Probably in those towns we just left."

"That's my thinking," Ben agreed. "We'll clear Hagerstown in the morning. I want us on full alert this night. The creepies know we're hot on their butts, and they probably also know Voleta and Monte and Ashley are somewhere behind us. They may try to form another alliance."

"You really think those thugs are following us?" Emil asked. Emil was slowly recovering from his one-sided affair of the heart with Michelle.

"Oh, yes, Emil. And on both sides and ahead of us, probably. They're wanting to get us in a box for an ambush. That's why I keep taking a snake's route getting home."

Thermopolis arched an eyebrow. He had wondered why the column was traveling like a bunch of wandering nomads.

"The creepies just might decide to clear out tonight rather than face us in the morning," West said.

"Personally, I hope they do," Ben told him.

Ben had his people up and fed and ready to roll while Dan sent his Scouts into the city well before dawn. It had turned colder during the night; winter was preparing to show them all it still held a punch.

"Tina reporting that the town definitely has creepies," Jerre told him. "No signs of other life."

"Order Tina and her teams out. Tell artillery to stand by. They will commence firing on my orders," Ben said. "HE and incendiary. Damned if I'll lose people when I can prevent it."

Less than a minute passed before Tina reported that her teams were clear and in position to act as forward observers.

"Commence firing."

The artillery rounds began singing their songs as they roared through the cold dark morning. In five minutes, portions of Hagerstown had been turned into a raging inferno, the flames caused by the incendiary rounds licking upward into the darkness. An old underground gasoline storage tank went up with a whooshing roar, balls of flame jumping high into the air like angry fingers of hate, searching to destroy.

The gunners began lobbing shells in with much more discrimination, setting one section of the town blazing, then moving to another. After an hour of pounding, Ben ordered the gunners to cease firing.

Dawn was just beginning to pierce the darkness with thin silver fingers, lifting up and pushing away the lid of night.

"If Monte and the others are within fifty miles of this area," Cecil said, "they'll sure know where we are."

"That they will. Jerre, order Tina and her teams back. Let's get ready to pull out."

The Night People finally figured out that Ben and his Rebels were moving westward, and nothing was going to stand in their way. The leaders ordered their kind to abandon any towns that stood in the way, moving either north or south until the Rebels had passed.

The Rebel columns bypassed the burning city and picked up Interstate 70, heading west, leaving the smoke and death behind them. Full dawn found them looking at the deserted little town of Hancock, Maryland.

"Less than two thousand people lived here before the Great War," Jersey said, looking at an old map.

"I had friends here," Jerre said. "Just up the road is a little town called Piney Grove. My suitemate at college was from there. I was so sick I couldn't even move off the floor of the room. I lay there watching her die. The thing that got me moving was when the rats came and started eating on the dead in the dorm. How come it didn't kill the damned rats? I crawled outside, found a car that was unlocked and passed out in the front seat. All around me people were dead or dying. Absolutely, totally gross. When I finally was able to see and sit up, and my eyes stopped seeing double, I found that the damn car didn't have any keys in it. The cars that did have keys also had dead bodies in them. I finally found a car that was empty and had the keys in it."

"Where was college?" Cooper asked.

"Salisbury State. Took me days to get home. I had to drive all the way up into Pennsylvania because Washington had taken a direct hit. I met people who had been on the fringe areas. They didn't have any eyes! They had looked at the blast and their eyes had melted. The flesh was burned off of others. I had never seen anything like that. I didn't know what to do to help them. Then it dawned on me that there wasn't anything I could do; nothing anybody could do. They were just walking around dying."

"You sure you want to do this, Jerre?" Ben asked, his voice soft, for he was remembering finding his own parents in Illinois, just after the bombing.

"Yeah," she said, her voice just as soft. "I need to do it."

Ben waved the column forward.

"Creepies have been here," Tina's voice came through the speaker. "But they've bugged out. It's pretty grim here, Dad."

"Hold what you've got. We're not far behind."

Jerre's eyes were busy as they approached the small city. But whatever thoughts and emotions she was experiencing, she kept bottled up . . . at least for the time being.

Ben halted the column just inside the city limits and walked back to Thermopolis's van. "Seems like I'm always asking you to do some unenviable job. So I'm asking again. This is where Jerre grew up. Would you people stay with her while she tours the area?"

"Don't you think she would rather have you with her, Ben?"

Ben blinked; looked shocked. "No. I don't."

Thermopolis cut his eyes at Rosebud, and both of them smiled rather sadly. "All right, Ben Raines. We'll look after her."

Ben and Dan took Tina and a team of Scouts and went on a quick tour of the town. It was just as Tina had reported: grim.

Mutilated bodies had been stacked in houses to rot and gather flies—after the choicest cuts had been carved from them. That the men and women had been carved upon while still very much alive was evident by the hideous expression on the still twisted and pain-filled faces, mouths still open in a silent scream, before death mercifully took them across that dark shore.

"Did you find any survivors?" Ben asked Tina.

"None, Dad. And no sign of any."

"The creepies took their meals with them," Ben said. "Twenty-first-century version of fast food."

They all looked at him to see if he was kidding. He wasn't.

"Large hordes of thugs and outlaws and warlords out west, Monte and Ashley and Sister Voleta operating here to the east, night crawlers all over the bloody place. We have long years of war ahead of us, General," Dan said.

"Probably more years than you and I have, Dan. Our children's children will be fighting to pull this land out of the ashes of barbarism and ignorance and savagery. It's up to us to see that they don't have quite as hard a battle."

Ben lifted a map and studied it for a moment. "We'll let Jerre get her fill of her old hometown—and it probably won't take her long; then when the birds land and get the rescued out, we'll cut south. I've got a hunch the creepies didn't go far. We'll check out this little town on the West Virginia line. It's just far enough off the beaten path for the crud to feel safe. If so, we'll see if we can't crash their party."

Jerre stood before a plaque that read: GOD HAVE MERCY ON THOSE WHO DIED IN THE GREAT WAR. TWENTY-ONE THOUSAND FIVE HUNDRED FIFTEEN SOULS. CUMBERLAND, MARYLAND.

"It was this way all over the nation, Jerre," Thermopolis told her. "The survivors scooped out great holes in the earth and buried them in mass graves. It would have been impossible any other way."

"I know. Well," she sighed, "I've seen it. Hell, I don't even know if my parents are buried here. They were pretty badly decomposed when I finally got back to the house."

"I thought that a neighbor was going to bury them?"

"He was too busy trying to get my pants off. No. They were still in the back yard when I popped that jerk with a poker and split." She shook her head. "I've seen enough. Let's go help clear the airport. The birds are on the way in."

"West, you take your men and cut south off the Interstate on this county road, Thirty-six. It's about ten or twelve miles west of our present position. Hold up when you get to this little town of Barton. We'll be coming down Two-twenty and we'll stop at McCoole. I want both our forces to hit Westernport together. I think the creepies have prisoners with them, so shelling is out until we learn different. You go ahead. We'll pull out thirty minutes behind you."

West nodded and left.

Ben glanced at Jerre. "How are you feeling?"

"I'm all right. In a way, I'm glad my parents died back then, rather than like . . . the creepie way."

"Let's start getting mounted up, people." He glanced up at the sky. He would like to travel through West Virginia, but he didn't want to get caught in the mountains in a snowstorm. The weather had turned decidedly cooler, but the skies remained clear. After Westernport had been cleared, if the weather still looked good, they would angle over and pick up the Interstate, take that south down to Charleston. After that . . . ? Play it by ear.

And where in the hell had Monte and the rest of that crud gone? Ben didn't think they had given up—although that could certainly be possible. They might well have reassessed the situation, found it not to their liking, and then pulled back to gather up more men. It seemed like for every decent person left in what had been America, there were ten times ten more crud. He shook his head. Time would tell.

He walked the line of vehicles, deep in thought and killing time until West was well on his way. He wasn't even sure what month it was. February, he thought. They had spent so many weeks in the city that all of them had lost track of time.

He looked up the line. The column seemed to stretch for miles. The trucks and tanks and APCs and jeeps and Hummers containing the only army in the world—that Ben was aware of—fighting to restore some type of democracy to the nation.

So much to do. And where in the hell did that large force out west pop up from? Had the nation been invaded by some foreign force? It was certainly possible. Khamsin had done it.

The Libyan had waltzed right in and caused a lot of grief before he elected to stick his nose in with the creepies in New York City.

Another force knocked down and out. But how many more to go? And would it ever stop?

"Miles to go," Ben muttered. "Miles to go."

NINETEEN

Jerre was very quiet as they rolled out, as could have been expected after experiencing one hell of an emotional jolt. Ben noticed that she looked back several times with tears in her eyes.

What could he say? He knew only too well the sense of loss when you have nobody left, all family dead. Kith but no kin.

"Recent fire right over there, General," Cooper broke into his thoughts, pointing to what was left of a house. The ashes were still smoldering.

"The creepies are just one jump ahead of us, that's for sure."

A mile farther down the road they saw another home that had been torched. Fat carrion birds were strutting around in the yard, too heavy to fly after gorging themselves on dead human flesh.

"Yuck!" Beth said, her eyes lingering on the bloated birds.

"All part of the plan, Beth," Ben said.

"You believe in God, General?" she asked.

"Oh, yes."

"Heaven and Hell?"

"Sure. But I also believe—rightly or wrongly—that there are levels, with the highest plane being very sparsely populated."

"And what level will you attain?"

Ben laughed. "I don't think I'll get very high, Beth. I'll probably be with the rest of the warriors. And I'm not at all certain that Valhalla is going to be a paradise. My punishment will probably be having to listen to Emil sing throughout eternity."

After the laughter, Jerre said, "Emil appears to be bouncing back rather quickly after his loss."

"Life goes on, Jerre. Emil is a sharp little guy and he'll be all right." *But,* he added silently, *I can tell you for an iron-clad fact that he'll never forget the woman.*

"So you believe that love fades after a time?" she asked.

"Sure. I don't know that true love ever really dies. It just loses its sharpness, dimming into a memory that one can live with."

After that brief exchange, the miles passed quickly and in silence. Ben was surprised that Jerre even brought up the subject of love; but then, she had always been full of surprises.

"Coming up to the junction, General." Cooper's words jogged him back to the present.

Ben pulled the mike from its clip. "Eagle to West."

"Go, Eagle."

"In position?"

"Setting on ready."

"We're turning west on One-thirty-five. Five miles to touchdown."

"I'm rolling."

"Eagle to Scout."

"In position, Dad. The town is populated, but it's iffy as to who or what lives here. Those that we have seen don't look like creepies."

"Ten-four, Scout. We'll be with you shortly. Hold what you have. Tank commanders, take your beasts to the point. Convoy slow, let them pass. Dan, block the road leading south out of the town. West, split your people and block the west end of One-thirty-five."

"Welcoming committee coming out," Tina reported.

"They're dressed in normal clothing, but they're all armed."

The tanks were in position as Ben pulled up. He stepped out of the Blazer and walked up to the knot of men and women. The first thing that caught his attention was the paleness of skin. Even though, he cautioned himself, that could be attributed to staying indoors during a very long and cold winter.

But he didn't believe that for a second.

"Welcome, General Raines!" a man called, a smile on his lips.

But he did not step forward to offer his hand in greeting.

"Thank you," Ben responded. "We just thought we'd drop in for a visit. Maybe stay a few days and rest up . . . if that wouldn't be an imposition on you good folks."

"Well . . ." The man hesitated. "We don't have much food. It's been a long winter and our supplies are almost gone."

Ben waved that aside. "We have plenty of food. We'll be happy to share it with you. As a matter of fact, I have an idea: Why don't we all get together for a potluck supper this evening? We'll all bring a dish and share. That sound good to you?"

"Just . . . wonderful, General."

Ben spotted a group of kids; they had the same flat look of hatred and contempt as the kids taken from Philly.

Stepped right into a snake pit, Ben thought, as his eyes caught faint movement on rooftops and second floor windows of homes. Riflemen waiting to open fire.

Ben and the spokesman stood and smiled at one another. And each smile was filled with contempt for the other. The creepies knew that Ben Raines would take no prisoners, so if this ruse didn't work, and the spokesman knew it wasn't, they would try to kill as many Rebels as possible . . . especially Ben Raines.

"Shouldn't your children be in school?" Ben asked.

"Well . . . it isn't every day that the famous Ben Raines drops in for a visit. We turned school out for the auspicious event."

"I'm flattered. But auspicious is a very heady word. Really, all we've been doing is killing crud. You folks been having any problems with the Night People?"

"Ah . . . no. We haven't seen any."

"You're a goddamn liar!"

The man brought his rifle up, his face mirroring his inner hate. He was shot all to pieces by Rebel fire just as the cannon on a tank boomed, the round blowing off the top of a building where the crew chief had seen creepies lurking.

On the road leading into town, the battle was very hot and very brief. The instant the spokesman brought up his weapon, several hundred Rebels opened fire into the knot of creepies, killing them almost instantly.

The children of the Night People ran away, disappearing into the buildings and the brush.

"Take the town," Ben ordered.

The retaking of Westernport was very short and very brutal, just as brutal as what the creepies had done with their prisoners, taken from the small towns and villages around the area.

The Night People must have sensed that the ruse would not work, for they had killed the prisoners, all the men and women and children, and hung them up on hooks, like hanging ducks.

And they had obviously told their own children to head for the timber at the first shot, for not a child could be found among the rubble that was all that remained of the little town after the Rebels had finished.

"Leave the bodies where they lie," Ben told his people. "It's too dry to burn them; we might start a forest fire. And there is no point in trying to chase after the kids. I don't know what in the hell we'd do with them if we did catch them."

Ben took a sip of water from his canteen. Even the water tasted of death.

* * *

The Rebels were back on the road without a backward glance at the shattered town and the bodies that littered the bloody streets.

They took Highway 220 out of Westernport and spent an hour in Keyser. Ben had expected to find somebody in the town that once held a population of over six thousand. But it was a ghost town.

"It hasn't always been," West said, walking up. "We've inspected several homes and found signs that people were here and not that long ago. There are graves that were dug maybe six months ago—no longer than that. And one hell of a lot of brass around. There was a fight here, and a big one."

"But against whom?" Ben questioned, not really expecting a reply. "And I doubt that digging up the bodies would tell us anything. Let's go."

A few miles south of Keyser the column turned west on Highway 50. They passed through small towns—all deserted. They saw no signs of human life as the Rebels pushed on into the unknown. With darkness just a couple of hours away, the Rebels moved into a small town and began clearing out homes and buildings to spend the night.

"Anybody see the city limits sign?" Cooper asked.

"Aurora, I think it was," Jersey told him. "Why, you want to mail a letter?"

"Funny, Jersey. Very funny."

"Double the guards," Ben ordered. "Just in case."

But the night passed uneventfully, with the Rebels catching up on rest. Ben was the first one up—except for the guards already on duty, and the cooks—and walked over to one of the buildings being used as a mess hall and poured a mug of coffee. He chatted with the cooks for a moment and then went outside, to sit on the fender of a truck until his butt got cold and he was forced to move around.

By that time he had some appetite and started back to the mess hall. A runner stopped him.

"General Ike on the horn, sir. They've docked and have

the equipment unloaded, ready to move west."

Ben turned just as the mess hall building exploded and the artillery barrage began.

The first explosion knocked Ben and the runner sprawling. He got to his knees and grabbed the ankles of the young runner, dragging him under a truck for protection, and then went racing toward his quarters.

"Everybody out!" he yelled. "Bug out! Bug out! They've got our range dead on. If we stay here, we're dead. Move, people, move!"

Grabbing whatever they could, the Rebels, in various stages of dress and undress, went racing for the vehicles as the deadly artillery dropped in around them. A deuce and a half went up with a whooshing roar as the incoming landed directly on the truck, blowing the gas tanks, the deadly debris killing several Rebels who had been working at frantically loading the bed of the truck.

Running without lights, the Rebels roared away from the small town, exiting east and west on Highway 50, and south on a county road, for the artillery was coming in on them from the north.

Ben took as many of his people as he could gather and headed north, up a county highway. He halted them a mile out of town, when the muzzle flashes of the enemy artillery could be seen from the road.

Flipping his radio on scramble, he lifted the mike. "Eagle to West."

"Go, Eagle."

"What's your twenty?"

"Couple of miles east of the town."

"Find a road north and take it. They're about a mile outside of the town. You may have to work across country on foot. I'm taking my people and heading for them now."

"Ten-four, Eagle. Moving."

"Cec, you copy?"

"Ten-four, Ben. I took some hits and bugged out south. Chase is with me, patching up the badly wounded."

"You hold what you've got and spread out. With any

kind of luck, we'll be driving them toward you."

"Ten-four, Eagle."

"Dan?"

"Right behind you, Eagle. What's the drill?"

"I think Monte found us. Now let's go find him and kick some ass."

TWENTY

Ben and Dan left their vehicles on the road, the keys out of the ignition, and began walking toward the artillery, while West and his men came cross-country from the other direction. Both advancing parties carried light mortars and rocket launchers. Just as the artillery ceased firing, Monte sure he had creamed the Rebels hard, he was hit from both sides with mortar, rocket fire and grenades fired from grenade launchers.

Ashley, being the cautious type, was not so certain he had done much damage to the Rebels and had pulled his people back about a mile and was attempting to see through night lenses. He saw the shapes of the Rebels closing the pincers and knew Monte was trapped.

"To help or not to help?" Ashley muttered.

"We don't need him," Sister Voleta said. "The man is a fool."

"Then it's agreed?" Ashley looked at the woman in the moonlight.

"Of course. There is always another day."

They faded back into the timber and joined their forces.

Monte and his men were, as one Rebel would later sum it up, getting their asses kicked.

With the Rebels closing with them from the west, and the mercenaries closing with them from the east, the warlord and his men went into a panic as the shapes seemed to materialize out of the darkness.

Monte's men were not accustomed to hand-to-hand combat, not on this scale, and not outnumbered. Like most bullies, they were cowards at heart, always being very careful to pick the people they bullied. This time they had tweaked the tail of a giant dragon, and the dragon was a many-clawed fire-breather.

Monte's men tried to run away. Only a few made it. Ben stepped around a light artillery piece that had been crippled by rockets and came face-to-face with Monte. Monte was standing by the cannon, one side of his face slick with blood from a minor wound.

The two men had never met, but each instinctively knew the other.

Monte lunged at Ben, a pistol in his hand. Ben kicked the man in the knee with a boot, and the pain caused the warlord to drop his weapon as he cried out, both hands grabbing his knee.

Ben stepped in closer and butt-stroked the warlord on the jaw with the stock of his M14. Teeth flew out of the man's mouth, and his lips were smashed to bloody pulp. Monte hit the cold ground moaning and rolling, trying to escape the rage of the man.

As the sounds of battle waned around them, Ben stood over the man, the muzzle of the old Thunder Lizard pointed at the man's chest.

"No!" Monte cried. "I'll deal with you!" The words came out mush-mouthed.

Then he saw Ben smile as a Rebel came to his side. "Tie this bastard up," Ben ordered. "I want him to stay alive—for a little while longer."

"Forty-seven dead, a hundred wounded," Dan reported to Ben as dawn kissed the darkness, the caress opening the mouth of light. "We're going to have to get to an airfield and open a runway for the birds to get the wounded."

Ben cursed at the totals. When he had profanely vented his spleen, he lifted a map. "There's an airport at Clarksburg. Send some people over there to check it out. If it's usable, clear a path and get the birds in."

"Yes, sir. About the prisoners we took this morning . . . ?"

"Keep them alive and well-fed and under heavy guard."

"Well-fed, sir?"

"That is correct, Dan."

"Very well, sir."

Ben walked over to West. "Ben, my people found signs where a large force waited and then pulled out, heading north toward Pennsylvania. Sister Voleta and Ashley, I'm sure. And they didn't show any signs of planning to stop anytime soon."

"They've had it for this run. I don't think we'll see them again soon." He glanced at Jerre. "Jerre, advise the forward teams heading to Clarksburg to clear the airport and advance no farther. Do not, repeat, *do not* enter the town. If there are creepies, leave them alone unless the creepies make the first move."

She looked at Ben, questions in her eyes. She nodded her head and relayed the orders.

West, too, had questions in his eyes, but they remained unspoken.

"Let's get our dead cremated and the wounded made ready for travel."

With creepies all over the place they had all agreed that cremation was the only logical way to treat any Rebel dead.

"Jerre, bump Katzman and tell him to contact Base Camp One. Send some planes up here for the wounded. We'll wait at Grafton until after the birds have taken the wounded on board, and then we'll move on."

"Yes, sir."

The convoy made the short run to Grafton and found the town a deserted death town—but only recently so. The signs and smells of creepies were all over the place.

Mutilated bodies lay about the streets.

"Burn them," Ben ordered. "And then stand down for the night."

"What's Ben got in his mind?" Thermopolis asked Tina, after the dead were collected and burned.

"I don't know. He's not talking and I'm not going to push him on it."

"Probably a wise choice."

Ben remained mostly by himself and very taciturn the rest of the day and all that night. He would occasionally walk over to the building where Monte and his men were being kept under guard, to stand and stare at them.

"You wanna deal, General?" Monte would ask each time Ben came over, the words mushy coming out of his busted mouth.

Ben would always mutter a low curse and turn his back to the man.

The planes began landing during the early morning hours and picking up the wounded Rebels.

Dan informed Ben that Clarksburg was filled with creepies. But they had made no move toward the Rebels, and the Rebels were leaving them alone as ordered.

"Keep it that way," Ben told him.

By eight o'clock in the morning, all the wounded had been transported out.

"Let's roll," Ben ordered. "All personnel out of the airport area. Link up on the Interstate and wait for me there."

The Rebels dismounted and stood on the Interstate, watching as Ben and his contingent stayed on Highway 50 and escorted Monte and his men to the city limits.

"Get them out of the trucks," Ben ordered.

On the pavement, Monte looked around nervously. "What the hell are you gonna do, Raines?" he demanded. "If you're gonna shoot us, get it the hell done."

"I have no intention of shooting you," Ben told the

warlord. "Strip!"

"Do what?" Monte screamed.

"Strip, you bastards! I want the creepies to see what's coming up for lunch."

"You can't do this to us!" Monte yelled.

Ben's reply was a tight smile.

"I ain't a-gonna do it," a man said.

Ben glanced at Dan. "Strip them and hogtie them."

Using rifle and pistol butts for clubs, the Rebels knocked the men down and stripped them naked, tying them up, leaving them on the cold concrete.

Monte lay on the highway, filth spewing out of his mouth until he was breathless from cursing Ben Raines.

"Creepies watching this," Dan said.

"Good."

Tina lifted her binoculars. "They're carrying knives, Dad."

"That's even better." He looked at Monte. "You're scum, Monte. Only God knows how many innocent men and women and kids you kidnapped, raped, tortured, sodomized, and then handed over to the Night People. It's payback time, Monte. You better start praying, because that looks like a hungry bunch over there."

"Goddamn you, Raines! This ain't decent. This ain't right. This ain't nothin' no human being would do to another human being."

"Call it justice, Monte," Ben told him. "Call it true justice at last."

Ben turned to leave.

"Wait!" Monte's busted and bruised mouth wailed out the one word of pure and nearly mindless fear. "You don't know them people. They'll torture us a long time 'fore they kill us. Them people is worser than anything on the face of this earth!"

Ben looked at the naked lot of scum and trash and outlaws. There was only contempt in his eyes. "I hope so, Monte. I really hope so."

The screaming from the mouths of the warlord and his outlaws began just as the long column of Rebels was pulling out. The screaming would continue throughout the very long day.

The Rebels made camp for the evening about fifteen miles outside of Charleston. Tina and her teams of Scouts reported that the city was filled with creepies.

"Do we clear the city, Ben?" Cecil asked, a haggard look around his eyes.

"We destroy it," Ben said. "Or as much of it as we can. We've been fully resupplied, so we're going to stand back and shell it and set it on fire."

Ben lifted a battered old map. "West, you take your people, this evening, and cross over the river down here at Interstate Seventy-seven. Cecil, take your battalion and cross over here, at Highway Twenty-one. At dawn, we'll commence shelling from three directions. That's it. You people get into position and get some rest. Tomorrow is going to be noisy."

When Cecil and West had gone, Ben turned to Jerre. "Get Katzman. Ask him if he's had any further word from Ike."

Katzman reported that Ike was well inland and moving toward Base Camp One.

"Advise Ike not to engage with the creepies. He isn't strong enough. Tell him to avoid the cities and head straight for the base camp and start setting up field supplies and vehicles for one battalion."

"All right, Ben." Her eyes touched his. "Your battalion, Ben?"

"That is correct."

He walked away while she was speaking with Katzman.

"When we get close to your camp, Thermopolis," Ben told him, "feel free to break loose and head home."

"We've talked it over, Ben Raines. We're going to

resettle in Arkansas. Until this creepie business is over, I have to admit there is strength in numbers. We'll settle near the Ouachita Mountains."

"Probably a wise choice. We'll set you up with good radio equipment and anything else you need."

"You won't run my community, Ben."

"I have no intention of running your show, Therm. I just want you properly equipped in case you're attacked or in the event we might need some help. Like I said before: We're not that different."

The hippie and the soldier smiled at each other and shook hands. "Well, I suppose I can live with that, Ben Raines."

"Good. I'll send a platoon of Rebels with you when you decide to break away. They'll escort you to your new base and help you get set up."

"That would be much appreciated. I suppose," he added dryly, "that Jerre will be among those assigned to escort us?"

"You're reading my mind, Therm."

"Maybe she won't want to go."

"She'll take orders or leave this outfit."

"In her own strange way, Ben, she cares very deeply for you. Surely you must know that."

"In her own strange way. Ships that pass in the night and all that crap."

"Yours is a strange combination of love, devotion, and anger, Ben Raines. She will never be subservient to any man."

"And you think that's what I want?"

"Of course it is. You have to control everything around you. I'm not faulting you; that's just the way you are. But you'll never control her. No man ever will. I think one did at some point in her life. And she will never permit that again."

"You might be right. But it's a moot point. Because I'll be pulling out and chances are very good that I'll never see her again. I have a suspicion that she'll stay with you and your group."

"She'll certainly be welcome."

"Take care of her, Thermopolis."

"I'm not her keeper, Ben Raines. She'll be free to come and go as she pleases. She's not a child."

Ben's smile was very sad. "That's where you're wrong, Therm. Because in a way, she is."

TWENTY-ONE

The shelling started at dawn, from three sides. Tanks and self-propelled artillery and mortars began their destruction of the city. They began dropping in HE, Willie Peter, and incendiary. It did not take long before sections of the city were blazing, the fires, unchecked, consuming the dusty old buildings.

Ben sat in an old service-station building drinking coffee, choosing to remain by himself and making it plain he did not wish to be disturbed. He had his boots propped up on the desk and was reading a paperback he had found when Jerre came in and sat down across the desk from him.

"Something on your mind, kid?"

"Thermopolis and his people are going to be leaving the convoy in a couple of days."

"Yeah, we talked about it earlier."

"You're sending a platoon of Rebels with them."

"That's right."

"I am formally requesting permission to be among that platoon." She stuck her chin out, getting set for an argument.

"All right."

She blinked, not believing what she'd just heard. "That's it? No arguments about it?"

"There is nothing to argue about, Jerre. If you wish to go, go. I'll reassign you right now. Dan is picking the team, isn't he?"

"Yes." She spoke softly.

"Then you're on your way. Pack up your gear and report to Dan. Tell him what I said. He'll verify it with me later."

She stood up and looked at him. "Well, I guess there is nothing left to say."

"I don't know that there ever was all that much to say, Jerre." He lifted his coffee mug. "Here's lookin' at you, kid."

She was gone amid the crash and howl of artillery shells.

Ben was not hearing the roar of combat. He was lost in memories, remembering that day years back when he had first looked into those blue eyes.

He sighed and closed the book, putting it in his jacket pocket. He stood up and walked to the door, opening it and stepping outside just in time to see Jerre get into a jeep.

She looked back at him.

He tossed her a salute.

"What's that all about?" she called, her voice small over the roar of the shelling.

"One always salutes the victor, Jerre. Protocol and all that."

"Nobody won, Ben. We both lost." She put the jeep into gear and drove off.

While it was impossible for a force as small as Ben's to completely destroy a city the size of Charleston, they did leave behind them a burning city. None had any way of knowing how many creepies they had killed, but for about eighteen hours, they had made life damned miserable for them.

The column crossed over into Kentucky without further incident, bypassing Lexington and taking Interstate 75 south.

It was just past Lexington that Thermopolis and his group split with the Rebels.

"We're not far from home, Ben Raines," Thermopolis

told him. "About a hundred fifty miles south and a bit east of here. So," he stuck out his hand, "I guess for a time, this is goodbye."

Ben shook the hand. "I'd like to say something to your following, Thermopolis."

"They are not my following, Ben."

Ben smiled. "Now who is bullshitting whom, friend?"

Both men laughed and walked toward the band of twenty-first-century hippies. The contingent of Rebels who were to act as escorts and to help with the move to Arkansas were already packed up and ready to go.

Ben made no speeches. He shook hands with everyone there and thanked them. Then he walked away. Without seeing Jerre.

As the columns split, Ben did not look back. Just told Cooper to take the country roads and to angle southwest; they were going down through Arkansas this time. And Ben also told his people they were not hunting trouble. They were going home.

They were lucky to make a hundred miles a day on the old county and state roads. Two hundred miles was considered good on the rapidly deteriorating Interstate system.

They followed Interstate 40 all the way over to Memphis. From there, the Rebels took 61 down through the delta of Mississippi. They saw occasional smoke from the chimneys of houses along the highway, but Ben made no effort to stop and inquire as to their well-being. Everyone in this part of the country, everyone in the deltas on both sides of the Mississippi River, knew that the Rebels' Base Camp One was located at Morriston, Louisiana. If they needed help, all they had to do was ask, it would be provided. They also knew not to screw up, or the Rebels would land on them hard.

And on a cool, very crisp and sunshiny midday, the Rebels pulled into Base Camp One to the sounds of a band playing and hundreds of people lining the streets, waving and cheering them home.

* * *

That evening after a very long and steamy and soapy shower and a good close shave, Ben was sitting in his favorite chair in the den of his home, listening to Gregorian chants on the CD player and having a vodka martini while his dogs lay around the chair, glad to have the master back home.

Of course, he was thinking about Jerre; she was never far from his thoughts.

A knock on the door brought him out of his reverie.

Ben waved Ike and Buddy inside and offered them a drink. Ike thought that would be just dandy; Buddy declined.

The CD player turned down and the drinks fixed, the men took seats. Ike propped his feet up on an ottoman and said, "I've had the mechanics working on vehicles for you, Ben. But since I don't really know how many people you're plannin' on takin' with you, I don't really know how many vehicles to line up."

"Four companies, Ike. All volunteer. And probably one short company of Dan's Scouts."

"The way our companies line up, you're talkin' about roughly eight hundred people."

"That's close enough."

"Your four-wheel drive has seen some rough use. I got you another lined up. People armor-plating it and replacing glass now."

"You're walking around something, Ike. What is it?"

"I'd like to go with you."

"Ike, you're a brand new daddy. And we've got several hundred new people to train. With Dan gone, that's up to you. You and Cecil are needed here."

Ike grinned. "I had to try."

"And I appreciate it." He cut his eyes to his son. "Your mother is still out there, boy. We could run into her on this trip."

Buddy shrugged his heavy shoulders. "Then so be it, Father. The woman is insane and for years has acted in a criminal manner. She must be stopped."

"Then you're volunteering?"

"Of course. Father, the entire base has volunteered

to go."

Ben had expected it, but it still filled him with pride. "I'll start picking names in the morning. Now then, the only outpost we currently have out west—the far west—is at Great Bend, Kansas. That's another reason for this trip. We've got to start stretching out and reclaiming territory, making it productive once more. I just went over the records here at camp. Jesus, Ike, we've got over ten thousand people around this area. We've got people coming in daily. So that means we've got to start pioneering some families. Pass the word that I'm looking for settlers to go with us."

Ike nodded. "I'm ahead of you, Ben. I got a list of more than two hundred families who want to go."

"Good. We're on the right track. Now then, as we go, we're going to start clearing small-town airports for the birds to use, to resupply settlers until they can get crops in and become productive. We'll probably be gone the better part of a year. Cecil is going to handle the administrative end of things while I'm gone. Everything else falls on your shoulders, Ike."

Again, Ike nodded.

"I'm not going to jump into this thing, Ike. I don't want to start out and find ourselves in the big fat middle of a blizzard on the plains. We're going to have very firm timetables as to when and where and how we resupply along the line. And down here, I'm going to go over everything from socks to bullets." He smiled at them. "But for this night, I'm going to listen to some music, have a few drinks, and relax. Get some sleep, boys; tomorrow starts a very hectic schedule."

Ben patted the track of a main battle tank, 105mm-cannon-equipped. "Ten of them," he said. "Ready to roll."

Beth took that down in a notepad.

"I thought you were going back to Lev and the cows, Beth."

"Lev got tired of waiting," she informed him. "There was a message waiting for me when we got back. It's just as well. I'd have gotten tired of wiping that ick off my boots." She jerked a thumb toward a very pretty blond woman, in her early to mid-twenties. "This is Corrie. She'll be handling the radio."

"I definitely approve."

"I thought you would," Beth said dryly.

Corrie smiled at him.

"I want a dozen hand-held vision scopes, Beth, and five tripod night vision scopes. Five grenade launchers per platoon."

Beth scribbled.

"I want Big Thumpers mounted on every vehicle that will take them. Five Dusters."

They walked on—Beth, Cooper, Jersey, Corrie, and Ben.

"Three eighty-one-millimeter mortar carriers, five-person crew."

Beth jotted it down.

"One five-point-five-six Minimi per platoon. One fifty per platoon. Two Puffs ready to fly at all times."

Beth noticed the absence of Ben's old Thompson. "What will you be carrying, General?"

"I'll keep the Thompson in a boot. I'll carry the old Thunder Lizard."

She jotted down .308 ammo.

"Tankers to keep us rolling and equipment to test gas and pumps to suck it up from storage tanks.

"Get everyone's boot size and make sure there are adequate replacements. I want all body armor checked and any defectives replaced immediately."

Beth wrote it down.

"One mini-MASH fully equipped. Find out what doctors are going along."

"Doctor Chase says he is leading the team of doctors."

"Doctor Chase is most definitely *not* leading the doctors," Ben countered.

"I just work here, General," Beth said. "Argue with

Doctor Chase."

"Put down Doctor Ling to lead the team. I'll deal with Lamar."

"Better you than me," Beth muttered.

"Umm?"

"Nothing, sir."

"Ike is seeing to the vehicles, so if any of them breaks down, we can blame it on him."

"Yes, sir. We can cuss him a thousand miles from nowhere, sitting on the side of the highway holding a busted U-joint. Right, sir."

"Make a note to recheck the transportation before we pull out," Ben said with a smile.

"Thank you."

"What am I forgetting, Beth?"

"About ten thousand things, sir. I have a list." She held out her hand and Cooper gave her a notebook about the size of the Bible.

Ben glanced at it. "Good God!"

"Yes, sir. Are you ready?"

"Do I have a choice?"

"No, sir."

"That's what I was afraid of. Where do we start?" He had discovered that Beth was very thorough.

"Five thousand pairs of socks."

"Can we start with the bras and panties?"

"We'll get to that later," Corrie said, smiling at him.

Ben arched an eyebrow. Might be a more interesting trip than he first thought.

TWENTY-TWO

Emil had settled back into his role as spiritual leader of his little group. The battle dress was gone and the robes had returned.

Emil had contacted the Great God Blomm, and Blomm, so the little con artist informed his following, had instructed him to keep his ass close to home from now on. But Emil was forced to admit, not aloud, that he did miss the excitement.

No more had been heard from Sister Voleta or Ashley.

Thermopolis and his group were settling in up in Arkansas. Ben had instructed the platoon of Rebels to stay with them for as long as they were needed.

At least that kept Ben away from Jerre.

And vice versa.

And Ben was stalling in pulling out, and he knew it. He had made up a dozen excuses for his delaying the trip west, some of them proving valid, most just no more than excuses and nothing else.

West knocked on his office door and Ben waved him in and to a seat. "What's up?"

"Ben, I lost two men last week."

"Lost two men? How? Desertion?"

"No. I've never lost a man to that. My people are professionals. But . . ." He spread his hands. "I thought at first that, well, hell, there is a first time for everything, so maybe they did desert. Now I find that two more are missing. Sometime last night."

Ben kept his face expressionless; but his first thought was of the kids of the Night People. "And your thoughts on the matter?"

"The same as yours, Ben," the mercenary said grimly.

"All the creepie kids accounted for?"

"Yes. But that doesn't mean a damn thing. The sneaky little bastards can almost slip out and away while you're looking at them."

"You think . . . ?" Ben let that hang.

"Yeah, Ben. I think."

"If they did the unthinkable and unspeakable, West, they didn't go far to do it. Come on."

The creepie kids would have few places to feast on human flesh, for there were no slums and no shacks in any town or outpost occupied by the Rebels. If there were unoccupied buildings or sheds on any land claimed by a Rebel, the buildings were repainted and kept up by the new owner, or they were torn down. Since building materials and nails and paint were free for the taking, the standing orders were: Just do it. Period.

When Ben said that Rebel communities were going to be models that would stand the test of time for future generations to build by, he meant it.

Morriston was rapidly becoming a small town that would have been the envy of anyone even when the nation was whole. There was no litter. If one littered and was caught, and the offender almost always was, the culprit spent a week, seven days, eight hours a day, doing community service work, usually cleaning out septic tanks, digging ditches, or some other unenviable type of work. There was no appeal. There just wasn't any litter.

But it was not an inflexible society. Ben knew that kids are kids and kids are going to break the rules from time to time. Loud mufflers and loud music of any type—rock to classical—was tolerated, to a point. Probably the most important thing was that the kids understood the rights of others. They were taught values not only in the churches and at home, but in the schools.

Members of the ACLU were probably spinning in their graves, and Ben hoped they kept on spinning, right out into another galaxy.

"Corrie," Ben told her, "have Doctor Chase get the lab ready to test for human blood on hands and lips and clothing. Tell Ike to take a team and go over their quarters like a Marine Corps inspection team landing on a recruits' barracks. They left something behind, bet on it."

"Yes, sir." They walked on toward the kids' quarters as Corrie completed her transmissions. She said, "General? Doctor Chase says that his goddamned, blankety-blank, I-refuse-to-say-that-word lab is always that-word-either blankety-blank ready."

"Thank you, Corrie. You have to remember that Chase was in the Navy. He was an officer, but he was a mustang. You'll get used to Lamar . . . eventually."

"If you say so, sir." But she looked very dubious about it.

"What are we looking for, Ben?" West asked.

"The last place those men were seen."

"They were pulling guard duty around our compound. The dog watch."

"We'll start there."

It took them several walk-arounds of the area, but West was the one who found the small splotches of blood. "Got it," he called.

Ben waved a lab technician over, and the woman lifted the blood onto slides.

"Now we have something to work on," Ben said. "Let's see if we can pick up a trail."

A dozen yards on and they found a thin blood trail leading toward a stand of timber across the old Interstate. In the timber, in an old shotgun house, they found the men, hanging up like sides of beef. What was left of them, that is. They were naked and had been carved on with very sharp knives.

"What's the drill now, Ben?" West asked, anger very plain in his tone.

"We either prove or disprove it was them. I have never believed in pampering kids. If a teenager commits an adult crime, they should be punished like an adult."

"And the punishment for a crime like this?"

"Death."

"What'd you have, Lamar?" Ben asked.

"Dried blood under their fingernails and on their skin and clothing. It's being matched up now. Did you find all the bodies, Ben?"

"All four of them. The kids ate their fill."

"If it was the kids," Doctor Holly Allardt said.

These were the first words she had spoken to Ben since his return to the base camp at Morriston.

"Right, Holly. If."

The doctor turned her back to him and walked away, to stand in her office doorway, glaring at him.

"Hell has no fury, and all that," Chase muttered, looking at Ben.

"I didn't scorn her, Lamar."

"You think."

A lab technician walked up to the group, which had now grown to include Cecil and Ike and Buddy and Tina and Dan. "It's a match. All the kids were involved. They all feasted. If that's the right word."

Ben nodded. "Dan, take their statements. I don't think they'll deny it. They're proud of what they ate."

"Yes, sir. And then . . . ?"

"Hang them."

"They're just kids!" Holly yelled at him. "The youngest is no more than fifteen. This is barbaric behavior."

"This is a hospital, Doctor," Chase warned her. "We have some seriously ill patients. So please lower your voice."

Holly walked up to Ben. "If you hang those kids, I'll resign."

"Turn your resignation in to Doctor Chase, then. And I'll be sorry to lose you. You're a fine doctor." Ben walked away.

*   *   *

The older cannibalistic offspring of the Night People were hanged, and Holly did not resign. But in the time Ben had left at Base Camp One, she avoided him whenever possible, and then spoke only when spoken to.

The younger kids were spared; they had taken no part in the killing and eating of West's men, having been housed in separate quarters. Most of Ben's medical personnel thought the younger kids had a chance to shake their earlier teachings. Only time would prove or disprove that theory.

On a cool early spring morning, Ben rose before dawn and stepped out of his house, a mug of coffee in his hand. He sat down on the porch and looked out at the quiet before dawn.

His dogs came to him and he petted them all. "Gonna miss you guys and gals," he spoke softly to them. He knew they would be well taken care of by the Rebels who stayed in his house whenever he was gone. "But the old man's got to go. I wish I could take you all with me, but that's not possible. I'll be back, and that's a promise, gang."

The dogs took turns licking the back of his hand.

Then they all ran out into the fenced yard to play.

Ben finished his coffee and went back into the house, to pack up a few last-minute things. He looked at the only picture of Jerre he had and picked it up; then he gently placed the framed picture into a drawer of the nightstand and closed it.

"You will never know how much I love you, Jerre."

Ben buckled his flight bag and walked out into the predawn darkness.

TWENTY-THREE

Ben walked up and down and through the lines of vehicles in the staging area, noting that a great many of the Rebels who had volunteered to travel west had been part of the forces who had fought in New York City. But still there were many new faces among the eight hundred Rebels.

Ben stopped and stared at a man from Missouri who had been with him since the beginning.

"Dammit, Jimmy," Ben said to the sergeant major. "When are you going to admit that you're just too damned old for the field?"

"The same day you do, General," was his reply.

Ben laughed and walked on, Beth, Corrie, Jersey, and Cooper walking with him.

He stopped at a truck and looked up at the line of Rebels seated on the bench. "Chuck, how are you feeling?"

"Good as new, General," Chuck said with a grin.

"Good to have you back with us."

"Thank you, sir."

Ben completed his inspection and looked at his watch. Ten o'clock. He walked back to his new Blazer, bullet-proofed and armor-plated. Cecil and Ike and Chase were standing beside the vehicle.

Ben shook hands with all of them.

Nobody said anything. There was nothing left to say. The three men backed into the throng of silent and watching Rebels who were staying behind.

Ben climbed into the Blazer and rolled down his window. "Corrie, tell the Scouts to move out and maintain a ten-mile lead."

"Yes, sir."

"Order the convoy out onto the Interstate."

The orders were given and the long column began rumbling and snorting and clanking out onto Interstate 20.

"Cooper!" Jersey spoke from the backseat. "Will you quit tailgating that damn tank. I swear to God, I only know one other person who's a worse driver than you!"

Ben laughed as everybody in the Blazer started singing "On the Road Again."